Brotherhood of Blood
Wildwood 2

Night of the
Nymph

BIANCA D'ARC

Copyright © 2023 Bianca D'Arc
Published by Hawk Publishing, LLC
New York

An ancient evil hidden among the trees...

Crystal is driving across the state for a job interview when she feels a pressing need to stop her car and get out. She's on the edge of a woodland and she finds herself drawn within to help the trees that are crying out for her attention.

An ancient vampire who treads the fine line between his nature and his duty...

Marco senses the trespasser and expects a confrontation. What he finds is something altogether different. A beautiful, magical woman walking through his woodland, talking to the trees. Enchanted by her innocent magic, he must discover why she is there and what she intends to do. The estate has an evil history and he's been working to reclaim it for the forces of Light, but he'll have to fight his own dark desires for this woman to discover if she is one of the good guys...or very, very bad.

A shared destiny bigger than either of them expect...

Crystal's unique abilities allow them to discover what has been sickening the trees, and they must work together to protect the entire world from the evil that lurks just below the surface. Will they prevail, and can they find a way to be together when she is a child of the daylight, and he is a creature of the night?

DEDICATION

To the friends who have helped get me through these past few months. Grief is such a hard thing. Different for each person, yet the devastation of losing someone we love is pretty universal. Thank you to my dear friends and readers who have commiserated with me and just silently stood by me through this sad journey from sorrow into... well... I'm not quite there yet, but I'm getting better as I go along. Thanks you all of you. <3

Special thanks to Peggy for helping track down those nasty typos and other boo-boos, and many thanks also to Jennifer for giving Brandt his name.

And, as always, my work is dedicated to my family, for encouraging me for so very long and never giving up on me.

PROLOGUE

Previously, in Wyoming...

"Will you take the gift of my blood to help sustain you while you rest, Leonora?" the Master vampire of the area, Dmitri, asked in a gentle voice. "Fair warning though—it could change you for all time." He winked at the dryad, Leonora, bringing a faint smile to her face. One of her eyebrows quirked upward in challenge, even though she was in terrible pain from a gunshot wound made with a silver bullet. Poison to her kind.

"An even exchange then?" she asked. "It's probably about time we expanded the bounds of our friendship to include that kind of trust."

Dmitri nodded gravely, the smile still touching his lips. "As you say, my old friend. I have long valued your presence in the woods near where I have made my home."

"And your empire," Leonora added with a weak grin. She was losing energy. Whatever they were going to do, they had to do it soon.

The dryad's distant relative, Sally, watched over them both, fretting. Sally's power flared along with her worry. That seemed to get Dmitri's attention.

"Right. Let's get on with this so you can rest more easily," he said, his gaze moving from Leonora to Sally.

Lifting one hand, he shifted the shape of just one finger into a wickedly sharp claw. Sally felt the rush of magic in a way she'd never before experienced and saw the glow of red increase around his hand as he willed it to change. Before she knew what he intended, he used the claw to slash a fine line over his other wrist. Blood welled, and he was careful to aim it directly into the hole in Leonora's shoulder.

From about twelve inches above, he dripped his dark red blood into the wound as Sally watched, dumbfounded by his actions. Leonora wasn't complaining, other than an initial hiss as the first drop found its way into the wound and sent up a sizzle as it began to react with her own chemistry. Sally had to trust that these two magical creatures knew what they were doing. She was totally out of her depth where vampire blood was concerned.

Even Leonora—who was her grandmother many times removed—was beyond Sally's understanding. Her blood wasn't red, but sort of clear tinged with the green of the forest. Like tree sap, maybe. That had shocked Sally when she'd first seen it after the attack that left Leonora so close to death.

Dmitri stopped at exactly thirteen drops. He removed his hand from over Leonora's body and licked at the small wound on his wrist. When Sally looked again, the wound was gone. Not even a faint scar remained. Amazing.

Leonora looked a little better too. Her wound was bubbling with pinkish light as her clear magical blood met and was aided by Dmitri's dark red. Leonora stopped fading, though she was quite obviously still in bad shape. Yet, the effects of the poison seemed to have stopped in their tracks. She wasn't getting any worse, which was a huge relief.

"You'll understand my inclination to wait until you are

completely healed of the poison to complete our exchange." Dmitri bowed his head in a formal manner.

Leonora nodded slightly, a faint smile hovering over her lips. "I look forward to the day I can fulfill my promise. For now, I must rest in the wildwood."

"And I will guard over your resting place by night, my old friend."

"The wolves and I will watch by day," Sally said.

"Already you speak on behalf of your mate?" Leonora seemed amused.

"I—" Sally hesitated.

"Don't worry. I approve wholeheartedly of Jason Moore. He's nothing like the creature my daughter Marisol chose to wed. He's a good and honest man, and you will do well with him. He will also support you on your quest, which could be useful. You two are a good match."

Sally was speechless. Leonora amazed her. She was at death's door, and here, she was reassuring Sally. Leonora was a trooper, that was for sure.

A tear tracked down Sally's face to splash onto the leaves that were hovering close. It sparked silver off the leaf. Only then did Sally realize the willow was weeping. It rained dew from its leaves onto Leonora, though none of the three within the circle of the willow's embrace were wet.

The silver sparkling dew was life. The tree's life force—perhaps the whole forest's life force—being given to the nymph who loved and sustained this portion of the wildwood. The dew landed on Leonora, and her body soaked it in. The dew seemed to be somehow preparing her body for what would come next, if Sally understood what it was Leonora wanted her to do.

"It's nearly time." Leonora's voice was fading as her own power ebbed. "You must deliver me into the willow. It will hold my body safe for as long as it takes."

Dmitri pressed a quick kiss to Leonora's hand then retreated a short distance. He nodded toward Sally, and she took his signal to mean that it was show time. Now, if only

3

she knew what it was she was supposed to do.

"Speak the willow's name in your heart," Leonora coached. Sally held tight to her hand, disliking the way her skin had cooled. Leonora was in bad shape. "Ask for its help. Send it your power to help it do what it must."

Sally tried to do as Leonora instructed. She searched for and found the willow's name. How? She had no idea. She only knew that when she sent her thoughts spiraling toward the tree, she knew exactly what to say. It was as if some ancient instinct kicked in and took her by the hand, showing her what to do.

Sally kissed Leonora's hand, much as Dmitri had done, then moved back a few inches to let the willow do what it would. It was in the tree's hands—or limbs, rather—now. As she watched, feeding her power to the pliable branches of the willow tree, small tendrils snaked down from above and wove a complex pattern under Leonora's pale body. In no time at all, it had woven a sort of basket around her. Sally and Dmitri stood as one when the branches lifted Leonora off the ground, raising her to a standing position before pulling her into the heart of the tree.

She blended with the trunk in a flash of golden, green and pulsing brown light. A blend of her magic and Sally's, along with a hint of the blood-red essence that Sally now recognized as Dmitri. The power flared to a high intensity. It was so bright Sally had to look away. When she turned back, Leonora was inside the tree, suspended in the trunk as it slowly faded from crystal clear to translucent then to opaque.

Before Sally lost sight of her completely, Leonora smiled. She looked stronger. Happy in the embrace of the tree's ancient wisdom. Sally had touched its heart, its mind, and knew it would hold Leonora safe for as long as it took, sustaining her life with its own. With the life of the very forest around it, if necessary. It was her guardian now and honored to be so.

Sally's quest was to find the rest of Leonora's long-lost descendants. It wouldn't be easy, but she would locate them, one by one, if she had to, and get their help in one day, restoring their ancestor to health and wholeness. One day, Leonora would come out of that tree and be healed by the conjunction of her descendants' magic and the forest that was her home.

CHAPTER 1

Present day, in Nebraska...

Even before he rose for the evening, the master vampire of this region, Marco, sensed something stirring in the forest around the old mansion. He had begun the work of cleansing the place with the help of a nearby group of shape shifters several months ago, and he still kept an eye on it. It was empty now, but the mansion and its grounds had been used for terrible evil. The outside pavilion, in particular, had been drenched in blood magic, and the gardens around it had been seeded with evil gargoyle statues that came to life, only to attack servants of the Light.

Marco might be limited to the hours of darkness because of his immortal nature, but he was a long-time servant of the Light and an opponent of evil. He had spent many years watching over the mansion and grounds on the edge of his territory in eastern Nebraska. He had rejoiced in helping rid the place of evil. But it remained a problem. It was empty, and the echoes of the evil that had been done there reverberated.

What the place really needed was new inhabitants. Good people with good plans for the place. He just hadn't found any to take it over yet.

Of course, Marco had crews there most of the day, working on the renovation, but nobody was living there full-time. And now, he wasn't sure it was completely safe. Something was going on there, and he needed to find out what it was. If evil had returned to the mansion, he was going to have to do something about it.

With that in mind, he rose in the darkness after twilight and headed out to check on the mansion. Although he was not strictly a mage, he had been able to forge some rudimentary wards around the property, and those were being tested by something. He wasn't sure what. He also wasn't sure if it was good or evil. All he knew, at this point, was that something had breached his wards, and he was going to find out who, or what, had done so and why.

He flew through the night air in the form of a black dragon. As an ancient vampire, he had the strength to transform himself into just about any shape he desired. It wasn't shape shifting in the traditional sense. He wasn't like those who had a beast living in their soul and could only transform into that one animal. No, Marco could do just about any shape he could imagine. Even mist.

But he enjoyed the dragon form. He liked flying, and if he kept his size down to a reasonable stature and his color very dark, then nobody could see him, other than those with magic of their own. Regular people, those with no magic, never looked up when he passed over and didn't see him. Of course, he could influence their minds to look away and not notice him as well, but he rarely had to resort to such methods.

As he flew over the forest that made up a large part of the mansion's property, he caught sight of something moving among the trees. He sensed magic, but it was a different sort than he was used to feeling. This felt almost...elemental. He couldn't be sure. He circled once again then landed not far from where he had sensed the intruder.

Crystal had felt compelled to stop her car and enter the woodland that was crying out for help. It wasn't normal for her to do things like this, but she'd never felt a call so strongly. She had discovered an odd ability to hear the whispering, musical communication of trees long ago. She had always considered it a secret quirk that she never discussed with anyone, but she listened to the trees around her and learned many things.

She was on her way across the state for a job interview, but something had made her take the exit ramp and come to this lonely stretch of road. She'd stopped her car and rolled down the windows, and a wave of despair came to her on the wind that nearly broke her heart.

Not really thinking about her actions, she'd gotten out of her car and walked into the woods, going deeper into the gloom as night fell. She wasn't afraid. The trees would warn her of any danger. They were her friends and would try to protect her. She didn't sense any wild animals that were big enough to hurt her or any other threats, but she felt the deep sorrow of the trees as a blow to her heart.

She summoned her energy and tried her best to soothe the trees, telling them that she was here and would do her best to help. She didn't know exactly what she could do, but she had to do *something*. It was a visceral need in her soul.

She walked among the trees, noting the presence of many oak and rowan seedlings that were doing their best to help their older friends of different varieties recover from whatever had been done to them and the land on which they grew. But the seedlings were too young, and too much had happened here for them to be able to cleanse the land easily or quickly. It was going to be a really big job.

Crystal kept walking, not needing light to see as the sun went down. It was a quirk of her power that all living things gave off a slight glow that allowed her to see in the dark, as long as there were living things around her. She walked to the heart of the grove and sank down to her knees as the despair of the trees nearly overwhelmed her. They were all talking at once, as if they had been waiting for someone like her to arrive. Someone who could hear them.

The Protector comes. The trees whispered the phrase over and over, but she didn't know what it meant. She didn't feel endangered. Far from it. The trees liked this being—whoever *The Protector* was. She wasn't sure she should be here. She was trespassing, after all, but if the trees trusted this person, then perhaps she could convey to *The Protector* the need she felt from the trees for cleansing of the land.

She held her position. *The Protector* would either find her or it wouldn't. She wasn't going to stop her work. She was busy summoning energy from the earth to cleanse the worst of the deep wounds suffered by the land in this area and, by association, the trees. It was the least she could do, and frankly, she couldn't go another moment listening to the wailing that only she could hear. The trees were in pain, and it hurt her to hear it.

Master Marco flew overhead, making for the spot on the edge of the forest nearest the road where he saw a thin golden glow through the trees. As he approached, the golden light shimmered, drawing him in like a moth to the flame. Intrigued, he circled, going lower to see if he could learn more before he landed, but the trees were too dense. He only got flickering images of a person standing in the center of the glow, seeming to command it with their hands.

It didn't look bad. It didn't feel evil. Instead, he got the impression that the being—whoever it was—wielded its power to try to help the forest in some way. Living things weren't his specialty. Especially not plants and trees. He had done what he could to try to help the land recover from the evil that had been done here. He had seeded the area with oak and rowan saplings, having heard that they naturally cleansed evil from the land.

Marco didn't know how long it would take, but time was something he had plenty of, and he often thought in terms of decades, or even centuries, rather than years or months. The little saplings were doing well. He checked on them regularly. But he had no way of knowing how long it would take those brave little trees to overcome the horrors that had been committed on this land.

Maybe the trees had gotten tired of waiting. Maybe they had somehow summoned one who could help them faster. He'd heard rumors through the Masters network that ancient elemental powers were starting to show themselves once more in the mortal realm. Just recently, he'd been told by his old friend, Hiram, about a fierce battle involving four water elementals and a whole host of Others, including an entire town of bear shifters, assorted mages from different disciplines and heritages, someone with sylph blood and even a part-dryad.

They had managed, between them, to send a creature of evil back to its own realm of existence before it could pollute the Earth's seas any more than it already had. If the creature had spawned here, for example, it would have meant centuries of incredibly powerful sea creatures—monsters, really—that would feed on any innocent traversing the oceans.

Hiram had nothing but praise for the people he had befriended in the new town in his territory that had sprung up a few years ago. Grizzly Cove was earning quite the reputation among magical folk. Both for the trouble it had encountered because of so much magic gathered in such a small place and for the social experiment of creating a town just for bear shifters, who normally roamed alone or in small family groups.

Bear shifters weren't like werewolves. They didn't form Packs. At least, not usually. However, the Alpha who had created the town had been a military leader. He had earned such respect and admiration from his men that they had followed him even into civilian life and the town he had created for them all. If Marco ever found himself traveling again, he thought he would like to see this town called Grizzly Cove. Hiram's description made it sound like a very interesting place.

But Marco's traveling days were behind him. At least, that was his belief. He had picked this area of the country because there were few people, and even fewer of his kind. He had lived far beyond his expectations. Centuries of living had left him feeling morose, if he was being honest with himself. He was just existing. He was protecting his little part of the world against evil. That was his only goal in life now. He had given up hoping for happiness, or a future with joy in it.

The years stretched ahead of him—and behind him—in a tedious line. He'd had an existential crisis of momentous proportions for a long time, until he just decided that he was here to protect his little area and help where he could to stop evil from hurting anybody else the way it had hurt those he had cared for in the past. He wouldn't let himself in for that kind of pain again. He wouldn't form friendships with the mortals around him. He wouldn't harm them, of course, though he needed to feed from time to time, but he also wouldn't befriend them.

Losing them was too painful, especially when they succumbed to evil. It had happened both ways to him. Someone he had trusted had been turned to evil and broken his heart. Or, most often, evil targeted those he had befriended, killing them without remorse, in horrible ways. Either way, Marco ended up mourning. Grieving for the people he had lost over the many centuries he had been alive. The only thing keeping him going, at this point, was his responsibility to try to stem the tide of evil wherever he could, so that others wouldn't have to feel the soul-deep sadness he had felt too many times to remember.

He circled over the light, going lower on each pass, trying to discover what he could before he changed shape and landed among the trees. He couldn't very well land in his dragon form, even though he could be a man-sized dragon.

The wingspan was always an issue among the tightly packed trees. But he didn't need wings to fly. He was vampire. He could become mist, if that's what he wanted. His magic was such that there was no limitation on the forms he could become, and flying was more of a magical operation than a mechanical one. At least, for him.

Maybe that wasn't the case for others of his kind. Marco didn't know for sure. He'd just always been able to do it, once he'd come fully into his power. That had happened sometime in the 1400s, when he had claimed mastery over his birth region in Italy, and he'd only grown incrementally stronger since then. Messina had been his birthplace and also the site of the start of the Black Death in Europe when three ships docked there from the Black Sea, bringing the plague to his homeland.

He'd watched throughout, knowing the plague for what it was—a magical attack by the Destroyer—who wanted, insanely, to *cleanse* the world of non-magical humans to make way for her twisted idea of an evil empire. Elspeth had sent successive waves of disease and pestilence against innocent human beings over many years of struggle while the forces of good tried so hard to gather their strength and fight her followers wherever they were found.

But Elspeth and her people were cunning. They hid in the shadows and preyed on the innocent. They killed so many in their attempts to gain ultimate power. Eventually, the forces of good had won the day and sent Elspeth packing, imprisoned and exiled to the farthest realms. Her followers had been killed or disbanded, and her time was at an end.

Or so the forces of Light had thought. Elspeth's followers—the ancient order known as the *Venifucus*—had not disbanded, as he had believed for so long. In recent years, it had come to light that they had kept going in secret. They had been working all this time to break Elspeth free of her prison and bring her back to the mortal realm.

Rumors abounded that they had in fact done just that. Marco wasn't sure, but he remained vigilant. He dreaded the idea that they would have to fight her all over again. He would do it. He wouldn't enjoy it, but he would do it. He had seen, firsthand, what she had done to the people of his beloved homeland and everyone else unfortunate enough to be in her path.

That's what kept him going. That was his reason for living. So few people alive today remembered what she had done. So few knew her tactics. He'd been a soldier on the side of Light. He knew what to expect from her and her people. It was his duty to be ready when his knowledge was needed again, and he very much feared that the time was drawing near.

Which was part of the reason he was so vigilant about this nearby mansion and its grounds. It had been fouled by blood magic and was susceptible to being misused again. He wouldn't let that happen. He had sworn to keep this place from being turned to evil once more. For lack of a better word, he was its caretaker. At least, until he could find people he could trust to inhabit the estate and watch over it for him.

The uninvited guest didn't seem to be doing anything bad. Marco would have sensed evil intent. He had set all sorts of spells and wards to warn him of just such an occurrence. When this person had crossed his ward, it had not flared with alarm. It had alerted Marco to the presence of someone, but it had not warned of malevolent intent.

For that matter, Marco didn't sense anything truly dark either. He was intrigued as he floated to earth, landing, by design, about twenty yards away from the glowing golden light. He wanted time to study the person at the center of the light. He intended to approach slowly, learning all he could as he drew closer, step by step.

Crystal sobbed as she reached for the earth energy, trying to cleanse what she could of the evil that permeated the ground here. It felt like some sort of blood magic had been soaked into every pebble, every grain of sand, every molecule of earth that surrounded the root systems of its suffering trees. It hurt so bad. It hurt the trees. It hurt the land. It hurt her to be in contact with it, but she must. She had to try.

Everything around her cried out for her help, but she had never faced anything this profound before. She'd never been so immersed in so much death and decay. Crystal began to doubt herself. She didn't know if she could handle this, but she had to try something. She couldn't just leave it this way. She couldn't just run away and pretend she'd never seen this blight.

Reaching deep within herself, she tapped the energy that lived within her soul. She had done it before, on a much smaller scale, to help save the life of dying plants. She knew she could give a little bit of herself to bring the plant back to life. She wondered if she could do the same here.

She would have to be careful. As far as she understood it, the power she used came from within herself. She couldn't leave herself too weak to walk or drive away. She had to have that out. If she opened herself up completely, this place might drain her dry and leave her comatose, or worse.

That in mind, she tried really hard to channel just a little bit of her energy into her hands. It manifested as a golden ball of light, glowing strong in the gloom of the forest night. She felt a little shaky. Maybe she had taken a little too much at one time, but she was committed now. She had to redirect the golden energy from her hands, down into the earth. She believed it would cleanse whatever it came into contact with, relieving some of the pain she sensed all around.

She knew she couldn't do much with just her own energy, but it was all she had to give. She wasn't very skilled with this sort of thing, having taught herself the little she knew. There just wasn't anyone around who had the same kind of power she seemed to have. She'd asked—very cautiously, of course. She'd talked to many people who claimed to know about the magic of the earth, but nobody had really been able to give her the knowledge she felt she needed. So, she had experimented. Trial and error had been her constant companion these past few years since she had discovered the energy within herself.

She really hoped this wasn't going to be one of the *errors*. Sending a quick prayer aloft, she placed one palm down on the ground transferring the golden ball of light from her hands into the earth.

"Oh, boy…" She had a moment of wobbly awareness that she'd gone just a little too far before she slumped, unconscious, to the ground.

CHAPTER 2

Marco watched the woman through the trees. He could see the glowing form was female as he drew closer. Shapely. Curvy. Lovely.

As he watched, she fell to her knees and touched the glowing golden energy to the ground, where it sank into the earth. He could just see it flowing out from her fingers, making the soil glow, revealing the web of tree and plant roots within for just a moment.

Then everything went dark, and the woman crumpled to the forest floor.

"Damn." Marco recognized the signs as he strode forward.

The woman given up too much energy all at once. If she was lucky, she'd only be out for a moment or two. If unlucky, she could very well have just magicked herself into a coma.

He knelt at her side, scanning her quickly. She was breathing, but heavily asleep. He didn't think it was a paralytic sleep, but she was definitely down for the count. He thought quickly about what to do. He couldn't just leave her here. It was going to rain later, and she needed to be under cover.

He decided to take her to the mansion. Nobody was living there right now, but he'd thoroughly cleansed the rooms as best he could, and he'd hired a human cleaning service to clean the place from top to bottom. It was ready for people, if he could just find the right ones to take it over. He'd bought the place outright and intended to be a good landlord to the right people, as long as they swore to never let evil onto this land again. That was his one and only condition, but it was a biggie, as they said in these modern times.

Marco listened to the slow whoosh of her blood flowing through her veins, the reassuring low thud of her heart. She was alive and not in too much distress. Just really drained after her foolish expenditure of energy. Had she no sense?

He almost growled then got himself under control. It wasn't like him to have such strong emotions anymore. What was it about this one frail human that had broken through his self-imposed reticence? He'd have to examine that…later.

For now, he had to get her under cover before the rain started. He reached out to touch her, and his skin tingled at the first touch. That was odd. He lifted her into his arms and stood, marveling at the way she felt against him. She was so soft. Rounded and lovely. And her scent was that of the forest. Intriguing.

Striding forward, he headed for the mansion. It wasn't too far away, which was good, since the rain was likely to start at any moment.

Crystal moaned as she came awake. Her head hurt, and she felt woozy, but she made herself swim out of the fog that had enveloped her. She had to wake up. She wasn't safe. Her last thought was of a forest, but she wasn't in the forest now. How had she gotten to…wherever she was at the moment? Had some Good Samaritan found her collapsed in the woods and taken her someplace? That didn't seem probable.

It was much more likely that some nefarious person had

found her and taken her to his lair. Oh, boy.

Would an evil doer's lair have a big comfy bed with soft cotton sheets? She had no idea, but a tentative stretch of her fingers told her she was in just such a position. A soft bed under her back and cotton sheets under her fingers.

She opened one eye against the pounding in her head. She was in a bedroom, and there was a man sitting in a chair next to her bed. She gasped. He was leaning back in the chair, sitting with one leg crossed over the other, as if waiting to hold a discourse like some old-world gentleman. Why she had that odd thought, she had no idea, but it seemed to fit.

"Hello?" she offered, her voice rusty with sleep. If he was Dr. Evil, she might as well find out and see where she stood.

"Ah. You are awake. Good. How do you feel?"

His voice was cultured and deep. It rumbled through her in a velvety caress. Surely, a man with a voice like that wouldn't harm her. And his face… It was all chiseled angles and classic elegance. He had wavy dark hair, just a little longer than clean-cut, and dark eyes. He looked Italian. Like one of those famous marble statues of old from the glory days of the Roman Empire. *Hubba hubba.*

She opened her other eye, just to be sure of her initial assessment and wasn't surprised when he was even more good looking in binocular vision. Yeah, if he was a bad guy, she was going to be majorly disappointed.

"I'm okay, thanks. Where am I?" She looked around the bedroom, a little uncomfortable now that she'd discovered Adonis sitting next to her and she was lying flat in a big bed. Her thoughts immediately went to naughty places. *Awkward.*

"You are in the mansion on the grounds where you fell. I found you in the forest and brought you here," he replied, as if he found unconscious women in the woods every day. Maybe he did, but she wouldn't bet on it.

"Mansion? I didn't see a house. Just the trees," she admitted. "I'm sorry if I was trespassing. I…um…" She didn't know how to explain why she'd been there. *Darnit.*

"Think nothing of it," he told her. "I'm just sorry you gave so much of your energy to the cleansing of the woodland that it caused you to pass out."

His words stilled her. They implied he knew about magic and what she'd done to end up unconscious in his forest.

"You, um… You know about what I did?"

"I *saw* what you did," he told her with a knowing expression. "But why did you give so much of your personal energy? Didn't you know better than to expend so much at once?"

"I thought I hadn't taken that much. I haven't done that…uh…very often."

This conversation was beyond weird. Aside from the few magic users she had tried to question, she had never really spoken openly about her abilities. They were something to be hidden. Only to be used in secret, lest she draw the wrong kind of attention to herself. The question remained: was this man's attention the wrong kind or the right kind? She fervently hoped for the latter.

"You must promise me not to attempt such a thing again until you have received the proper training. Anybody could have happened across you, and as you can surmise, this land has not always been used for good. I am attempting to rectify that situation, but I believe it will take time." He shook his head, as if in resignation.

"You're *The Protector*." She realized, as she spoke the words aloud, how strange they must sound, but she was convinced. She blinked, trying to explain herself. "The trees told me you were coming. They call you *The Protector*."

"They do?" His aristocratic brows raised in question, as if he was flattered by the news. "I have not had the good fortune to run across one of your kind in many years. What is it that brought you to these woods tonight?"

His words brought up a number of questions, but she decided to tackle the easiest first. "I was driving through and had to stop when I felt the despair coming from your forest. I've never felt such sorrow and pain coming from a living wildwood. Something bad—really bad—must have happened

19

here. The trees were crying out for help, and it compelled me to stop to find out what was going on."

"You should not take such risks, milady." His dark brows drew together in concern. "As I have said, this land was not always free of threat. I have endeavored to make it safer by ousting any who would try to reclaim this place and turn it to evil once more, but not every place has someone looking out for it as I look out for this one."

"So, you're saying you're one of the good guys?" she challenged, starting to feel a bit stronger and more sure of herself. He didn't seem like such a bad guy. She would not take him completely at his word, but it wouldn't hurt for him to claim to be on the right side of things.

"Forgive me. My name is Marco, and I serve the Light as, I believe, do you." He paused, waiting for her to reply.

Crystal nodded. "I oppose evil, if that's what you mean. Though, I admit, I'm kind of new at this and haven't had a lot of experience in the field, so to speak. My name is Crystal."

"Have you only just come into your power then, Mistress Crystal?"

The way he said her name sent a tingle down her spine. She did her best to ignore it.

"The magic has been with me for a long time, but I haven't really used it until recently. I always thought I was some kind of aberration. I met a shaman a few years ago who finally explained to me that I wasn't alone in my perception of the magic all around me. It was reassuring to finally learn that Others existed, but the shaman couldn't help me learn anything specific about my abilities. He'd never met anybody who could do what I can. I've asked around, very carefully, but have yet to learn of anybody like me, or anyone who might be able to tell me more about my kind of power." She didn't mind admitting to this, even if he was lying to her. There was little he could do with the information, she figured. He might as well know she was a novice with not a whole lot of power that she could use in any way.

"Ah. I begin to understand. As it happens, I have heard

tell of other wood nymphs recently discovered. Perhaps I can put you in touch with one of them. They may be able to help you more."

"What did you call me?" Had she heard him correctly? Some kind of nymph? Weren't those the naked cherubs floating around in Renaissance art? She shook her head. This didn't sound kosher.

"Wood nymphs are earth elementals with a special proclivity for growing things. They spend a lot of time in forests, from what I have heard. I don't think you're a full-blooded nymph, but from what I witnessed outside, you certainly have that kind of power. What do you know of your ancestry?"

This conversation was getting stranger and stranger, but she would play along.

"Nothing," she answered truthfully. "I was raised in foster care. I was orphaned as a baby, and nobody could tell me anything about my parents." The pain of that knowledge had dimmed to a dull ache over the years.

"I am sorry to hear it," he replied, looking apologetic and truly contrite, which she hadn't expected. A little bit of her hardened heart softened toward him. "Though, I have heard there is a way wood nymphs can bring forth their family tree, so to speak. Perhaps one of the others will teach you."

"Are you sure there are others? And are you sure that's what I am?" She wasn't convinced of any of this.

"Yes, to the former, and I am fairly convinced of the latter just by what I witnessed you doing in the woods. Giving of your own energy to the healing of the land is something very few beings would feel compelled to do," he told her. "It demonstrates a degree of open-heartedness toward the earth and its forests that most people do not feel."

She shrugged, shaking her head slightly. "There something…" She grimaced and tried again. "Something isn't right out there. I did what I could, but before I passed out, I got the distinct impression that it wasn't enough. It was just a bandage over an open wound, so to speak. I think there's something wrong. Something buried, perhaps."

Marco sat back, thinking about her words as she continued. Crystal looked confused, seeming to test out the soundness of her theory as she spoke.

"There's something out there that needs to be fixed. The forest will not be happy until it is discovered and nullified."

She scowled but somehow still managed to look beautiful. Marco hadn't responded so strongly to a woman in more years than he could remember. What was it about this frail mortal? True, she had power, but he was an ancient. To him, she was nothing but a child, magically speaking.

"I've been over this land many times since expelling those who had done such evil here. I've never come across anything that would indicate a problem like that which you describe." He shrugged. "Of course, my magic is not tuned to the earth the way yours is. You likely have a much closer bond with the earth and growing things than many other beings. If you say there's something there, I believe you. Now, the question is, will you help me discover what it is, where it is, and how to fix it?"

"I was on my way to a business meeting that I should still try to make tomorrow, if possible, but after that, I'd be happy to help." She shifted, as if uncomfortable.

"What kind of business meeting, if you don't mind my asking?"

"It was a job interview, really." Now, she looked faintly embarrassed, a blush of blood rushing to her cheeks that made him catch his breath.

He would not think of her blood. He *could not* think of her blood. That way lay madness. The blood of certain magical beings was like a drug to his kind. Shifter blood endowed a vampire with certain magical abilities that came from the shifter, though the effect was temporary. Fey blood was said to be so incredibly strong they could drive a vampire mad. The kind of rush he could get from drinking magical blood was like a drug. It would be too easy to get addicted to the power.

Marco had no idea what dryad blood would do to him, though he found himself all too curious. For his own good, he would have to control himself. The last thing he wanted to do was get hooked on her. She was mortal. She would die. They always did.

But he also recognized that he needed her help in this instance. Her connection with the land would go a long way toward fixing whatever it was that she sensed was wrong. The naked truth was that the land had not responded the way he had expected it would. It was taking too long to recover. It hadn't made sense until she had just said what she felt. Now, in light of her information, it made a great deal more sense.

The evil ones had left something behind. Something he hadn't sensed. It would take someone of her skill and ability to pinpoint the problem. The forest had done its own work of bringing her here. Marco would be a fool to let her go before she had shown him what the problem really was. And Marco was nobody's fool.

"You are between jobs then? What is it you do for a living?" He kept his tone polite all the while, the gears in his mind were turning swiftly.

CHAPTER 3

"I work in the hospitality industry. Until recently, I was managing a specialty hotel and conference center, but the place was bought out by a conglomerate, and they wanted their person in charge. I got a nice settlement and severance package, but I really do need to find a new job."

Crystal hated admitting that she was unemployed. She'd held a job ever since she was old enough to work. Having an income meant being free to do as she wished. Money was security to her. Without a steady income, she felt like a failure. A frightened, anxiety-ridden, failure. But she was keeping it together. She employed positive self-talk whenever her mind threatened to spiral down into fear and hopelessness. She had skills. She would find a job suitable to them. She would be independent, and secure. No other outcome was acceptable.

"You know," Marco looked around the large room, his eyes focused on the ornate trim along the ceiling, "I had given some thought to converting this place into a kind of

NIGHT OF THE NYMPH

retreat. It would need a large staff, of course. I wouldn't run such a thing by myself. Perhaps, you would be kind enough to give me some advice." His tone was light, but she got the impression he was working his way toward something. Was he going to offer her a job?

"What sort of advice?" She tried to keep her own tone equally as light.

"Well, for example, if I were to open this place to the guests, what sorts of amenities might they expect or be interested in?" He gestured toward the window, but it was dark out, and there was nothing to be seen. "There are several tennis courts that could be refurbished. There's even an abbreviated golf course. Putting greens. Nine holes, I believe. You've seen some of the forest. I could put some hiking trails within. There's also a small lake adjacent to the formal gardens which are on the other side of the house. There's a rather complex shrubbery maze and an outdoor pavilion that can seat a few hundred people. I believe there used to be outdoor concerts held there, when the place was first built."

Crystal's mind filled with possibilities. She'd had no idea the woodlands surrounded an actual estate. It seemed almost too good to be true that the estate was also empty and looking to be repurposed by its owner. Perhaps this was the hand of Fate, stepping in? Crystal wasn't sure. Marco hadn't exactly made her an offer, though she suspected he might be working his way around to one. What she would do then, she wasn't quite sure.

"I would have to see more of the grounds to give you any solid ideas. Perhaps on my way back, I could stop and see the place during the day," she suggested.

Crystal noted the way he cringed just the tiniest bit. He hid it well, but something she had said had distressed him in some way.

"Did you have a firm offer from this potential employer, or was this just a speculative meeting?" he asked, not quite addressing her suggestion.

"It's just a first interview. They're seeing a few candidates, from what I understand. It's a well-established conference center that needs a new head of development. To be honest, I'm not quite sure my resume is strong enough to be a real contender for that position, but I had to try. It's a field I've always wanted to go into, if given a chance."

She felt as if their discussion had, indeed, taken a turn into a job interview of sorts. If he was really serious about opening this place up to guests, even from the little she'd seen, she would be interested in the position. If he was offering one, that is.

"It's just possible that Fate brought you to my doorstep tonight," Marco said with a charming smile. "The house has been empty since the last occupants were evicted. I've been doing renewal and cleansing of the area for the past year or so. The former occupants were dedicated to evil and had done some terrible things on the grounds. I stepped in, with the help of a number of Others, and put an end to it. Magically, I've been taking care of the place for a long time, trying to put it to rights. Legally, I became the owner of the estate and its lands not too long ago. I've been trying to figure out what to do with it ever since."

"Then, you don't live here yourself?" She had to ask. If he could own a place like this, he must be loaded.

"I reside nearby, but this place was too soaked in evil to be comfortable. I'm rectifying that, little by little, and time, of course, helps. Still, it's not the most comfortable place to be for long periods of time." His grin invited her to agree. "But I think we're at the point now to take the next logical step. I've been looking for caretakers until now, but I think, instead, I should find a way to put this house and its land to good use. The emphasis being, of course, on *good*."

"I don't know how large this house is, but generally, it will take a group of people to run such an endeavor. I can help with the development and planning, if you like, but running the place will take staff." There it was. She had done it. She had put herself forward for the job—if there was one.

Boldness wasn't her usual course of action, but

sometimes, she knew, she had to take a chance and be brave. So far, this man hadn't done anything threatening to her. In fact, he had helped her when she had lost consciousness. And she hadn't forgotten the fact that the trees called him *The Protector*. They trusted in him. They looked to him for protection. That said something very profound.

"This house has twenty-seven bedrooms. Most are comparable to this one, though there are slight variations in size and decor." She caught her breath. This was some kind of mansion, indeed. "There's a music room, a ballroom, an art studio, a chapel, the usual breakfast and dining rooms, along with a very large kitchen. And the indoor pool is adjacent to the house. It's very luxurious by any century's standards. I believe most of the construction was completed in the early 1900s. The original owner was one of the early transportation tycoons. I believe he dabbled in railroads." Marco stood abruptly. "If you're feeling up to it, perhaps I can show you around the house a bit. There is a bathroom through that door, if you wish to freshen up. I will leave you for now. If you wish for a tour, just meet me at the bottom of the stairs when you are ready. I will be making calls in the front room, but I will hear you when you come down."

Crystal was surprised by the quick change in mood, but she felt silly lounging around in bed during what had turned into, essentially, a job interview. Perhaps he had come to the same realization.

"I'll meet you down there in a few minutes. Thank you for everything." She met his dark gaze and felt the impact all the way down to her toes. Her tummy fluttered with awareness, and her blood heated in her veins. The man was potent.

He swept from the room, and suddenly, it felt empty. He had such a big presence that he had filled the space with it, and she only just realized how large and empty the place was when he left.

Crystal got out of bed, moving slowly, at first. She was still a little weak from her expenditure of energy, but she was feeling stronger every moment. She usually bounced back pretty easily, which was why she been able to hide her abilities so well. Even when she'd been learning and had made miscalculations, like the one she'd made tonight.

She went into the bathroom, finding it every bit as luxurious as the bedroom. Plaster molding on the ceilings, period art on the walls, and fixtures from the early twentieth century. The whole place was just lovely, and everything worked as it should. Somebody had taken very good care of the place. Either the former owners or, perhaps, the mysterious Marco had been renovating with an eye toward authenticity.

Crystal freshened up, looked at herself in the mirror, and realized she was feeling much better. She straightened her clothing and went out to meet her Fate.

Master Marco decided he needed more information before he went any further with the gorgeous creature currently moving around upstairs. He'd met someone with similar powers, but he hadn't wanted to mention Maria without her permission. He had to contact the woman, who was now mated to a werewolf Alpha, and discuss his next move. In all likelihood, Crystal was somehow related to Maria, and he shouldn't wait to alert the lady, for whom he had the greatest respect.

Maria and her new mate had come to the rescue of two werebears who had been kidnapped and used in a sinister ceremony in the outdoor pavilion. Followers of the Destroyer had been trying to drain the considerable magical power of a pair of werebears—husband and wife—to fuel some evil plan. Maria and her mate, Jesse Moore, who led a paramilitary organization of shifters known as the Wraiths, had arrived to free the werebears. Marco had intercepted them and added his own considerable power to their attack, managing to free the mansion of its evil inhabitants once and for all. Or so he hoped.

He would do his best to prevent the place from falling into the wrong hands again. Part of his plan might just include Crystal, if he could convince her to stay.

He hadn't meant to offer her a job when the evening began. He'd wanted to help her and figure out why she'd been in the woods. But as he spoke with her, he'd become hopelessly intrigued. She fascinated him on a deep level he hadn't expected.

Not looking too closely at his own motivations, he placed the call. He would call Jesse and relay through the werewolf. Approaching an Alpha's mate directly wasn't considered tactful, and Marco was nothing if not a man of surpassing tact.

"Jesse, my friend, it has been too long. How are you doing?" Marco asked when the werewolf picked up the call.

"Doing well. How are things with you, Master Marco?" came the guarded reply. Marco knew the werewolf was still a little uncomfortable with bloodletters, though they had worked together quite well during the action in the pavilion.

"Please, call me Marco. So few do, these days. I am calling to get the advice of your lady, if she is available. Someone very much like her has shown up on the grounds of the mansion and claims the trees called to her as she was driving, and she felt compelled to stop." Marco knew he'd have to give Jesse the briefing first. Alpha wolves were very protective of their mates, and Jesse would want to know all the details before he passed the call on to his mate. "I observed her and saw her raw power as she gave it to the earth in an effort to heal it. She overdid it, I'm afraid, and fell unconscious. I brought her back to the mansion, and I've just had a very interesting discussion with the lady. She doesn't know what she is and was raised in foster care, so she does not know her ancestry. I believe she is at least part dryad, which is why I thought I should probably speak to your mate."

"I see." Jesse's tone was only slightly suspicious, but he seemed satisfied with the explanation. "Let me get Maria. I'm not sure if you knew this, but she has been searching for other members of her extended family. It's just possible that your guest is one of them, which could prove helpful since the rest have been much harder to track than anticipated."

Now, *that* was interesting. Marco knew a little bit more about Jesse and his brother, Jason—two very strong Alphas who managed to share space within the same Pack—and their mates. Their ladies were cousins. Both had dryad ancestry, from what Marco had been able to learn. It was just possible that the lady Marco had left upstairs was somehow related to them.

"Hi." Maria's bright voice came on the line. Marco noted that Jesse did not leave the call. "Sorry. I was just tending to one of the pet dogs that ate something it shouldn't have," she explained. Marco knew that Maria was a veterinarian by trade and that she usually specialized in exotic animals and their rehabilitation. Maria had a very big heart. Marco had seen that firsthand when she'd visited this estate, helping to free the werebears and defeat the enemy.

"It is good to speak with you again, Maria. I have a guest at the mansion," he told her, launching into the story about how he'd discovered Crystal and what she'd been doing. Maria listened, gasping a few times as he described what he'd observed.

"Oh, my goodness," she finally said when he'd completed his recitation of the facts. "I think she might be one of the ones we've been looking for." Excitement colored her tone. "I have to call Sally and see if she has any more information. Is Crystal going to stay with you?"

"I'm not sure. I am considering offering her the job of developing the mansion and grounds with an eye toward making it a resort for those trusted souls among us who need a place to get away. I wasn't certain what to do with the place, but that seems a reasonable use. Plus, Crystal seems convinced that something evil was left here, on the grounds, though I sense nothing. I'd like her help in discovering it, if it is really there. I want all traces of evil eliminated from this place before I go any further." Marco thought through what he'd said and clarified. "Crystal said she was on her way to a job interview when she was driving past, and I got the impression that she needs employment somewhat urgently. If employing her will make her more likely to stay, then I will offer it."

"Please, Marco. Please try to keep her there, short of kidnapping her." Maria chuckled, even though her words were urgent. "Would it be possible to set up a video call with her? I know it's getting late, and she must be tired, so maybe we can schedule it for tomorrow or the next day? I'd like a chance to meet her and talk with her," Maria said. "I'll get Sally in on it too."

"I will do my best," Marco told her. "Though, I will not keep her here against her will, and I am not available during the daylight hours. I will, however, ask some of my friends in the local shifter population to keep her company, if she agrees to stay. I have employed them to refurbish the house and grounds, and there are several ladies who would make good companions among the local wolf Pack."

"I can talk to their Alpha, if you need me to," Jesse volunteered. "This is important to my mate and to my brother's mate. It's family," Jesse said with a special emphasis on that last word. Marco knew that Pack was all important among werewolves.

"Thank you, Jesse. I will let you know if that becomes necessary, but I do have a rather good relationship with the Pack. We've been neighbors for a while." He didn't go into the close bond he had with the Pack. Jesse didn't really need to know that he'd come to a deep understanding with his neighbors in recent months. They worked together to keep this area clear of evil.

"I'll call Sally," Maria said decisively. "Then I'll get back to you. May I text you? And maybe you can text me back the moment you know if she'll stay or not?"

"I would be glad to do so," Marco agreed readily, rattling off his cell number. He might be an ancient vampire, but the modern age had some true conveniences that he'd adopted readily. A moment later, his phone dinged, and he looked to find that Maria had sent him a smiley face. Now, he had her number as she had his. "Got it," he reported. "I'll let you know what her plans are, once she's made them."

CHAPTER 4

Marco was aware of every movement Crystal made in the house. His hearing and other senses were finely tuned, and he knew that she was moving about. Time to end the call.

"She's coming down the stairs. I will be in touch," Marco told Maria.

"Thank you so much," Maria replied, and Marco felt the earnestness of her words. He was glad now that he'd reached out. Maria and Jesse had good souls, and Marco was happy to do them a good turn.

He ended the call a moment later after exchanging goodbyes with the couple and went out into the hall. Crystal was descending the stairs, and she took his breath away. Her golden-brown hair fell in waves, and her green eyes shone like her namesake in the dancing incandescent light of the chandelier. She had an unconscious grace that woke something deep within him that had lain dormant for centuries.

Surprised by his own reactions, he didn't question them

too much. This was no time for introspection. He had to convince this lady to stay. His allies had asked him to do so, and so, he would try.

"This foyer is magnificent," Crystal said as she arrived at the bottom step. Her head was craned upward to take in the large crystal chandelier that twinkled in the artificial light.

"I have been restoring the house to its original grandeur," he replied. "There are some local craftspeople that have been working on the place for me, but to be honest, I've been leaving them to their own devices more often than not during the day, as I have other business interests to see to. I could really use someone to supervise the renovations each day while I am occupied elsewhere."

No time like the present to begin to convince her to stay. He only had a short window of opportunity. He had to act fast.

"I don't suppose you would consider taking on that task?" he asked, point blank. "You did say you had management experience."

She paused, her head tilted to one side. "I do, but..." She shook her head slowly. "This is all very fast. You don't know much about me, and I really don't know what I've fallen into here."

"Are you a believer in Fate, Crystal?" he asked, his voice dropping low as he looked deep into her crystal green eyes.

She nodded, just once. "I suppose so. And you're going to say that it was Fate that brought me here today." She sounded knowing, and he had to admire her courage. Of course, she didn't know what he was. Or, at least, she hadn't figured it out yet. He wondered how long he could keep her in the dark—or if he should.

"I believe that the hand of Fate had something to do with it, yes. But as to what you believe, that is up to you. The fact is, I need someone to oversee this place, and you have the relevant experience. You also seem to think that there is something on the grounds that needs attention. I have not or, possibly, cannot sense it," he admitted "If there is a problem,

I believe you are the only one who can tell me what and where it is, and possibly, you will be a large part of the solution, if you are willing to help. To solve this problem, you need to be here. You have also told me that you are in search of a job. I just happen to have a job open for which you are qualified. Ergo, this all fits nicely together. If you want the job, it is yours on a trial basis. And I mean that both ways. I fully expect you will be trying this out to see if it works for you. If it works for both parties, then I say Fate definitely had a hand in getting you here and bringing us together."

"Maybe so." She still didn't look convinced, but she was listening.

"Let me show you around, and perhaps you can get a better feel for the place." He had to be a better salesman. He had to sell her on the idea of working for him and staying here.

To that end, he took her through the rooms that had been renovated first. The ballroom was a wonder of twinkling light when he switched on the main fixture—another antique chandelier that glittered with crystal drops. He heard her breath catch in her throat as she beheld the room that was straight out of another era.

"This is gorgeous," she breathed, walking to the center of the room and looking up at the shining fixture.

He couldn't help but notice the long, elegant line of her throat and the pulse that invited him to sink his teeth in and drink. But no. Not now. Not yet. Perhaps, not ever. Crystal was someone special, and not just to him, but to the Wraiths' Alpha and his mate and the Alpha of their home Pack and his mate as well. There were a lot of high-powered Others who cared what happened to this woman, though she didn't realize it yet. Marco would have to tread carefully.

He was tempted to sweep her into his arms and whirl her around the empty ballroom in a breath-stealing waltz, but now was not the time. He had to play it cool, though it was difficult with the things she was awakening with him. Things that had not been awakened in too long to remember.

"This room is done. It didn't need much work physically, though we did upgrade all the electrical and put in LED lights to add to the twinkling effect. If you look closely at the plaster, you can see them here and there. Besides restoring the place to its original grandeur, I've also planned to make it energy efficient and self-sustaining. There is a large array of solar panels on the roof and batteries in the basement. The physical plant was the first thing we upgraded, and now we're going room by room to upgrade all the fixtures." He paused, ushering her into a gallery off the ballroom that had doors to the outdoor esplanade. "We're restoring the original fixtures, where they still exist, by upgrading the wiring in them to modern standards while keeping the vintage look. Where the original fixtures were removed, we're searching for period replacements online and in antique shops. I have someone tasked to do just that, and she's been remarkably successful in finding what we need."

"Is she an interior decorator?" Crystal looked interested now. Good. Maybe she was coming around.

"She wants to be. She is the eldest daughter of one of the local werewolf couples and is studying design in college. I gave her a job for the summer, and she's surpassed all my expectations," Marco admitted. He had to be honest about the magical component of the people he employed, at least in a general way. Crystal had magic of her own, and she needed to know that she'd be working with Others if she took this job.

"Werewolves?" she fairly squeaked.

"Have you never dealt with shifters before?" Marco asked as he opened one of the many glass doors that led out onto the esplanade.

Crystal shook her head vigorously. "I've heard they exist. The shaman I told you about mentioned it to me when he first told me about the magical world. He thought I might have shifter blood, but I never believed it." She stepped out into the night, and once again, she paused to look up at the starry sky, and he had thoughts about the beating pulse at her neck that he must not act upon.

"There is a wolf Pack nearby that now counts this estate as part of its territory, though it is not owned by them. I give them free run of the forest and grounds. At least, for now. If I end up with human tenants—which I don't really foresee as probable—I'd have to ask them to be more discreet, but for now, they help keep the place free of intruders," Marco said, realizing only then that it was odd that Crystal had not encountered one of the wolf patrols. Perhaps that was more evidence of the hand of Fate in play. "In fact, most of the craftspeople who are doing the work on the place are members of the Pack. There are a few other shifter species working on certain parts of the renovation, but everyone I've employed to work here is magical in some way. The vast majority are shifters, though I do have another mage who comes in, as needed, to help with casting out the evil that has seeped into some of the structures from the former owners."

"Nobody has been working on the forest?" she asked in a low voice as the night air surrounded them.

"I planted rowans and oaks to help, but as I told you, I didn't sense anything else I needed to address," he told her. "If there is something that lingers, we need to oust it and set the earth to rights, as well as the trees." He spoke the words like the vow they were. He had promised to cleanse this place of the evil that had been done here and protect it with his immortal life. It was a sacred duty.

"I noticed the young oak and rowan saplings, but they are overwhelmed by the problem," she told him as they walked slowly along the wide esplanade.

The night was deep and turning toward morning, but she didn't seem tired, though she still had that residual weakness from her earlier power output. He supposed she would crash later, but that was all to the good, as far as he was concerned. She would sleep part of the day away, at least, and miss that job interview. It wouldn't matter, though. She would have a job with him and stay here, just as the Alpha couple had asked. And…as Marco himself desired.

"Then, I must beg your help in discovering what the problem truly is and rectifying it," Marco pressed, then relented. "If you look down this main path, you can just see the roof of the outdoor pavilion. I've been doing a lot of work to cleanse that building, because that's where the former owners were doing the worst of their blood rites."

"Blood magic?" She looked aghast, as well she should.

"Yes, I'm sorry to say. They were some of the worst of the worst. Followers of Elspeth, Destroyer of Innocents. They sought to return their mistress from her imprisonment in the farthest realms. We stopped them, but I'm sure there are other groups out there striving toward the same goal, if they haven't achieved it already. My task, as I see it, is to ensure that this place is never used for evil again. At least not while I still exist."

"A noble calling," she agreed, nodding as she looked out over the dark garden toward the structure just visible in the distance. "These grounds are really extensive. It's a lot bigger than I'd have guessed." She kept looking, as if she could see well in the dark. He wondered if that was the case. "Is that the maze? Off there, to the left?"

"Indeed, it is," he confirmed. "You see well in the dark," he observed, wondering if she would admit to her ability.

She shrugged. "It's a side effect of my power, I think. I've always been able to see things in the dark that others could not. I learned to hide the ability. I wanted to fit in, not stand out, in the foster homes I lived in."

"That must have been tough," Marco commiserated in a low, soothing tone. He sensed her sadness but didn't want to pry into her past. Not unless she invited him in. He would listen to whatever she wanted to tell him, but he had no right to pry.

She shrugged. "It was okay. I survived and grew up and found my independence liberating." He sensed the hurt under her bright words but didn't miss the bravery behind them either.

It was time for a topic change. He had to get her to agree

to stay, then he would get to know her better, and perhaps later, he'd be more deserving of her confidences.

"I've had some of the local lads refurbishing the esplanade. Many of the stones had been pushed up over the years, making for uneven paving and dangerous walking. Just that last section still needs attention." He pointed to an area that was roped off with yellow caution tape at the far end of the area, then turned to reenter the mansion at another of the many glass doors that led from the long gallery. "Now, let me show you some of the indoor areas where work is ongoing."

They spent the next hour walking slowly through the rooms where construction was happening or about to start. He outlined his plans and saw her eyes light up, room after room. It was as if she could see it the way he could—when it was all restored and beautiful again.

She was beautiful. The most beautiful thing he had seen in many a century.

But that was not a good thing to be thinking about. Not now. Possibly, not ever.

"So," he turned on her as they made their way up the grand staircase about an hour before dawn, "will you stay? I will pay you double your last salary, and there are other benefits. You can talk to Martine tomorrow. She has all the details. She runs HR for me and works out of the downstairs office from about noon until after dinner. I'll tell her you're a new hire, and she'll take care of the rest, shall I?"

"I suppose..." Crystal looked around the hallway and changed direction to face the room he'd put her in before. She was already getting acclimated to the mansion, which was a good sign. "I'm so tired. I'll never make it to that interview tomorrow. I'll call them in the morning and let them know, but I'm inclined to take you up on your offer. On a trial basis, as you mentioned. I'd like to see the place in the daylight before I commit fully."

"Certainly," he said, keeping his glee carefully to himself as he escorted her back to her room. "This room is yours for as long as you need it. Consider it a perk of employment. The house is usually left open at night because I come over and check things after I'm done with my other business of the day, but we can change that since you'll be in residence. I can have security in the house, as well as the patrols that are already working outside, if that will make you feel safer. The cooking staff arrives..." He made a show of checking his watch. "Actually, they arrive right about now and start on bread and breakfast for the construction crews. Everybody eats in the large dining room. Three meals a day are part of the compensation, and the kitchen is staffed until they're done cleaning up after dinner, so you won't be alone here most of the time. I usually swing by after dinner to catch up on the day's progress. We can meet tomorrow at that time and talk over any concerns or ideas you may have. Is that acceptable?"

They were at the door to what had become *her* room, so he paused. He would not go inside with her. Not now. Not again. If he entered her room again tonight, he would not be able to hold back the desire that was awakening within him, and the last thing he wanted to do now was scare her off.

CHAPTER 5

Marco left her at the door to her room, waiting outside while she opened the door and entered. She muttered a quick goodnight and closed the door with him still standing there. It felt awkward, but she didn't know what else to do. She was attracted to him. *Very* attracted to him. But they'd only just met. She couldn't act on any of the impulses coursing through her veins. Not without violating her own, somewhat old-fashioned, rules of propriety.

She closed the door and leaned back against it for a moment, savoring all that had just happened. She'd spent more than an hour with the most intriguing man she'd ever met. He'd offered her a job, and she'd accepted it—on a trial basis. She had never been so impulsive before, and she hoped she didn't live to regret it, but everything about the evening had a surreal edge to it—from the moment she'd felt compelled to stop her car and enter the woods to this moment, standing here, thinking about Marco.

Marco. A strong name for a compelling man. His

personality was one of the strongest and most masculine she had ever encountered. She liked the way his strength rubbed up against her independence, not striking sparks, exactly, but definitely creating an awareness that they could both be forces to be reckoned with. Yes, indeed, she liked that a lot.

She was a woman who felt comfortable managing a staff of hundreds and overseeing a budget in the millions. Some of the men she'd encountered in her career had chosen to see her decisiveness as bitchiness, or even more unflattering terms. She'd long ago decided those men were weak, and if she was ever going to partner up with a guy, he'd have to be as strong of character as she was. A weak man would never do for a woman like her. She wanted a lover she could respect and admire, who found her stronger qualities attractive rather than intimidating.

So far, she hadn't found a guy like that. She'd kissed more than her share of frogs but had never found her prince.

Crystal stood up straight and looked at the lock on the doorknob for just a minute. She should lock it. She was alone in a big empty house. Or, if there were others in the house, she certainly didn't know them…except for Marco. But he wouldn't be here during the day. He'd already told her that. He had work elsewhere and lived someplace else as well. He only checked in here at the mansion at night, after he'd finished his other work for the day.

With a decisive snick, she turned the lock and went into the room. Much to her surprise, she found her overnight bag and pocketbook lying on the bed with a folded piece of paper on top. She reached out to look at the note.

Marco asked me to find your vehicle and park it in the employee lot. I also brought up your stuff in case you needed anything. I'll be in the kitchen when you wake up. No rush.

It was signed simply, *Marci*.

Marco had asked this unknown woman to rescue Crystal's car? Had the man thought of everything? Not that she wasn't grateful. It was nice to have her own things, but she also felt a little odd about someone else driving her car and bringing her belongings up here. She would be intrigued to meet Marci, but first, Crystal needed sleep. The tour and talk had kept her going, but she'd had a long night. She'd planned to spend the night at a hotel and then be fresh for the interview in the afternoon, but her plans had been derailed.

She'd have to remember to call the interviewer tomorrow as soon as she woke, to explain that she wouldn't be able to make the interview after all. She cringed, knowing it was rude, but it was only a first interview, and she knew she was just one of many contenders for the position. And not even a strong contender, at that.

Shrugging and too tired to worry that Marci might have gone through her stuff, Crystal went to her overnight bag and got out her pajamas. Might as well sleep comfortably, even though most of the night was already gone. She planned to wake mid-morning to take stock of her situation. Maybe she'd be more clear-headed then.

Crystal woke at noon, much later than she'd planned, but she felt much better. She'd been running on empty last night after that unplanned expenditure of magical energy. She hadn't really felt its full effect, because once she woke in the guest room, she'd been faced with one startling thing after another.

Crystal gathered her clothing—a suit she had planned to wear on the interview she had decided to cancel late last night by sending them email via her phone—and went into the attached bathroom, showering quickly and getting ready for what remained of her day. Her tummy started to rumble, and she realized she was starving just about the time she was finishing doing her hair. She left the room, heading down that grand staircase toward the kitchen Marco had showed her the night before.

"Um…Marci?" Crystal asked, pausing in the large doorway to the enormous kitchen. A young woman was stirring something at the stove but turned when Crystal arrived. She was smiling.

"You must be Crystal," the woman said, putting down the big spoon and striding forward. The center island worktable was between them with an array of empty serving dishes on it. "I'm just about to start dishing up lunch if you're hungry."

Crystal became aware of the scent of roast and something savory. It smelled delicious, and her stomach rumbled again so loudly that Marci must have heard it. She laughed outright, and Crystal blushed in embarrassment.

"Of course, you're hungry," Marci said, not waiting for a verbal reply. "Just go on through to the dining room. My helpers will be back any minute, and we'll bring everything out. Don't be concerned by the crowd. The work crews will be descending on the dining room over the next half hour, but they've all had their shots, and Marcus briefed us on who you are and your new role. They'll be curious but will mind their manners. Oh, and Martine needs to talk to you. She'll be in the dining room too. Tall, blonde, dressed sort of like you. Everybody else will be in working clothes, so she should be easy to spot."

Buoyed by Marci's pleasantness, Crystal walked toward the door to the dining room as a small group of teens and young adults trooped into the kitchen from the other end. They must be Marci's helpers. Crystal nodded and said hello to them on her way out, going into the dining room as Marci had directed. It was empty, but that didn't last long.

An elegant blonde in burgundy slacks and a cream silk blouse strode in with all the confidence in the world. She was gorgeous. Lustrous pearls gleamed around her neck, and she was tall and absolutely stunning.

"Hi," she said, smiling dazzlingly at Crystal. "I'm Martine. And you must be Crystal." She held out her hand for a shake as she came closer, and Crystal accepted the gesture absently.

As their hands touched, Crystal felt a little tingle of magic pass between them, and Martine tilted her head to the side, as if intrigued. Crystal suddenly remembered what Marco had told her. The wolf Pack. Many of the local werewolves worked for Marco, and the way Martine had just tilted her head… She was probably a werewolf, but Crystal didn't feel fear. Rather, she was intrigued. Martine looked equally intrigued, if Crystal was any judge.

"Marco said you had magic, but he also warned us not to talk too much about it, in case it makes you uncomfortable," Martine went on. "Does it make you uncomfortable to talk about magic?"

The wide-eyed innocent look seemed just a little overdone, but Crystal decided to give the other woman the benefit of the doubt.

"I'm not accustomed to talking about it. I don't really run in those kind of circles. I was raised without magic and only learned about what I could do when it started manifesting. At first, I thought I was going crazy. Until I happened to meet a Cherokee shaman who told me a few things and set me straight," Crystal revealed.

Martine shook her head. "That had to be tough. Well, if there's anything you want to know, Marco told me to give you the full brief. Just ask me, though I should warn you, most shifters don't respond well to direct questioning about their animals or their magic. We have a special situation here with Marco. We are allies, which is something that hasn't happened between the various races of Others in centuries. But Marco is a good guy, and we're happy to help him. Plus, the working conditions here are great. He gives us the run of the place, and it's really nice to see it coming back to life after the terrible things that have been done here. We're washing all that away." She nodded, a satisfied look on her face. "Lunch will be served in a few minutes. Will you sit with me?"

"Of course. Thanks for the invitation." Crystal allowed Martine to lead the way toward a smaller table at the side of the room.

The dining room was huge. There was a grand central table with many chairs, but also, smaller tables had been placed around the periphery of the room. The wall nearest the kitchen entrance was set as a buffet, and even as they walked toward the smaller table, the kitchen crew began bringing out platters to put on the buffet.

"We'll just let them get set up," Martine said, taking her seat and nodding toward the bustling kitchen staff. "We can talk business while we wait. Marco told me that you had accepted the position on a trial basis." Again, her head tilted to the side in a somewhat canine way, as if puzzled by the idea. "I've been instructed to explain the benefits package and the terms of employment. It's all very standard, since we do live in the mortal world and have to adhere to human labor laws and the like. The thing is, we also have this other awareness, if that's what you want to call it. We're all magical folk here. Most of the employees are shifters. Many are members of my own Pack. There are a few outliers, of course. Different kinds of shifters and a few specialty mages Marco brought in to help with the cleansing of the buildings. A lot of evil had seeped into the very walls, but it's almost all gone now."

Crystal kept silent. She wasn't really sure how to respond to any of this. It certainly wasn't like any other job interview or briefing she had ever had before. But she had to admit she was very curious about what other kinds of shifters there might be in the world and working on this estate. Of course, Martine had warned her that shifters weren't really amenable to being asked about their wild sides. The shaman she had met years ago had warned her of the same.

Seeing as Martine was the first shapeshifter Crystal had ever met, to her knowledge, she wasn't about to be purposely rude during their first conversation. Even if Martine had said Crystal could ask her anything, Crystal was going to save that option for when something came up that really mattered. Just being nosy about what kind of animals might share souls with the people that worked here wasn't really important enough to Crystal's way of thinking. Everybody deserved a little bit of privacy, and Crystal wasn't eager to pry just to satisfy her own curiosity.

"Marco says you're a specialist in earth magic. Frankly, I'm glad you're here, if that's the case. We've all been sensing something not quite right out in the forest, but we can't pinpoint what it is. Maybe you'll have better luck." Martine looked both friendly and hopeful.

"I can tell you right now that there definitely is something wrong out there. Something hidden. Something…buried? Possibly?" Crystal shook her head. "I'd like to have a closer look outside, if that's possible."

"Yes," Martine agreed. "Marco asked me to give you a guided tour of the grounds and fill you in on what we've done so far and what remains to be accomplished. He has a master plan for the renovation and restoration of just about every inch of this property. He's had a lot of time to think about it. He brought us in as soon as he secured the title to the property, and we've been working hard ever since." Martine stood, looking over at the rapidly filling buffet as a group of men walked in. "We better get our food before everyone else gets here. I had hoped you might be up to the tour after lunch. Does that sound good?"

"Sounds like a plan."

Crystal followed the tall woman toward the buffet, noting the easy camaraderie she had with everyone present. She introduced Crystal to a few people as they filled their plates with a truly outstanding selection of food. Crystal would have to remember to compliment Marci later.

CHAPTER 6

As it turned out, they didn't go straight to the tour right after lunch. They stopped off in the front office so Martine could go over the traditional employee benefits package with Crystal. There was an open-ended contract for her to sign that included a nondisclosure agreement. It was all pretty standard, except for the fact that it was stipulated that they were both on a trial basis.

"Marco asked me to add that clause into the contract especially for you," Martine said with a grin. "He seemed incredibly amused about it. I haven't seen him smile so broadly...probably ever. I think it's good for him to have somebody around who doesn't ask *how high* when he says *jump*." She chuckled. "Of course, my Pack mates will never admit to it, but we're all a little afraid of him. Not that he's a tyrant or anything. He's just really powerful, even compared to our Alpha. A lot of us know about what he did here when the big battle between good and evil happened out in the pavilion. We didn't get involved until later, at the request of our leadership. Some of them had fought alongside Marco during the purge of this estate and vouched for him. We'd always been aware he was nearby, but we all kept our distance from each other in the old days. Things have certainly changed. I never thought we'd be allies with him, much less working together."

"I didn't realize..." Crystal wasn't sure how to phrase her thoughts. She tried again. "I mean, I knew he was wealthy and probably powerful, but I didn't realize just how powerful." Her voice dropped to a whisper. "Is it safe?"

Martine held up a hand and smiled. "He's behaved honorably with us ever since we started working together. Our Pack has kept track of him and his business dealings over the years. There was nothing questionable in his past actions, and what he did on this estate proved his allegiances beyond a shadow of a doubt. He's definitely one of the good guys, but you'll get to see that for yourself, I think. He asked especially if you would stick around after dinner to work with him on some of the magical aspects of your new position. He wants to be in on whatever you discover and help plan how to neutralize it. Nothing happens on this property that he doesn't have a hand in. I hope that's okay."

"Since I'm pretty much a novice when it comes to using my abilities, I don't mind at all. And to be honest, I don't really sleep much normally. Sleeping until noon was very out of character for me, and I don't mind staying up tonight." Crystal remembered something Marco had told her last night. "Is it true that most of you work a later shift than usual?"

"Yes, most of the crews have leveled off now that the really heavy lifting is mostly over. Back when this project first started, we had an early morning crew that would work from before dawn until midafternoon, then the regular crew that would start around noon, overlapping with the tail end of the morning shift, and go until after dinner. The morning crews usually worked with a mage, cleansing the area they worked in of evil, as they went along. Now that most of the buildings have been purified, we've cut back on that early shift, though occasionally, they might come in for a special project. Since most of us like to roam around at night, the later shift works better for us. And we also get to see Marco when he comes over after dark and makes sure we're still working to plan."

"I guess I'll stay on that schedule as well. It sounds like Marco wants to be in on whatever I find out in the forest, and I don't mind the dark."

"That's probably a very good thing, considering who you're working for," Martine said, a speculative expression on her face. Crystal wasn't exactly sure what the other woman meant, but Martine got up from behind her desk and ushered Crystal out of the room before she could comment further.

They toured every inch of the grounds, excluding the acres of forest. Neither woman had the right footwear to be trekking through the trees. But even so, the tour took the rest of the day. Crystal got to see the outdoor pavilion, the many outbuildings, every inch of the main house that she hadn't seen the night before, and the ongoing work on the esplanade.

A crew of handsome, bare-chested men were digging on one end of the esplanade, taking up old stones and relaying the groundwork before replacing them. Making them level and even. Some of the old stones were cracked and needed complete replacement.

There was a stonemason working off to one side, making stones to fit. His name was Eugene, and he explained that they had matched the original stone, tracing it to a nearby quarry, and he was able to replace the originals in such a way that they would never be noticed. He pointed out examples of stones he had already cut and that had already been put back in place by the work crew, and Crystal marveled at the craftsmanship.

It was clear to her that no expense of time or materials was being spared in the reconstruction of this beautiful estate. Even though there was a lot more work to do, she could already see how lovely the place must've been in its heyday. And it would be again. Marco, apparently, wanted to restore it to its full grandeur.

As she toured the grounds with Martine, Crystal became more at home with every step. It was an odd thought, for a girl who had never really had a place to call home. She had been moved around to various foster homes during her youth and, as an adult, had moved to wherever she needed to be for work. She had a small apartment and a few belongings that could be packed up and moved with relative ease.

Crystal had already been contemplating moving to wherever her new employment turned out to be. If she stayed here, this could be it. More and more, she wanted this to work out. She sensed no ill will from the buildings or the people. The only problem was the forest and its continued pleas for help.

The urgency of its tone had gone down several notches. Trees were nothing if not patient. Now that she was here, they would wait for her to figure out the problem and address it. Their cries had been enough to make her pull off the road, stop her car, and venture out into the dark forest the night before. Seldom had she ever heard anything like it. The only thing she could figure was that they sensed her power and made that almighty racket in order to make her stop and listen. Now that they had, the alarm had toned down considerably.

She was more than grateful. The cries had been almost painful to hear. Compelling. They had literally stopped her in her tracks. As Crystal and Martine returned to the office in the mansion, one thing was clear.

"If I'm going to take on this job, then I'm going to need a pair of sneakers," Crystal muttered.

Martine laughed out loud as she sat behind her desk. The room was large, and there was another desk on the other side of the space. Martine gestured towards it.

"If you're going to take on this job," Martine echoed Crystal's words, "then you can have that desk. Or, if you'd rather have a private office, just pick out one of the other rooms, and we'll set it up for you."

Crystal walked over to the other desk and sat behind it.

She looked at it, checked out how far the chair tilted back and if it was comfortable, then looked around. She could live with this.

"It would probably be easier to work alongside you for the beginning, at least," Crystal thought aloud. "I'm sure there's a lot I still need to learn about this place and the people. As long as you don't mind having an office mate, I think it would be nice to have the company."

"All right then, neighbor." Martine smiled broadly. "Looks like we'll share this space for a while, at least. I won't take offense if you change your mind later. I should warn you that some of the work crews do come through here to discuss HR matters from time to time. Wolf Packs tend to like togetherness. We like to be around one another and check on our Pack mates. If it gets too annoying for you, I will totally understand."

"I don't see a problem," Crystal told her honestly. "I was a foster kid. I learned early how to get along with all sorts of people. If I hadn't, I would've been miserable. And, honestly, I'm very intrigued to meet more of your people. I've never been able to discuss my abilities openly with anyone, so it's kind of cool."

Martine's expression was amused then turned serious. "If you meant what you said about needing a pair of sneakers, I should mention the storeroom by the kitchen entrance is full of clothing. When we shift, we can't bring our clothes with us into the shift, and since public nakedness is frowned upon in the human world, we've learned to have stashes of clothing in certain places. We also have locker rooms—which I showed you. When someone wants to run in his or her fur, they can disrobe in the locker room and leave their stuff there while they go out the back entrance to run around. But if someone comes here in wolf form and then needs to be human, we have spares in that storeroom. I'm sure there's something there you can use, including sneakers. Marco has been very generous in providing a nice selection of new things there for us. I think he has investments in a few different clothing manufacturers. There's an entire wall of shoe boxes to choose from in all sorts of sizes. I'm sorry I didn't realize it before, or I would've taken you inside and gotten you a pair of more comfortable shoes before our tour."

"Oh, that's all right," Crystal told the other woman. "My flats were fine for the walking we did, but I was thinking more about trekking into the forest. I still need to find out what's going on out there, and these shoes aren't quite right for that kind of terrain." She held up her foot and showed the sensible black flat with the gold buckle. Fine for indoor or paved walking, it wouldn't hold up to hiking in a forest—as she'd learned the night before on her first trek into the woods.

"There are boots in the storeroom as well. Maybe look for a pair of hiking boots? I'm sure if there's nothing there now, we can get it delivered by tomorrow. Why not go take a look, and if we need to order in, we can do that before quitting time," Martine suggested

"Okay," Crystal said, rising. "If you're sure."

Martine rose as well, but Crystal gestured for her to relax. "I can find it. You've given me more than enough of your time, and I thank you for the tour, but I need to start going around on my own and making sure I know where things are. If I have to, I'll leave a trail of breadcrumbs," she joked, and Martine laughed, sitting back down.

"Just yell if you need help. Somebody will hear and come get you," Martine told her. "We all have really good hearing, in case you didn't realize."

"Ah, that explains a few things," Crystal said as she neared the door. She'd have to remember to watch her muttering when around shifters. They could probably hear everything.

Crystal found her way to the storeroom and opened the door. She was amazed at the array of clothing inside. Martine hadn't been kidding when she said there was an entire wall of shoeboxes. What she hadn't mentioned was that the wall was at least twenty feet long. It looked like the stock of an entire shoe store.

As she looked closer, she realized that everything was organized by size. Crystal found her size and then looked through the boxes. Most had a small image of what was inside, and the shoes were mostly sneakers, hiking boots, or other casual styles meant for comfort. She settled on one pair of sneakers and one set of hiking boots, placing them aside.

If she was going to go into the forest, she needed the equipment, and she didn't want to wait until she had arranged to have her own belongings packed up and shipped to this location. The trees were being patient so far, but she didn't want to make them wait too much longer. Crystal would gladly repay Marco for the shoes, and the clothing she planned to take after seeing the offerings. The fact was she needed the items, and they were here. Convenient. Necessary.

Moving to the racks of clothing, Crystal picked out a pair of black yoga pants, and a loose dark green T-shirt. Two pairs of socks, some underwear still in the package, a lightweight dark-gray hoodie, and she was all set. Everything was brand-new, still with the tags on.

She took her finds up to her room, just dropping them off for later. She was planning to stay in her work clothes until after dinner, then change when she went out into the forest to take a closer look at what was going on with the trees. She found, when she entered the room, that someone had been in to make the bed and tidy up. There was even a chocolate mint treat on her pillow.

Crystal would have to find out who the housekeepers were and thank whoever had been so thoughtful. Plus, she needed to know what services were routine in this place, and what were optional or had not yet been added. She might be able to suggest things that had been done at other places she had worked, once she knew how they were running things here.

She dropped off the clothes and headed back down to the office, nodding to the workmen she passed on the stairs. She'd seen them at breakfast but hadn't yet been introduced. They all seemed friendly enough and more than a little curious about her, judging by the way they looked at her, but she was the new person here. It would take time for them to get to know her, so the curiosity wasn't unexpected. She'd been in such situations before as the new manager coming in to a team that was already used to working together. She'd have to prove herself to them, which she took as an interesting challenge, rather than something negative.

Martine was on the phone with a supplier when Crystal returned to the office they were now sharing, so she settled in behind her new desk and began moving things around to her liking. She switched on the computer and looked at the options available. Someone had thoughtfully left a sticky note on her screen with her new login and temporary password, so she got on the system and started poking around.

It was an hour later when she finally came up for air, surprised to find that much time had passed. A glance out the front window told her that the afternoon was starting to turn into evening as the sun's rays lengthened. Martine put down the phone that she'd been on almost constantly all afternoon and sat back in her chair with a long sigh.

"Almost dinner time," she said happily. "Which is also quitting time for me. Some of the indoor crews will continue working for a few hours longer, but most of the outdoor work and office stuff shuts down before dinner. We all break and eat together just before sundown, then those of us who are done for the day go home, and the rest go back to work for a bit, usually after consulting with Marco. He shows up after sundown to see how far we've gotten during the day and take a look at what still needs fixing. He is very hands-on with this project, and of course, he knows what everything is supposed to look like, so he's a valuable resource for the authenticity of our renovation work."

"He's something of an historian then?" Crystal asked absently as she put away the few papers she'd used for notes. She looked up to find an uncertain expression on Martine's face, but the other woman didn't say whatever it was she was thinking.

"You could say that," she answered, sounding odd.

Crystal got the impression Martine wanted to say more but decided not to. Crystal frowned a bit, but she was still the new girl, and she had to tread lightly. Martine was an important link here, and Crystal needed to be friends with her if she was going to succeed in this position, so she let it go.

CHAPTER 7

They walked to the dining room together to find it filling up quickly. This time, Martine led Crystal through the buffet line before taking a seat at the large central table. Crystal had Martine on one side and a man introduced as Bruce seated on the other. Bruce told her he was the foreman of one of the crews that had been working on the outdoor pavilion. They were completely renovating it from top to bottom, he said, and was particularly interested in Marco's future plans for the maze, which had not been touched yet.

They talked about that through much of dinner, and others joined the conversation, each introduced in a very natural way. A few pointed questions were asked about Crystal's previous jobs and the kinds of projects she had worked on, and she was glad to answer them. This was a great, informal way to get to know the people she would be working with, and Crystal thought whoever had set up this communal meal situation was a genius. Everybody really seemed more like family than just coworkers.

Crystal recognized the silliness of her thought when the meal was nearing its end, and she realized many of them *were* blood-relations who talked about driving home together because they lived in the same house or neighborhood. They were also mostly werewolves, she remembered, and she'd heard from her shaman friend that they traveled, lived and worked in Packs.

She wanted to know more about them and the way they lived, but also remembered the caution her shaman friend had given her about being too nosey. She didn't want to alienate or insult anybody on her first day. She was very much the outsider, despite how welcoming they'd been so far. When the meal was over, Martine stood and stretched, as did a few of the others.

"Well, I'm going for a run over the grounds before I go home. Marco will be here any time now. You can wait for him in the office or, if you want to check out the forest, just be aware there will be wolves prowling. Nobody will give you any trouble, but don't be frightened if you see one of us," Martine had warned. "Maybe for your first foray, you should wait for Marco. He's used to us."

"Yeah," Crystal had replied. "Although I wouldn't want you to think I was a chicken."

Martine smiled cunningly. "I would never think that. Chickens are prey. You, my friend, clearly are not. Though what, exactly, you *are* remains a bit of a mystery."

"To me as well." Crystal laughed, surprising Martine. Crystal could tell by the way Martine's eyes widened and then a pleased expression crossed her face that the other woman liked Crystal's answer.

Martine left, and Crystal followed suit, heading back to the office. She'd wait there for Marco. She had considered changing into the new casual clothes, but she wanted to make a good first impression. She figured taking five minutes to change later would be better than appearing in casual dress— worse, casual clothes he'd supplied—for her first official meeting with her new employer.

When she entered the office, the light was on, and Marco was already there. Night had fallen completely while they'd been eating dinner, and Marco must have arrived at some point and just gone to the office, rather than interrupt everyone's meal. Maybe he didn't like eating with his employees, or maybe he'd just gotten there. She wasn't sure.

"Good evening," she said, greeting him formally as she entered.

Marco was seated at the large table to one side of the room. There were the two desks placed opposite, but there was also what Crystal had assumed was a conference or worktable to the side with six chairs around it. The room was large enough to support that much furniture and more. Crystal assumed this room had once been a front parlor or living room prior to Marco's purchase of the property.

"Good evening, Crystal," he said, his warm voice washing over her senses. It *was* as sexy as she remembered. She'd thought maybe she'd been dreaming about his impact on her senses, but she'd been wrong. He was every bit as handsome as she recalled. It had been no dream. "How did you find your first day?" he asked solicitously, putting down the tablet on which he'd been reading.

"Very good, thank you. Martine has been wonderful and showed me every inch of the house and grounds, except for the wild areas. As you know, I need to inspect the forest if we're going to get to the root of the magical problem. The trees have quieted now that I'm here, but there is definitely something wrong out there." She gazed out the dark window, seeing only her reflection but feeling the call of the forest deep in her soul.

Marco stood. "Very well. I would like to go with you, if you don't mind. Do you have any objection to walking through the woodlands at night?"

"None at all. That was my plan, in fact. I just need to change into something more practical. I hope you don't mind, but I borrowed some clothing from the storeroom Martine told me about. I needed better footwear, for one thing, but also something more comfortable for hiking through the woods." She felt a bit sheepish, but his expression was indulgent.

"I'm glad you found something in the storeroom. Feel free to take whatever you like from there. It is for the convenience of all who work here," he said magnanimously. "I will wait here while you change, if you like. Then we can go out and see what may be seen."

"Sounds like a plan."

She grinned at him and left the office, feeling the impact of his presence down deep in her soul. The man was a force of nature, she thought, as she mounted the stairs and went into her room.

She changed quickly and was zipping back down the stairs in a matter of minutes. Marco was waiting for her at the bottom, and her breath caught when she saw him. He was so...*Compelling* was the only word she could think of. It was more than just his wavy dark hair and classical features. More than the sexy dark eyes and chiseled shape of his jaw. More than the muscles his clothing couldn't quite camouflage completely. It was the sparkling intellect that flashed in the depths of his eyes. The integrity she sensed in his actions and the way he treated his people. She'd learned a lot about him from the people he'd hired and the time she'd spent touring the grounds today.

Marco was universally respected by those who worked here. She got the impression that they saw him not as their boss, but as their ally. She didn't know why she thought that, but it likely had something to do with the fact that everyone she'd met were probably werewolves. She sensed that such beings didn't subjugate themselves to anybody. At least, not easily. There seemed to be a definite hierarchy among them, but outside of their species, she didn't think they took orders from just anybody.

Everyone she had spoken with today had praised Marco's plans and vision for this place and talked like they were working together, not as master and subordinate. Marco gave her that impression as well. He talked about consulting with the crew chiefs, not ordering them around. She liked that. A truly strong man didn't have to throw his weight around. It was clear Marco—and everybody else—knew he was in charge here and footing all the bill, but he didn't act like a tyrant. Far from it. That garnered her respect.

Marco was enchanted by the sight of Crystal coming down the stairs. In another time, she would've been wearing a ball gown, and he would have been proud to offer her his arm and take her into the ballroom where they could dance the night away in a swirl of music, laughter, and delight. He had to remind himself that this was the modern world where such things were no longer common. For a moment, he entertained the fantasy of throwing a ball, as in the old days, just so he could dance with this lovely woman who was somehow becoming more important to him with each passing moment.

She was dressed casually in soft fabrics of dark colors. A good choice for roaming the woods at night. She had tied her golden-brown hair back in a ponytail. His fingers itched to release it from the velvety band that held it back, but he resisted the impulse. He had to tread lightly around this woman. She stirred things in him that he had not felt in centuries.

If she was meant to be important to him, he didn't dare scare her off by revealing himself too soon. So far, it seemed she had no real idea of what he was. Surprisingly, she had not commented on the fact that he was only about at night. Certainly, he had laid the groundwork many years before to project a normal human appearance to the outside world. He had the wolves keep up the pretense that he was occupied elsewhere during business hours, and that's why he only came around here at night. Not that anybody asked.

Occasionally, the mail and package delivery people might ask questions about the new owner of the property. Marco had discussed it with Martine and some of the others, and they had agreed to casually spread the story that the new owner was much occupied elsewhere during normal business hours. That seemed to satisfy the curious folks from the post office and the inspectors who came to issue permits and verify that the restoration work was proceeding according to local codes.

Martine dealt with them on Marco's behalf. She was an excellent organizer and kept everything humming along at a brisk pace. They were already far ahead of the projected goals he had set out when he'd first proposed the Pack do this work. All around, it had been an excellent deal for all concerned. The Pack kept its people employed in high-paying jobs, and Marco had people he could trust working on the property, setting things to rights much faster than he'd hoped. People who understood about magic and the true nature of good and evil.

The alliance had forged a stronger bond between himself and the Pack as well, which he thought was probably a good thing considering the increase in *Venifucus* activity. That evil brotherhood was up to its old tricks, if Marco was any judge, and things would be coming to a head sooner rather than later. Goddess help them all.

Crystal arrived at the bottom of the stairs, and Marco joined her. His impulse was to offer her his arm, but he knew that wasn't quite done in these modern times. Instead, he just smiled at her.

He kept to himself the fact that he had found it difficult to rest knowing she was in the mansion. For the first time in centuries, he had wanted, so much, to be up and around in the daylight hours so that he could spend them with her. Alas, his fate was much different. His limitations kept him away from her, but even so, his usual rest was disrupted by the knowledge that she was nearby. He had come as soon as he was able, anticipating the moment when they could be in each other's presence again.

Such thoughts made him wonder if perhaps she was more special than he'd originally thought. The strange yearnings she had awakened within him felt more significant than just the recognition of a novel sort of magic. He began to wonder if she might be...his One.

No. It couldn't be. He had lived so long and searched far and wide. He had resigned himself to never finding the other half of his soul. He had given up. Deciding to dedicate the rest of his very long life to eradicating evil. Fighting it wherever he found it. He had stopped looking for his soulmate. It would be more than ironic if she just happened to arrive on his doorstep. If such was the case, Fate was having a good laugh at his expense.

He simply didn't think he had earned such an honor. He had not done anything to distinguish himself so much that the Goddess would deliver his mate to him without any effort on his part. It just didn't seem possible.

Then again... The divine was said to work in mysterious ways.

All this conjecture amounted to a mass of confusion for Marco. He had resolved himself to just see where things led, and proceed with caution. Not easy, when every fiber of his being was pushing him to be with her. It didn't matter if it was day or night. The position of the sun made no matter. Even if it finally killed him, he yearned to be with her.

Marco would not examine that much more closely. Not yet. Not until he knew more about her and what she desired for her future. He would not harm her in any way. He would not ask her to give up the sun and deal with his limitations no matter how much he might wish to do so. He had to be a better man than that.

But, he realized, he was getting way ahead of himself. First, they had a job to do. He had set out to cleanse this estate of evil, and she had arrived at the behest of the forest itself to help make that happen. The eradication of evil had to come before all else.

"Shall we?" he asked gently, gesturing toward the front door.

Crystal smiled back at him and preceded him toward the

wide entry. They went outside together and headed for the trees lining the long front drive.

"I thought we would start with the front area," Marco offered. "As you can see, the grounds are rather extensive. I suspect, we'll have to do this in parts, and it will likely take more than one night to cover it all."

CHAPTER 8

Crystal was resigned to spending the next few nights walking through the woods around the estate. It would take as long as it took. All she knew was that she had to find whatever it was that was causing the trees such distress. She had the time now to do a thorough search. And walking through the woods was never a hardship for her. It was where she felt most at home. Day or night, it didn't matter. The forest was always her friend and always protected her as she cared for it.

She set off across the small area of mowed lawn that fronted the house, Marco at her side. Although it felt good to have green grass under her feet, she didn't feel truly happy until they crossed over into the wildwood. The trees greeted her with joy and hope. She noted that they also marked Marco's passing with respect. She already knew they thought of him as *The Protector*, but there was more deference toward him then she would've expected. She had never seen any forest react to a person the way this one reacted to Marco.

Even the oldest trees seemed to treat him as they would an elder, which seemed odd to her. She didn't understand it, but it was clear they respected him, which pleased her enormously. She liked him a little too much. If the forest had rejected him, she would have been very disappointed. She knew from past experience that she could not be friends with anyone that the trees did not like. The trees saw everything. Even into the depths of a person's soul, she believed.

They started to the right of the driveway, covering the area from the right corner of the house forward, to where the driveway met the road. They walked straight down to the edge of the property and back several times, moving a bit more toward the driveway with each pass until they had covered the whole area.

"Do you sense anything?" Marco had asked her as they walked along.

Crystal shook her head. "There is definitely something on the grounds, but I don't think we're close to it here. Still, we're going to have to cover every inch of the estate until we find it. For all I know, there could be more than one problem. I'd hate to find something, fix it, and then realize I missed something in another section."

"Good point," Marco said, frowning. "I guess we just keep walking until we've covered every part of the estate. I did so, when I first took over here, but I don't have your sensitivity. I am more than happy to accompany you on these little forays into the forest. I suppose Martine warned you that her people patrol the grounds in their fur?" He looked over at her as they walked, his dark eyes flashing in the night.

"She did say something to that effect, though she didn't use the word patrol. Do they contribute to the security of the estate as well as the restoration?"

"In fact, they do," Marco said, nodding. "Several of them have military experience as well as their natural instincts to fall back on. And in their wolf forms, their stealth is excellent. The casual observer would never even see them."

"Very clever," she complimented him. "I've never seen a

werewolf in its wolf form. For that matter, I've never even seen a wolf in person."

Marco smiled at her. "Then, you're in luck. If I'm not much mistaken, the Alpha will be waiting for us when we finish this next section."

"How do you know?"

"He and I often confer at this hour. After all, I currently employ a large portion of his Pack. We are allies, though this alliance is somewhat new. For that reason, I am happy to speak with him whenever he wishes to cement the relationship between myself and his Pack."

Crystal didn't really understand everything about what Marco had just said, but she let it pass. He was her employer. She didn't want to seem overly curious about his private dealings. She would watch and observe, learning what she could from what she saw. At least, for now. She was still getting to know Marco. Everything she had seen of him indicated that he was open to her questions, but still, she hesitated. Her position here was too new, and she didn't want to annoy the man so early in their employer-employee relationship.

Even if her secret heart whispered that she really wanted to be more than just his employee. She pushed that thought aside ruthlessly. She had no right to be thinking of him like that.

They came out of the trees back at the top of the driveway in front of the house, and Crystal gasped when she saw the wolf—the giant wolf—waiting there for them. She clutched Marco's arm reflexively as a jolt of fear went through her body. The trees had not warned her. She didn't understand, at first. Trees always told her when predators were near so she could avoid them, but the trees here hadn't done that.

The wolf padded forward, and Crystal found herself hanging back just the slightest bit, behind Marco. She tamped down the fear response. Clearly, Marco was not concerned. The trees were not concerned either. Perhaps, there was nothing to be concerned about.

Only a giant freaking wolf.

"Good evening Alpha," Marco said as they approached the wolf who was sitting on his haunches. Even sitting, he was huge!

The wolf nodded its furry head almost regally and then shifted its gaze to her. Crystal felt suddenly, as if the spotlight had been turned upon her. She didn't like it.

"Alpha, this is Crystal, whom I suspect you've heard about already from Martine. She is concerned there is still something evil on the grounds, and I will be walking over the estate with her for the next several evenings, making an inspection of every part of the woodlands," Marco informed the ginormous wolf. Again, the creature's head dipped regally in acknowledgment.

Well, that was news to Crystal. It certainly sounded as if Marco would be with her every step of the way. That was both comforting and a bit intimidating. Did he not trust her? Or was he feeling the same attraction she was fighting?

No way. Couldn't be. A guy like him could have any woman he wanted falling at his feet. He wouldn't be interested in a frump like her. Not with the gorgeous Martine around. Or any of the women Crystal had seen here. They were all so incredibly gorgeous. Shifters seemed to all be tall, fit, muscular and handsome, both the men and the women. She felt at a bit of a disadvantage around them, but they'd all been polite so far.

Crystal cleared her dry throat before speaking to the wolf. "Nice to meet you, uh, Alpha, sir."

The wolf yipped quietly, as if chuckling, and when she looked at Marco, his handsome lips were lifted slightly, and his eyes were sparkling. Were they laughing at her? *Hmph*. She stepped out from behind Marco and touched the rose bush that was planted just to the side of the path.

Just like that, the pale roses started to bloom in response to her touch. The wolf looked startled then bowed his head. It looked like respect, and that made her feel marginally better. She didn't want the wolf to think she was weak, even if her type of magic wasn't especially useful for anything other than showy tricks like making flowers bloom.

"Yes, that rather confirms my theory that you have dryad blood," Marco said, coming to stand next to her. "Milady Crystal appears to be at least part woodland nymph, Alpha," he said, addressing the wolf once more. "We both know how rare that sort of power is. And how potent."

The wolf nodded once and tilted its head at Crystal. She felt as if she'd just received a blessing of sorts. Or maybe permission or approval. She wasn't sure which exactly. She wasn't too good at deciphering the silent gestures of the werewolf yet. If she stayed here though, she suspected she would have to learn.

The wolf stood and padded off, disappearing into the woods they had just left. Marco turned to her and smiled.

"You did well for your first meeting with an Alpha wolf," he told her, looking pleased.

"I did?" She was incredulous. She wasn't sure what had prompted her to display her power, but she'd been running on instinct.

"You most certainly did. Alpha wolves have been known to reduce some people to quivering silence. You must have felt the power of his personality. His dominance. He leads his Pack due to the power of his wolf and the surety of his character." Marco escorted her to the other side of the driveway so they could begin the second half of their search on the left side of the long drive.

"I admit his size scared me a bit. I'm not very good with giant predatory animals. I've never even had a pet dog, so seeing a wolf like that…" She shook her head and shivered. "He's just scary."

Marco chuckled and put his hand on her elbow as they navigated a rough patch of ground. His touch felt so good, though a layer of cloth separated them from actual skin-on-skin contact. She liked how solicitous he was of her. How old-world his manners were toward her. He made her feel special, and that was simply enchanting to a woman who'd

never had a man treat her as if she were made of spun glass—
a treasure to be cherished and protected.

They entered the woods and repeated the search pattern
they had done on the other side of the driveway, walking
together companionably. Crystal enjoyed being with Marco.
He was good company, even if she did have to fight the
attraction she was feeling for her very compelling, very
powerful new employer.

"You see very well in the dark," Marco observed as they
walked along.

Crystal shrugged. "I always have. And I don't need much
sleep. A few hours, and I'm good to go usually. Especially
when I have access to a healthy forest. I feel like it sustains
me somehow." She'd never told anyone that before, but she
thought Marco might understand.

"All the more evidence that you truly are a nymph," he
said, nodding. "Or at least partly."

She shook her head, a smile on her face. "That word still
sounds kind of funny to me."

"The woodland nymphs were also called dryads," he
offered. "Is that any better?"

"As a matter of fact, I think I like that better. It doesn't
sound so potentially naughty." She looked up at him out of
the corner of her eye and saw the dawning amusement on his
handsome face.

"I hadn't thought of that. I was thinking more of the
classical nymphs depicted in art," he said.

"Oh, the famous nymphs painted by Waterhouse," she
said, thinking back to the art she'd seen in various museums.
"They're all naked. Not sure if that's better or worse than
what I was thinking." She chuckled as they continued to walk
and survey the land.

"Now, you have me curious. What exactly were you
thinking?"

Crystal felt her cheeks heating with a blush. "It's the word,
I guess. Nymph. You know, like *nympho*?"

Marco burst out laughing, the sound deep and rich. She

liked his laugh. It sent shivers of appreciation down her spine. When he finally stopped laughing, he turned to her. Merriment still danced in his eyes.

"Oh, my dear lady, I'm sorry to laugh at your expense, but that had not occurred to me. I will endeavor to remember to call you a dryad, henceforth."

"Thanks," she told him, shaking her head. She would have said more, but just then, a wolf howled in the distance. The sound was haunting. A primal fear struck her heart, and she paused in her steps.

Marco came up beside her and put his hand on her shoulder in a comforting way. "Fear not. It's just our allies. They will not harm you. I promise."

She rubbed her own arms and shivered as more wolf voices joined in the song. It certainly sounded as if they were surrounded. She'd had no idea there were so many wolves in the woods prowling nearby.

"I'm sorry. It's just somewhat unnerving. I've never heard anything like it before." She felt unaccountably vulnerable walking in the dark woods with Marco and wolves, unseen, all around.

Marco moved closer, his nearness bringing her comfort. "It's all right. I suspect there is much for you to get used to here, and you've had little time to do so. On my honor, you will come to no harm on my land. You are under my protection, and my allies know that. They will not attack. Far from it. They will protect you."

"If you say so." She continued rubbing her arms, peering into the woods, wary now as the wolf song started to die down. Marco was still close, and she longed to lean into his embrace, but that wouldn't be proper. Not at all.

Marco put both of his hands on her shoulders and turned her slowly to face him. "Be at ease, Crystal." His voice was almost hypnotic, and she felt her tension fall away as her gaze met his. "You are safe."

"I haven't felt safe in a very long time." Now, why on the world had she just admitted that? She'd never said that aloud to anyone, and she certainly shouldn't have told Marco. She'd only just met him, but there was something so…compelling about him.

His brows drew together in a frown as he searched her face. "That is at an end. Do you understand, Crystal? You are under my protection now. I will keep you safe. You need have no more fear on that account."

He drew closer, and she didn't object when he put his arms around her. In fact, she let go of her own arms and reached for him, resting her head on his shoulder and hugging him back. It was ridiculous, but he felt so warm and safe and…perfect.

All the tension drained from her body as she rested her head on his shoulder. She could feel the hardness of his muscles beneath her cheek.

"I don't know why I feel so safe with you," she admitted, resigned to the way her mouth seemed to just spout deep truths to him whenever he was near. "You should scare me, but you don't."

He sighed, and she felt it against her body. "I terrify many people, but I do not want to ever frighten you, dear heart."

"You don't. Far from it," she replied, whispering her truth as he held her gently.

He drew back slightly, looking down to meet her gaze as she lifted her head from his shoulder. Their eyes met and held. And time stood still. His mouth hovered near hers, and then his head moved closer, and his lips were on hers in a kiss as sweet as wine.

Time had no meaning, and everything else faded from memory. All that mattered was Marco's arms around her. His lips on hers. His body surrounding hers and making her feel things she had never quite felt before.

No other man had ever been so masterful. So tempting. So incredibly alluring. He made her want to do wicked things with him. The fact that he was her boss was forgotten in the most delicious kiss of her existence.

She didn't know how long it lasted. Only when the

renewed howling of wolves sounded in her ears did she slowly come back to herself. The canine song didn't frighten her this time. No, this time, she was surrounded by the mystique of Marco. The most intriguing man she had ever met. And, by far, the best kisser.

She drew back from him and moved out of his embrace, a bit embarrassed now that the moment was over. He was her boss! What had she been thinking?

Actually, she admitted to herself, she hadn't been thinking. That was the problem. One look from those mysterious dark eyes and all responsible thought had fled from her mind.

"This is awkward." There she went again, saying exactly what was in her mind. It was as if she had no filter around this man.

"Why?" he asked, giving her space but keeping up with her as she began walking slowly forward once more.

"Uh. You're my employer, for one thing," she pointed out. "There has to be something in the employee handbook about fraternization."

CHAPTER 9

Marco chuckled, and the earthy sound zinged right through the most intimate parts of her body. Damn the man. He affected her senses on a cellular level.

"We don't have an employee handbook. I assume that's a mortal thing, but we have no need of it since everyone who works here is magical in some way. We all know our places, and if there is attraction between two consenting adults, then that is between them."

He sounded so earnest, his deep voice causing tremors of attraction to run down her spine even as they walked. She had to look at him, catching a concerned expression on his handsome face. She stopped walking and turned to look at him.

"How does that work, exactly? How can you avoid office romances turning ugly without rules laid down ahead of time in a handbook?" Not that office romances didn't often cause problems, even if there were rules against them. Human nature being what it was. But she didn't mention that.

"Any fraternization, as you put it, among the wolves is governed by their social rules. Most shifters search for years to find their one true mate. Once they find that person, they are true for the rest of their lives. Unless they are mates, they all know any liaisons can only be casual ones, with no hearts broken on either side because they are not true mates. Only a true mating involves the heart and soul. And true mates are rare. There is only one for each person, and sometimes, they never find each other."

"True mates? I've never heard that term. Of course, I know next to nothing about shifters," she admitted. "It must make things easier to have both parties know exactly where they stand."

"I believe it does," Marco replied. "But it's also difficult to know that the person you like and are enjoying spending time with is not your mate and can never be your permanent companion. The longing to find love—true love—can be devastating and very lonely."

The look in his dark eyes was haunted, and her heart went out to him. "You sound like you speak from experience," she said quietly.

"I do," he replied just as quietly. "I have searched many years for my One. My kind also has only one true mate, and we search our entire lifetimes to find them. To be honest, I had given up and dedicated myself to fighting evil, but just lately, I find hope reasserting itself."

What was he implying? Was he saying that *she* was making him rethink his decision? No way.

"How do you know if you find your One?" she asked, her voice the merest whisper.

"There are ways," he said, turning cagey and sly. "For shifters, I've heard that some can identify their true mate by their scent. Some from a single kiss. Others have a harder time, and it may take a few days of exposure to be certain."

"Do you think nymphs—" She stopped herself. "I mean *dryads*, have a similar thing? Could there be just one true mate for someone like me?" That might explain why she'd never had much luck in the relationship department.

"I cannot say for certain, but it seems likely. Most of the magical races seem to follow a similar pattern. There is someone we could ask, if you want to know for certain. A colleague of mine has had dealings with a full-blooded dryad and some of her descendants." Marco paused. "In fact, it seems likely that you might also be related to her. I happen to be on friendly terms with one of the ladies in question. She and her mate were key to freeing this estate from its former owners. We all fought together to rid the place of that evil. Full disclosure—I called her when I first brought you in from the forest. I was concerned about your welfare and wanted to ask her if she had any advice. She really wants to talk with you and suggested a video conference. If you are amenable, I will set it up for tomorrow."

Crystal caught her breath. "I don't know where I came from. I tried searching for records, but there were none. I gave up hope of ever finding any relations." Hope filled her heart, but she dared not let it get out of control. "I'd like to talk to this friend of yours. If nothing else, she might be able to tell me more about dryad magic."

"She can absolutely do that," Marco reassured her. "She is definitely a daughter of the dryad, Leonora. A many times great-granddaughter, in fact, but she has dryad magic and is mated to an Alpha wolf. She could advise you on how dryad magic affects mating, perhaps, as well as other things."

Crystal nodded, biting her lip as she thought through the possibilities. "When can we video chat with her? If she's a friend of yours, I'd kind of like to have you there. I hope you don't mind. Can we do it after dinner tomorrow? Do you think she'll be free then?"

"I will set it up. I am almost positive that she will make time to speak with you whenever you wish. She is eager to discover more of her family. From what I understand, many of the dryad's descendants were unaware of their heritage and are only just being discovered and united with their extended family. I believe three of them have been found so far, my friend, Maria, among them." They started walking slowly, the forest night surrounding them in a peaceful cocoon of intimacy. At least, that's how it felt to Crystal.

"Maria." She repeated the name, testing it out. Could she have a relative named Maria? She was both eager and scared to find out.

"The two others are sisters who grew up separately, not knowing about each other. Sally is the elder sister, who is mated to Maria's mate's younger brother, so they are cousins as well as sisters-in-law now." Marco chuckled wryly. "They recently found Sally's younger sister, Sunny, and she is now mated to a cougar shifter."

"All three are mated to shifters?" Crystal mused.

There must be something to that. If shifters had only one mate, then perhaps dryads had the same. If so, could it be possible for a dryad to find a true mate among another magical race? She hadn't felt drawn to any of the handsome shifters she'd met here, but there was something about Marco that pulled her in like an iron filing to a magnet.

She assumed he was some sort of magic user, though she didn't know the exact nature of his power. It would be rude in the extreme to ask. The shaman had taught her that much. She was hoping to discover more about Marco and his particular brand of magic in a more natural way. He was still her employer, but she was discovering that things were different in the magical world. Maybe they could get involved and not worry overly much about the rules of the mortal world, as he'd called it.

That thought stopped her. She hadn't quite realized it when he'd said it, but if he called regular people *mortals*, did that mean he was *immortal*? And, if so, what *was* he? She didn't think he was fey. The shaman had described the fey to her, and Marco didn't really fit that description. But what other race could be considered immortal in this realm? Shifters were very long-lived compared to humans, but nobody considered them immortal. Some mages lived magically-extended lives due to the nature of their power, but they weren't really immortal either. It was a puzzle, but Marco drew her attention as they walked, and she put it aside for later consideration.

He had taken a cell phone out of his pocket, and the screen lit as he tapped it.

"There. I sent a text that Maria and Jesse will get when they wake. I've requested a video chat for eight p.m. tonight." He put away his phone as they continued walking.

Eight p.m. She had until then to wonder about the woman who might be related to her somehow. Even if they weren't related, this Maria could probably tell her a lot more about dryad magic—if that's really what Crystal had. Either way, she figured she would learn something.

"Thank you, Marco. Truly." She couldn't say more around the lump in her throat at the thought of possibly finding family.

They walked along in silence for a time. Crystal was deep in thought, though still paying attention to her surroundings. The trees here were content for the most part. Wherever the evil was hiding, it wasn't necessarily in the immediate vicinity.

Completing their search pattern, they arrived back at the front of the house. So much had happened during their walk. He had set the groundwork for a video chat the next evening with someone who might actually be related to her. They had talked and walked companionably. She'd become more comfortable with him. And…they had kissed. Her body still tingled with aftershocks from the simple touch of his lips on hers.

He had talked a lot about the concept of true mates. Why would he tell her about such things if he was just playing with her? But how could he possibly be even the tiniest bit serious when they'd only just met? She wasn't sure if she believed in his claims about fated mates and magical people searching years for the one and only. She wasn't sure about any of it, but she did know that she was growing even more attracted to him the longer she was around him. So far, there was nothing about him that turned her off. Quite the contrary.

"Did you sense anything at all?" Marco asked, turning to her as they reached the grassy expanse between the woods and the front of the house.

Crystal shook her head. "Nothing in the front of the house. If we had more time tonight, I'd suggest we try another area, but it's getting late."

It was long past *late*. It would be dawn in an hour or two. They had been out in the woods for hours.

"After the video call tomorrow night, we can try again," Marco offered as they walked across the grass, heading for the front door. Soft lights lit the exterior of the mansion, creating a lovely tableau, though neither of them needed light to see in the dark.

"I thought I might do a little exploring on my own, during the day," she countered, but Marco shook his head.

"I've been thinking about this, and I would prefer to be with you when you search. Just in case you find something. I don't want you to be caught on your own with something potentially dangerous," he said quietly. She could feel some sort of repressed emotion in his voice that touched her deeply. He sounded as if he actually cared—maybe just a little—about what happened to her.

"That's sweet, but I've been on my own a long time. I can usually handle myself pretty well." She felt the need to protest, a little uncomfortable with the idea that he wanted to watch over her. Nobody had ever taken care of her like that. She didn't know what to do with the idea.

"Humor me," he said, escorting her up the wide front steps. "Besides, I would like you to prepare some ideas for further improvements to the estate now that you've had a chance to see most of it."

He might have phrased it as a question, but it felt more like a directive from the boss, albeit a very polite one. Still, she had to remind herself, he *was* the boss. Much as she'd like to assert her independence, she did owe him a duty as his newest employee.

"All right," she agreed as he opened the door for her, and

they walked through. "I'll do it, though I'm not happy about waiting. The forest needs my help, and I hate making it wait."

"Understood," Marco acknowledged seriously, nodding once. "I have only your safety in mind, I assure you. I will spend the night in your company, and we will search the estate as long as it takes to pinpoint the problem. Does that suit?"

Grudgingly, she nodded. "That'll work," she agreed.

Marco left her at the door to her bedroom with just the lightest kiss on her cheek. It was nothing she could object to. It was simply polite and mildly affectionate. She might have wished for more, but even if there was no employee handbook to object, she still had to remember her place. She was the new girl. She was still getting the lay of the land. This position had come to her in a very odd way, and she still wasn't really sure what she was doing here or why she had accepted it.

Except for the trees. They had called her here, and they had never once steered her wrong in her entire life. It was Marco's presence, and that of the werewolves, that made her feel odd about the whole situation, but she was determined to come to terms with it. She had to help the forest here. It was imperative somehow. Part of her nature that she could not ignore told her she had to do something to help, and to do that, she had to be here. On this estate. If that meant working for Marco and with all those werewolves, then she would do it.

So far, everyone had been very nice to her. The compensation package was far and away the best she'd ever had. She couldn't object to the working hours, either. Although, she did stay up half the night with Marco, she didn't mind that at all. Far from it. Something about him made her want to spend as much time as possible with him.

He was mysterious and sexy. Intelligent and knowledgeable about things she didn't fully understand. He seemed to know a lot about magic. She sensed she could learn a great deal from him, but she didn't see him as a teacher figure. No, the woman inside her saw him as a potential lover. No matter how much she reminded herself that he was her boss, she just couldn't help but see him that way.

She hoped she didn't live to regret it.

CHAPTER 10

The next day, Crystal woke about midmorning. She showered, dressed and went downstairs to find Martine already hard at work. Crystal spent the rest of the morning sketching out some ideas for the estate. At lunchtime, she and Martine went down to the dining room together. They sat at the large table with everybody else and conversation flowed around her.

After lunch, Crystal put her ideas into a more official format so she could present them to Marco when he arrived later. She tried really hard not to get her hopes up, but all afternoon, she kept thinking about the videoconference to come. She had never had family. Never thought it was possible that she might find some. She had done well enough on her own, but it would be the sweetest kind of magic to find that she wasn't alone in the universe anymore.

She wasn't sure she could be so blessed, but the thought that she might find some actual blood relations made her just the tiniest bit giddy. She kept tamping down the bubble of hope that wanted to rise. She kept telling herself not to get too excited. This might just be a dead end. At the very least, she would at least meet—virtually—someone who might know more about her brand of magic. If nothing else, that would be a good thing. She would like to know more about the unique powers she had discovered by trial and error. Maybe they could straighten a few things out for her.

By the time dinner rolled around, Crystal could no longer concentrate on her work. She practically jumped up from her seat behind the desk to join Martine in the short walk to the dining room. She didn't really pay attention to the conversation flowing around her. Her mind was on the videoconference to come. She ate, enjoying a small portion of the many dishes on offer while the people around her ate their fill. She was getting used to the idea that these shapeshifters could eat massive quantities of food and never seem to get fat. Must be nice.

When she was done eating, Crystal made her way back to the office, leaving Martine and the others behind. She stopped in the ladies' room to freshen up and check her hair. She wanted to make a good impression on the people she would be meeting by video. Not to mention, she would be seeing Marco again. That thought made her just the tiniest bit breathless.

Arriving back at the front office, Crystal found Marco already there, waiting for her. He was seated, as he had been the night before, at the conference table. This time, however, he was pressing buttons on a panel that had been hidden inside the antique-looking table. As she watched, amazed, a large flat-panel display rose from the center of the table.

Marco looked up as she entered the room, meeting her gaze. A smile lit his dark eyes, and she felt warmth flow through her veins at the intimacy that sprang up between them, pulling them together with unseen bonds.

"Ah, good. I was just about to test the connection. I received word that Maria and Sally would be available any time tonight. They told me to just initiate the call, and they would answer. Are you ready?"

Ready? For a split second, Crystal panicked. They had been supposed to meet at eight o'clock. It was only six. She shook her head, chastising herself internally. It would be better to get this over with. She had been obsessing about the call for most of the afternoon. Time to put herself out of her misery and see if these people really were her relations. Or not.

Though, how they could settle the question completely just by meeting over a video chat, she wasn't sure. Maybe there was some magical way to tell. She had a lot to learn about her own powers and was hoping to at least get some guidance on that. If that's all that came from this meeting, then so be it.

"Sure." Crystal walked forward to the conference table, trying to project self-assurance. "We might as well." She took a deep breath for courage and joined him at the conference table.

Marco put the call through, and it was picked up on the first ring. Two women appeared on the screen. One of them smiled and greeted Marco.

"It's good to see you again, Master Marco," she said, her voice melodic, even over the computer interface.

"Good to see you, too, Doctor," he replied politely.

"You remember Sally, of course," Maria went on.

"I do," he said. "You're looking well, Detective. May I introduce you both to Crystal. She came across the estate on her way somewhere else and, as I mentioned, felt compelled to stop." He turned to Crystal and smiled encouragingly.

"Hello," Crystal ventured, her throat suddenly dry with nerves.

"Hi," Maria replied. "If you don't mind my asking, what made you stop at the estate?"

"Uh…" Crystal cleared her throat and knew she had to be honest with these women if she wanted to go any farther down this path. "It was the trees. They were crying out for help. I was compelled to stop and see if I could do anything. As it was, I overestimated my stamina and gave too much of my power. That's how Marco found me."

Both women looked alarmed when she admitted that. "You were lucky it was Master Marco who found you and not someone else," Maria told her.

That was the second time Maria had used that title— Master. Crystal didn't know why the other woman referred to Marco that way, but he seemed to take it in stride. She'd have to ask later, if the opportunity presented itself.

Crystal shrugged. "So many points of convergence. It seems like maybe Fate was playing a role here. The fact that Marco had an opening on his staff in exactly my field, and I've been searching for a job. That's just a bit too coincidental. And that he knew what I was doing when I was trying to help the forest, and how to help me when I gave too much of my own energy. That was pretty big too," she pointed out. "And he knows you, which means he is familiar with my kind of magic. I've never met anybody who knew what I was. I didn't even know what I was until Marco told me, though I'm not entirely convinced, even so."

She was babbling. She knew it. Nerves were getting the better of her, so she ceased talking and hoped she hadn't made a bad impression on the other women.

"Oh, I think we can settle the question about whether or not you're a dryad descendant pretty easily," Sally said, looking at Maria and back again. "Have you ever been able to call up your family tree?"

"I'm an orphan. I don't know anything about my kin," she told them.

"We both have similar backgrounds," Sally assured her. "What I mean is, have you ever seen your magical family tree?"

"Uh...no. Not even sure what you mean, to be honest," Crystal replied, shrugging.

"That's okay. I didn't know how to do it until Leonora showed me," Sally said not unkindly. "Leonora is a full-blooded dryad I met a few years ago. She is our ancestor many times removed. Apparently, dryads are close to immortal, though I'm not sure how that would apply to us, since the dryad magic is very watered down in our cases." Sally gestured to Maria and herself. "Let me know if you can see this."

Sally held up her hand within view of the camera and made a gesture. Immediately, a glowing treetop appeared under her hand.

"I see the top of what looks like a hologram of a tree in glowing gold," Crystal reported, unsure of what exactly was appearing.

"Oh," Sally looked at Maria, "would you tilt the camera down so she can see the whole thing?"

A moment later, Maria tilted the camera, and the rest of the tree was visible. A glowing apparition that appeared to have information along the branches, though Crystal couldn't make it out over the video connection.

"This is my family tree. Maria's branch is right along here." Sally pointed with her other hand to something Crystal couldn't quite make out. "Leonora tasked me with finding as many of her descendants as I could, but even with this tree, it's not that easy to find others like myself and Maria. I was a police detective and even with my skills and contacts, it's been difficult. I found Maria first and sent my brother-in-law after her, to keep her safe. They ended up mated, which is great because now we live close and get to see each other all the time. I also had a lead on my sister, which panned out, and she's now happily mated as well. We found another cousin recently, and now, you've appeared." Sally frowned. "Only I don't know where you fit on my tree. It's been filling in as we find more of our relatives. Same for Maria."

Sally let her hand drop, and the tree faded from view, but Maria raised her hand, and another tree began to form. This one glowed a slightly different color that was more brown and green than gold. It was also shaped differently.

"Can you see this one?" Maria asked.

Crystal nodded. "I see it," she replied.

"Great. Mine isn't nearly as filled in as Sally's, but each

time we locate another relative, more of it becomes clear. We were sort of hoping that if you could manifest your own tree, that would not only prove that your magic is dryad magic, but it would also allow our trees to fill in, so we'd see where you fit."

"If I fit," Crystal couldn't help but say. She wasn't going to get her hopes up. No siree Bob. She shook her head to clear away her thoughts. She had to go into this with an open, receptive mind. "So, how do I make the tree show?"

Crystal held up her hand as the other women had and nearly jumped out of her skin when, at the merest thought of a tree, one started to grow out of thin air, made of light and energy swirling together to form an elaborately curling branch system.

"Would you look at that," Maria marveled. "She's a natural."

"So, definitely a dryad then," Sally agreed, grinning. "Do you see either of us on your tree?"

"Uh... Let me look." Startled greatly by the ease with which this magic had come to her, Crystal nonetheless began to examine the tree in detail.

Some of it was in sharp focus. She saw a representation of herself among the lowest branches. And at the tip of the tree, she saw what must be the dryad ancestor represented not with a clear image of a face or a written name, but an image, of sorts. Crystal couldn't really make it out, but she had a sense of *knowing* who it was and what that person meant to her.

She tried to follow the branches down from the tip of the tree but could not make out much until one branch showed itself, untwining from within to reveal two joined presences. One was Sally, she felt, but the other...

"I see Sally and... You said you had a sister?" Crystal said.

"Sunny," Sally said. "My little sister, Sunny. We never knew about each other until just a short time ago."

Another branch revealed itself as the tree turned under her hand. She felt more than saw the branch that held Maria. And then other branches revealed themselves.

"I see Maria and another two."

"Two?" Sally jumped on that. "We only know of one other for certain, though there are many branches that are still unclear. Is one Cecelia?"

As Sally spoke the name, the image came clear in Crystal's mind. "Yes, one is named Cecelia, though I have no idea how I know that. The branch just belongs to that name, now that I know it. The other is someone..." Crystal tilted her head to one side. "Someone we will meet soon."

"The next one," Maria murmured. "It happened like that for me each time we were about to add one to our number. You must be the link to the next one we find."

Crystal shook her head. "I don't think I understand this at all. I've never had family," she whispered.

"Neither have we," Sally agreed.

"But we do now," Maria put in. "*We're* your family."

Crystal felt the words deep in her heart. Tears started behind her eyes, and the glowing tree under her hand intensified for a brief moment before stuttering out. For a split second, she was afraid it was gone forever, but she felt strongly that she would see it again. Many times. Now that she knew it was there and how to call it, she would do so later, to study it further.

"This is a lot to take in," Crystal said to the other two, shaken to her core by the course of events.

"We understand," Maria replied calmly. "It was for me too."

"Take the time you need to figure things out," Sally put in. "Now that we know who you are and you know us, we have time to get to know each other and talk about our mutual ancestor. One last thing I'll mention before we sign off. You have an open invitation to Pack lands here in Wyoming. I'd like for you to come here so we can meet in person and so you can see where Leonora rests. I hope you'll consider coming sooner rather than later. I'd really like to see you in person. In the meantime, I'll email you our contact numbers so you can call me or Maria anytime if you have any questions. Marco already gave me your new email address on his system. Now that we've met, I don't want to lose touch. Maybe we could schedule another video chat for later in the week?"

Crystal agreed, and they ended the call a few minutes later. She sat back in her chair and breathed out a heavy sigh. Marco sat silently beside her, just letting her process. It was a lot to take in all at once.

"Well, that went well," Marco said finally after a long moment of quiet had passed.

"It did," Crystal agreed.

CHAPTER 11

Marco escorted Crystal outside after the call. She was quiet, appearing to be in an introspective mood as they walked toward the forest that bordered the more sculpted land around the house. The plan was to explore the woods on the left side of the house, near the area where Crystal had first entered the property the night she'd been driving past on the road that bordered the estate on one side. They had decided on this course of action the night before, hoping to pinpoint whatever it was that had drawn Crystal here from the road. Perhaps it was on that side of the house. It was worth a try to look there, even though they would have to search the rest of the grounds, no matter what.

The last thing Marco wanted was to leave some sort of evil undiscovered on the grounds. Even if they found something tonight, he would still want Crystal to check the rest of the place thoroughly. However, finding and dealing with the threat took precedence at the moment. If the problem was big enough for the forest to cry out for her attention, then it had to be something important. Something he had missed. Even worse, something he and all the others who had worked to free this property from its evil previous owners had not seen.

That thought worried him more than he liked to admit. Of course, it could just be that the specific kind of magic was something he hadn't been looking for, or just couldn't see. That happened sometimes. Marco had lived a long life and had learned that even he, with all his learning and experience, just couldn't see certain things. If the problem was, as he suspected, something hidden by the earth, then it made sense that they would need someone in tune with the earth to find it. As far as he knew, there was no being more in tune with the earth and its magics than a dryad.

He suspected divine intervention. No way was it just a coincidence that someone with dryad magic—which, after all, was incredibly rare these days—showed up on the estate. Marco had been suspicious until he realized that Crystal was likely one of the long-lost relations of Leonora. It made a certain sort of sense to him that these daughters of the dryad were starting to appear when and where they were needed.

Crystal didn't really know it yet, but her ancestor needed her help. Leonora was trapped between worlds. She would need as many of her descendants as they could find to try to rescue her. Marco knew that Sally and Maria had been trying to find their relatives for a while now. They had been putting a lot of energy out into the universe toward that task. Sometimes, that kind of concentrated search brought things to the surface. In this case, it brought Crystal to a place where she could be identified and united with the family she had never known.

Marco saw the hand of the Goddess in this situation. Some people might call it Fate as well, but Marco had always been a servant of the Lady of Light. No matter how much mortals vilified creatures like himself, Marco had never turned to the dark side. He had been a religious man in his youth. He had seen terrible things in his homeland of Italy.

He had traveled the world many times over the centuries of his immortal existence, but he had never lost his faith. It had changed, in subtle ways, of course, but he had stayed true to the teachings of his *strega* ancestors.

His mother had been a witch who believed in the Goddess, cloaking her devotions in the trappings of the church that was so powerful in their homeland. It wasn't until long after his mother had died that Marco had become immortal. He had not inherited much of the magic of his mother's line, but he knew enough to do small things, back before he had been changed. Now, of course, after centuries of living as what some called *vampire*, he had learned a great deal more and could command magics stronger than anything his mother had ever imagined.

But he had always stayed true to those initial teachings. His mother had taught him to be a good man, and to serve the Light. Even though he lived in eternal darkness now, he knew the Light existed in his soul. It was the only thing keeping him sane.

He had long ago given up on ever finding his One. It was a curse of his kind that, without the right person to share his eternal life, a bloodletter would often go mad. That's where the myths and legends of the vampire had come from. Beings of such power gone insane could be terrifying. Marco would stake himself out in the sun to burn and die rather than let himself become the monster that preyed on innocents and killed indiscriminately.

But so far, his purpose in life had been to fight evil wherever he found it. That had been enough to keep him sane when many others he had known had ended their immortal lives once they saw themselves going down a dark path. Others had been killed by their brethren to prevent a bloodbath among mortals, which would expose them all. Bloodletters policed themselves.

The Master of each region ran it as he saw fit. Marco knew several of them in this country and called them friend. Others, he wasn't so close with. He also wasn't sure if they served the Light or simply their own interests. Some of the younger Masters, in particular, had not gained his trust. However, there were certain elders that he respected and knew, for a fact, were fighting on the right side of the eternal struggle between good and evil, like himself.

Master Hiram in Seattle was one of those. Not only a friend, but a respected elder, Marco kept in contact with Hiram from time to time and exchanged information with him. Dmitri Belakov was another Master whose territory was somewhat closer. In fact, Dmitri was very near the mountain in Wyoming that the Wraiths called home. Dmitri was closely allied with the wolf Pack lead by Jason Moore and the Wraiths led by his brother, Jesse. Both men had mated recently, to Sally and Maria, respectively.

If Marco was going to remain involved with Crystal, bonds would be forged between himself and that wolf Pack as well. Because, as amazing as it seemed, Marco was beginning to believe that Crystal just might be his One.

"Let's start over there," Crystal said, breaking into his reverie as she pointed to the left.

They were approaching the tree line, and even though Crystal still seemed a bit distracted, she was leading the way toward the farthest most point they had searched the night before. It made sense. They would pick up at the boundary of the area they had already searched and go from there.

"A good plan, milady," Marco replied, bowing his head slightly in her direction. For some reason, she brought out all his old courtly manners that he had not used in quite a long time.

She smiled somewhat absently at him and then set to work. He walked beside her, well aware that her mind was still on the meeting they had just had. He tried to imagine what it would be like to discover that she did, indeed, have blood relations after thinking for so long that she was all alone in the world. He couldn't quite wrap his head around it. He had always known where he'd come from.

He'd had a good family with magical ties. He had known

about the unseen world through his mother, who taught him as best she could in secret. It had been dangerous to have such knowledge in the old days, but it was hereditary knowledge in her family, and she had passed it on to his sisters.

His beloved sisters had followed in his mother's footsteps. They had been powerful witches. *Strega*, as they were known in Italy. His three sisters had lived long lives, escaping the worst of the plague that had hit their hometown so very hard. Those had been horrible years, and they had changed him forevermore.

The year had been 1347 when the ships had landed in Messina, carrying the plague. The Black Death had taken so many, but the *strega* had not fallen. They fought against it with everything in their arsenal and did all they could to protect their neighbors. What most did not realize, even to this day, was that the Black Death had been a weapon sent against the forces of Light by the followers of Elspeth, the Destroyer.

Elspeth and her army of *Venifucus* sycophants had been trying to take over the world, little by little. Many plagues and catastrophes could be traced to their evil efforts. They had killed so many people. They had almost killed Marco, himself.

While his sisters had been fighting the plague, Marco had been doing battle with the *Venifucus* agents who had been spreading it. With his knowledge of magic and his ability to fight, he had been one of the few who could try to stop the evil at its source. He had gone, with his family's blessing, to try to stop the spread of the plague by the *Venifucus*.

But the *Venifucus* were too strong for him at that time. He had been able to prevent one of their agents from spreading the plague to a small town, but he had been mortally wounded in the battle. It was only as he lay dying in a dark alley that Fate had sent him salvation in the form of a bloodletter who had witnessed his fight with the *Venifucus* agent.

Marco had managed to kill the other man, but he had been left for dead as well. The battle had taken place during the day, close to the supper hour. Marco understood now why the bloodletter had needed to wait until after dark to come to him. She had offered him a choice. To thank him for saving her town, she offered to heal his wounds by sharing her immortality.

Bella had been a conflicted creature. She had seen her eternal life as a curse. She had been created as a plaything a mere hundred years before by a nobleman in a city far away who had been on the edge of going mad and turning into a serial killer with no remorse or conscience. He had been destroyed by the local Master when his madness had become apparent, and Bella had been freed. She had moved around quite a bit in that century but had returned to the place of her birth, living on the outskirts, watching the children of her brothers and sisters, aunts and uncles, grow old and die for generations. She had become their protector, of sorts. Which was why she had offered to save Marco's life in return for what he had done for her town.

He had been nearly delirious with blood loss at the time, but he had agreed, and she had gifted him with a portion of her own immortality. She had turned him that night and spent the next few weeks teaching him how to exist only at night. She had pleaded for him in front of the Master of the region, explaining why she had turned him. Marco learned then that creating more bloodletters went against the Master's rules.

However, Bella had been granted leniency, and Marco had been accepted among his new brethren. The Master of that area of Sicily had been a good and just man. While he hadn't exactly been a servant of the Light, he also hadn't been a proponent of evil. He had let Marco go, and after getting used to his new life, he had returned to his hometown of Messina.

He couldn't stay there, of course, but he had to tell his sisters what had happened. They deserved to know, even if it had broken their hearts. But they had surprised him. They had wept for the changes, but also in thanks for having him still among them, even if he could only see them at night. They had made it possible, after the plague had left the countryside almost barren, for him to live on the outskirts of town. They would visit him. They would keep him as part of the family while he learned how to deal with the new instincts that rode him hard.

He would hunt among the city dwellers for the blood that he needed to survive, but he learned how to control his hunger and not to take too much from any one person. He left them with a smile and no memory of what he had done.

Eventually, his sisters grew old, and mortality caught up with them. But he knew all their children, and their children's children, and so on, to this very day. He kept track of his family, even as spread out all over the globe as they were. He had multiple companies under his control, and all of them were run by distant relatives of his. His sisters' children and their descendants. He took care of them all, though only a few of them knew it. The few that still followed the ways of the *strega*.

"There is definitely something here, but the trees are remaining quiet." Crystal's voice brought him back to the present.

Seeing her meet her family had brought him thoughts of his own. He supposed it was a night for introspection, but Crystal's words reminded him that they had a job to do.

"When you say *here*, do you mean right here? Or someplace nearby?" he asked gently.

She shook her head. "No, not right here. Sorry. I mean someplace on the estate. In the woods connected to this area. But I can't pinpoint it exactly. We're going to have to keep walking." She smiled over at him, and he felt his heart lift. She was so good for him. It felt good just to be around her. "Good thing you stocked these comfortable shoes. Thank you again. Nothing I had with me would've been suitable for this kind of hiking."

"Think nothing of it. I'm glad they were available to help you."

"You're really good to your people, you know? I've worked for resorts that had all kinds of perks for their employees, but they were usually things that could be written off on the taxes or that weren't too difficult for the employer to accomplish. What you've done here—these little things like the storeroom full of clothes—these things are above and beyond. Thoughtful gestures that mean a lot to your people. You're a good boss." She smiled at him and kept walking, her words touching his heart.

"I just try to make things comfortable for everyone," he said quietly, unsure how to respond.

Not many people talked to him this way anymore. The way friends would speak to each other. Even the wolves treated him with kid gloves. They always seemed so aware of his station.

While it was true he was Master of this region, he didn't lord it over anybody. At least, he didn't think he did. Occasionally, he had to lay down the law to others of his kind when they transgressed his rules, but he tried to be fair. He didn't make anybody bow and scrape to him. He wasn't born to the nobility, and he'd always thought it was an outdated arrangement.

"Well, you do a very good job of that," Crystal told him as they walked along. "It's clear your employees respect you greatly. Though, I'll be honest, I do sense a wariness from some of them, but the rest really do have genuine affection for you, even if they don't show it."

Marco was floored by the idea. He wondered if she could be seeing things correctly or if she was misinterpreting something. Regardless, he was intrigued by what she saw that made her think the werewolves might be coming to accept him. It had been a long road to get to this point with them, and although they were officially allies, he wasn't always entirely sure if they actually liked him, or not.

Marco knew he didn't have to be liked in order to have an efficient and profitable alliance with the Pack, but the part of him that had grown up human wanted friends. Ancient as he was, he still hungered for friendship. Unfortunately, with his limitations, it had been very hard to find.

He would've said more, but at that moment, Crystal stopped in her tracks and bent to touch the earth with her hand. He watched, instantly on guard. Did she sense something? Had she found what they were looking for?

CHAPTER 12

Crystal stopped walking and dropped to one knee, reaching out to feel the ground. "Something happened here." She shook her head, closing her eyes, trying to let the information flow into her consciousness, but it wasn't really working.

She stood and looked around. There was a large maple tree about five feet away. She walked up to it and placed her hand on its bark. Would it speak to her? She wasn't sure.

A flood of images screamed into her mind. Violence. Anger. Death.

"They chased somebody into the woods and caught them here." Her eyes were shut against the images, even as they flowed into her consciousness. It was hard to watch, even as disjointed as it was. Crystal opened her eyes and met Marco's gaze. "Somebody died here."

She removed her hand from the tree trunk and let it fall to her side. Sorrow engulfed her. Someone had died, and their life force had been drained for evil purposes. A tear ran down her cheek, unchecked as despair came over her like a wave.

Marco moved the spot where she had knelt and raised his hands about waist high, holding his palms downward toward the earth. He was doing something. She could feel energy shifting and moving about him. Then he began to speak in low tones, saying words she didn't understand. It was another language. It sounded faintly like Latin, though she really had no expertise or knowledge of other languages.

She felt energy rise, and then release. As it dissipated, a feeling of joy washed over her. She didn't understand it.

"What did you do?" she asked Marco.

"I cleansed the area, releasing what remained of the soul who had died here." He looked down, his face solemn.

"You can do that?" Crystal was impressed.

He shrugged, standing to his full height. "My mother and sisters were *strega*. I learned quite a bit from them over the years."

"What is *strega*?" she repeated the strange word.

"In the simplest terms, that is the Italian word for witch, but there's actually a lot more to it. Each *strega* line descends through the female side of the family. Some go back eons. My own family had a long history of the power, and my mother made sure my sisters were trained, since they all carried that same power."

"What about you?" she asked.

"I learned most of my skills elsewhere and long after I had left my family. Things were very different in those days. There was little equality between women and men, and the *strega* knowledge was preserved only for the females of a family. It is that way to this day. But even if it weren't, it wouldn't have mattered." He shrugged. "I had little to no power of my own as a youngster. I was aware of what my mother and sisters could do, but I couldn't share in it. My own power didn't come until later, and I learned from those I lived among when it came to me. I have added to that knowledge over the years as I traveled from place to place."

"What about your family?" He sounded so alone in the

world. She knew that feeling very well.

"I'm still in contact with most of them. Some of them run various parts of my business holdings, in fact."

"Your sisters?"

"No, they're long gone, I'm afraid. But I look after their descendants, and many of the girls still follow the way of the *strega*." He looked proud of them for a moment, and it warmed Crystal's heart to think that he still had family and cared for them deeply.

She wondered if she'd have a chance to get to know her newfound family and how they could connect their lives. She hoped she would be able to be part of her cousins' lives and have them be an active part of hers, but she wanted to get to know them better. That would have to be the first step. When making new friends, people either meshed or they didn't. She really hoped they would hit it off. She wanted desperately to have family. To belong. Crystal had thought she'd gotten over that childhood longing, but apparently not.

They walked for another hour that night but found nothing more. Crystal was a bit frustrated with the lack of progress, but Marco was patience itself.

She felt closer to him now that he'd shared a bit about his family. It was sad that he had lost his sisters, but she was warmed by the idea that he looked after their children. She suspected that, being a mage of some kind, his life had been extended by his magic. The shaman had told her that some forms of magic did that, but not all. So, the *strega*, as he called them, must not have had that particular brand of magic.

Marco walked her up the stairs and left her at the door to her room with a peck on the cheek that left her wanting more. So much more.

Marco found it hard to walk away from Crystal after sharing so much of himself with her. He hadn't spoken of his family in too many years to count, but something about her invited confidences. He *wanted* her to know the real him. The Marco who had grown up in Messina and had loved his vibrant, magical mother and doting sisters. So much so that he kept track of every last descendant and helped them however he could.

Some worked directly for him, heading up companies he had developed over the years or, in some special cases, companies he had bought and nurtured specifically for one of his relatives' special talents. A few of them—mostly the newer generations of *strega* who understood magic—knew what he was and who he was to them. They accepted his help and remembered him as part of their extended family, but it had never been the same since his sisters had died. Their children had been close to him, but as generations passed and he moved around the globe, the emotional connection had become more and more tenuous.

He wanted so much to kiss Crystal and hold her close, but he also didn't want to rush her. She was too important to him—and to Others. She was related to two powerful Alpha females who were mated to two very influential Alpha werewolves. The last thing he wanted was hard feelings between himself and those particular wolves. Scaring Crystal off could cause a political rift that would be hard to mend, but it would also break his heart.

A heart that had not beat in centuries for anyone or anything other than the cause of Light and defeating evil. He had dedicated his immortal life to that service, not thinking he would ever be so blessed as to find his One. Yet, if he wasn't much mistaken, here she was.

That Crystal had stumbled onto his land, drawn here magically by a plea of the trees that apparently liked him enough to label him their *Protector*, seemed a minor miracle. That she might very well be his One and Only was even more miraculous.

He had simply stopped looking for his mate a very long time ago. That she had very possibly come to him, when he'd given up the search... He saw the hand of the Divine in that and counted his blessings, sending up a silent prayer to the Mother of All as he walked down the grand staircase and into the main hall of the mansion.

Dawn would come all too soon, but he had just enough time to check in with one of his favorite relatives of this generation. It was already daytime in Italy, and Philomena would be at the office by now, running her fashion empire. He didn't often call her to just chat, but she was one of the few members of his extended family that wasn't over-awed by him just because he was ancient and immortal. She respected his abilities as he respected her *strega* power, for she was the most like his older sister—whom she had been named for—than any of the offspring had ever been. If he believed in reincarnation, he would think maybe Philomena had come back to this realm to keep him company, if only from a distance.

He went into the office at the front of the house and sat down at Crystal's desk. He liked sitting there, just knowing it was her area. It made him feel close to her somehow. Shaking his head at his own silly thoughts, he picked up the phone.

Philomena answered on the second ring. He had used her private number, so he didn't have to talk to her secretary.

"Good to hear from you, Uncle Marco. How are things going for you?" she asked, her tone friendly.

It warmed him even more than usual. Crystal's influence, no doubt, bringing his feelings to the fore when they had been mostly dormant for ages.

"Very well, Mena. How have you been?"

They exchanged pleasantries for a while, both speaking in Italian. Marco had picked up the more modern way of speaking, though he did occasionally lapse into the antiquated phrases of his youth. Mena didn't mind and didn't really tease him about it. She was a very patient woman. Much like her namesake had been.

"I realize I haven't called in a while and just wanted to catch up with you. I was talking about my family with a…new acquaintance this evening." He didn't know quite how to explain about his new and strange feelings for Crystal, but he suspected Mena would figure it out. She was very intuitive, and she knew he rarely spoke of generations past except under very special circumstances.

"You were?" Mena sounded intrigued. Marco breathed a sigh of relief. Mena understood everything he couldn't really put into words. "Who is this new acquaintance?"

"She is a magical woman who only learned of her true heritage a short time ago. She is descended of a dryad, and the trees—believe it or not—called her to my land. There is still something evil here, she says, that we must find and eradicate."

"She just showed up on your land?" Mena sounded suspicious. "Where, exactly?"

"At the estate," he clarified, realizing Mena might think Crystal had somehow found his lair—the place he slept during the day that was ultra-secure and as top secret as he could make it. "She was driving past on the road that borders the forest and heard the pleas from the trees. She stopped and followed the sound, trying to give of her own energy to help the forest. She gave too much and passed out just as I found her."

"Are you sure she's not an agent of the enemy sent to lure you out?" Yes, his little Mena was ferocious when she went into protective mode.

"I'm sure. She checks out. I know two of her relatives. They have been searching for more of their kin for a while now, and one by one, they've been coming out of the woodwork, so to speak. Crystal has already spoken with them, and they have verified by magical means that she is one of theirs. I hired her to work on the estate—she has valuable experience and was on her way to a job interview anyway—and she's been here two days. Martine is working with her during the afternoons, and I walk the grounds with her at night, looking for whatever it is that's still here causing problems."

Mena paused, and Marco knew she was being cautious. Just as his sister had been.

"I have been meaning to go over to the States for business

for some time now. Would you mind if I dropped by? I think I'd like to meet this new employee of yours and just make sure she's what she seems."

"She is, Mena," Marco assured her with a sigh. "But you know I always love to see you. Come whenever you like. There's plenty of room at the estate if you wish to work from here."

"I believe I will take you up on that offer, Uncle." Her voice was rich with satisfaction, and Marco had to shake his head even as he smiled.

He didn't fear that Mena would be difficult or insulting to Crystal, but she would definitely check her out. Mena had a protective streak a mile wide. Probably due to the fact of her mixed heritage. One of her ancestors had been a bear shifter, and as he knew, bears tended to look after their own. That Mena put herself in the role of the mama bear with him made him chuckle.

"Although I am restoring much of the mansion to its former grandeur, there are a few areas that will need to be entirely redecorated. Maybe you could consult on that with my team while you're here?" Mena's style sense was off the charts. Everything she touched turned to gold in her business, and he could have no one better working on this project.

"I'd be happy to take a look," she replied, as he had suspected she would. Mena loved a challenge and was always ready to help her family.

They hung up after a little more small talk, and Marco suspected he would be seeing her sooner rather than later. She was successful enough that she owned her own private jet. She could fly over here anytime she wanted, and he thought maybe she would be gassing up that jet as soon as possible.

He hadn't meant to make her so curious that she wanted to come visit, but he didn't mind at all. She was a powerful *strega*. She could help safeguard Crystal during the day while he had to sleep. She could also be of some use if, and when, they found whatever it was that had brought Crystal here. Of course, he just liked seeing her. It was rare, these days, for him to be around his blood relations.

Marco had become more or less a hermit in recent decades. As his emotions shut down, he hadn't felt the need to be around his extended family as much as he had in the old days. But meeting Crystal had reawakened his heart. She had brought him back to life when he'd least expected it. She was a blessing to him in so many ways.

Marco got up from the chair and headed outside. There was one more person he had to speak with before dawn chased him back to his lair. Marco had decided to enlist the aid of his strongest ally in this area—the Alpha wolf.

CHAPTER 13

Brandt Bennet was waiting for Marco at the bottom of the stairs, just outside the front door of the mansion. He was impeccable in a custom-tailored suit. The glint of gold cuff links sparkled in the moonlight as he raised his hand in greeting. He was the epitome of the well-dressed man about town, which wasn't the usual way Marco saw Brandt. Usually, he was wearing a fur suit and had sharp, pointy teeth. When he wasn't furred or naked, he wore whatever came to hand, usually something stretchy from the storeroom in the mansion.

Marco didn't do a double take, but it was a close thing. He thought he knew Brandt well enough by now to speak plainly.

"What are you all dressed up for?" Marco asked as he came down the steps to meet the other man on the walkway.

"Business meeting ran late. Figured I'd stop by and see if you were still here," Brandt said casually.

Marco sensed a woman's perfume clinging to the Alpha wolf's skin and clothing, but he didn't mention it. Marco just supposed the *business* meeting had included a lot more than just business. He'd gotten used to the lusty ways of the werewolves since he'd started working so closely with them, but Brandt was always more discreet than his fellows.

Come to think of it, werewolf women didn't wear perfume. Their senses were so acute they didn't even like scented soaps. Marco had let them choose what to put in the employee areas of the mansion, because it didn't matter to him and they were concerned about strong scents.

That being the case, Brandt had probably been dallying with a human woman. Or, at least, not a shifter. Marco wouldn't pry, but he was intrigued, despite knowing it was probably none of his business.

"I'm glad you stopped by," Marco said, carefully not asking anything he'd just been thinking about. "I wanted to talk to you about Crystal. It turns out she is definitely related to the Moores' new mates. We verified that tonight in a video call with the ladies."

Brandt tilted his head in that canine way of his as he took in the information. "That's interesting. I suppose it's safe to assume you're going to suggest that we watch out for her even more during the daylight hours? You want us to go from surveillance to protection, right?"

Marco nodded. "Indeed, yes. And not just for the Moore family's sake. You are my strongest ally in the area. I am loath to admit this to anyone just yet, but you need to know. Crystal is very important to me, personally. If anything happened to her, I shudder to think what I would become."

"Whoa, there, friend." Brandt met Marco's eyes with concern. "This sounds serious. Is she—"

Marco held up a hand. "I'm not entirely sure yet, but I believe it's possible. She could very well be my One. If so..."

It was Brandt's turn to hold up his hand. "Say no more, Master." The Alpha wolf rarely used Marco's proper title. They had decided to consider themselves equal and work together, rather than compete to find out who was the stronger of the two. That Brandt used the honorific now was significant. "I and my Pack will watch over her when you cannot. You have my vow."

Marco paused for a moment, feeling the strength of Brandt's words. "Thank you, Alpha," he said finally, sealing the deal, but he felt he had to issue a bit of a warning, nonetheless. "You know what happens to a bloodletter when his One is destroyed, right? Because if that happens, you have to get help before you try to end me. Call my family in Italy, or Master Hiram in Seattle. He's closer and probably one of the only ones of my kind who could take me. I don't want to be the cause of any loss among your Pack."

"Then the old legends are true? You guys really go insane when you lose your mate? I mean, among shifters, most do not survive the loss of their mate, but it's sorrow that usually takes us. We lose the will to live without our mate. You guys take it to the extreme, huh?" The Alpha was clearly looking for confirmation of something bloodletters were usually loath to discuss with Others because it was a terrible vulnerability and put a target on the backs of their mates.

"I once knew a Berserker, back in the old days. I've also seen more than one of my kind lose it over the centuries. Like the Berserker, they went after anything in their path. Friend, foe, stranger. It didn't matter. They just killed anything and everything in their insanity. It's not pretty, and it's where the legends of the vampire came from. You're right about that." Marco stared into Brandt's eyes, hoping to impress upon him the import of what he was saying. "I have walked this earth since the Middle Ages. It will take another of my vintage, or older, to take me out."

Brandt looked at Marco consideringly for a moment, as if he was wondering who would win in a true test of strength. Brandt was ex-Special Forces and had soldiered all over the world, but Marco had centuries of craft and skill behind him. Marco knew it wouldn't even be close, considering the magic Marco could wield, but he let the wolf keep his pride.

"One more thing," Marco said, changing the subject. "One of my extended family will be arriving shortly. I'm not sure exactly when. She is coming from Italy on a private jet, and she will be staying here and working from the mansion for a bit."

"When you say family, do you mean another bloodletter or something else?" Brandt asked, his gaze shuttering with suspicion.

Marco had to chuckle. "Something else. I actually still have family. I was born in Italy in the 1400s. Philomena is a descendant of one of my sisters, and she knows exactly what and who I am. We spoke on the phone tonight, and I suspect she's already making plans to come here and check out Crystal. Mena is very protective of me, though she has little reason to worry as she does. She's just that kind of mother hen. So was her ancestor. My oldest sister, the mother hen of the family after our mother passed. She kept track of all of us, even after I...became what I am."

"You've never talked of your origins before," Brandt said, looking both pleased and perplexed.

"Meeting Crystal has reawakened something in me. I realize now that I had grown cold over the centuries. I wasn't feeling with my whole heart, though I did keep track of my sisters' children. They all work for me in one form or another, though few of them realize it." Marco shook his head. "I'm trusting you with this information, Brandt. I value our alliance, and I've come to really enjoy working with you and your Pack."

"Likewise, Marco," Brandt replied with genuine warmth. "And I have to say, I think it's awesome that Crystal has been able to affect you this way. If she's not your mate, I'll eat my hat, but I suspect your kind has rituals or something to figure that part out. Just let me know when it's official, and we'll throw you a party the likes of which you've never seen." Brandt's grin was wide, and Marco felt himself smiling in return.

"I'll do that but give me a few more days to settle things one way or the other. If Mena shows up, can you tell your people to sort out her accommodation? I've left a note for

Martine, but just in case…"

"It shall be done," Brandt said formally. "If your Mena shows up on the doorstep, we'll treat her like royalty and entertain her until you rise."

"Thank you, Alpha." Marco paused before turning to go and looked at Brandt from the corner of his eye. "Oh, and a word of warning. Mena is a very powerful hereditary witch. Have you ever met a *strega* before?"

Brandt looked surprised but intrigued. "Can't say that I have," he admitted.

Marco chuckled. "Just don't upset her or she'll turn you into a newt or something."

And with that, Marco launched himself skyward in a cloud of mist, heading back to his lair. It was getting too close to dawn to dally. Brandt's laughter followed Marco into the sky, and if he could have laughed in this form, he would have joined in.

※

Crystal woke early, despite the late night. She seldom needed much sleep and found herself wanting to get out into the morning sunshine. She put on her new sneakers and headed out, grabbing an apple from the basket near the side door. A few of the men were already at work in the house. She greeted them as she passed, biting into the tangy apple as she headed outdoors.

She hadn't gone more than a few steps when she stopped short. There was a woman on the esplanade, looking out at the garden. She wasn't anyone Crystal had ever seen at the estate before, and a quick glance told Crystal that nobody else was in sight. Crystal took a deep breath and decided to be brave, even if the woman gave off a bit of a creepy vibe.

"Hi there," Crystal said as she drew closer. She stayed about ten feet away from the stranger, just for her own comfort. "Can I help you with anything?"

The woman turned and pinned Crystal with fathomless black eyes that almost made her shiver for a moment. Then the woman smiled and blinked, her gaze going clouded, as if she was hiding her true self.

"Oh, I just came here to deliver this." The woman walked forward, holding out a large envelope. Crystal took it and frowned a bit. "I hope you don't mind. I couldn't resist taking a look at the garden. The pavilion on this property is the talk of local legends. I'm from the Chamber of Commerce, and we have a proposal in there," she nodded to the envelope Crystal was now holding, "for an event we have upcoming in a few months. Can you make sure it gets to the property manager or whoever is in charge?"

The woman looked Crystal up and down and apparently decided that Crystal was just some sort of errand girl. That was fine with Crystal. She didn't mind at all. In fact, if it would get the woman out of here faster, she would be happy to pretend she was part of the cleaning staff, a waitress or anything else this woman probably disdained in her haughtiness.

"I'd be happy to pass this along to Martine. She handles that sort of thing, I believe." Crystal forced herself to smile at the woman. "But you know, it's a little dangerous out here. They're replacing a lot of the stones, and I don't think any of us are supposed to be walking around the grounds unless the work crews say it's okay. I just was looking for the foreman to pass along a message," Crystal lied, pretending to look around.

When she looked back at the woman, she was gone. Disappeared without a trace. Shivers ran up and down Crystal's spine, and she backtracked quickly to the door of the house, trying to look casual.

She closed the door behind her and felt like breaking into a run but forced herself to walk slowly down the wide hall. A tall man passed her and stopped short. He touched her shoulder, and she paused.

"What is that?" he demanded without preamble, pointing to the envelope Crystal held.

"Uh…" Crystal tried to gather her scattered thoughts.

"There was this strange woman on the esplanade. She said she was from the Chamber of Commerce and handed me this." Crystal held it out to the man, and he moved back, much to her surprise.

"Sweetheart, that package reeks of dark magic. Why don't you just put that down on the side table, there," he suggested, pointing to the half-round table against the wall.

Crystal put it down and immediately felt lighter. Only then did she realize she'd felt sick to her stomach, as well as scared out of her wits.

"Oh, my goodness!" Crystal took a few deep breaths, wiping her hands on her pant legs, as if to rid them of some dirt.

The man whistled through his teeth and immediately a number of burly men poked their heads out of the rooms in which they had been working. The man talked to them in terse sentences.

"Intruder on the esplanade," he told them. "Be careful. I scent evil on the package. See if you can pick up a trail. A lone female, but there might be more."

The men were already on the move out the door, jogging without a sound past Crystal and the tall man.

"Who are you?" Crystal asked him. He seemed familiar, but she'd never met him before to her knowledge.

The man smiled. "Brandt," he answered easily. "We met before, but I was in my fur. I'm the Alpha of this lot, and I told Marco not four hours ago that I'd look after you." He took her elbow and guided her to a chair that was just down the hall. She sat as he watched over her. "And here I am, letting you get into trouble first thing. Marco's going to be upset."

"Why? You couldn't control that woman. She disappeared like magic. I hope your people can figure out how she did that," Crystal said absently, looking down the hall toward the door through which the men had left.

"It probably was magic," Brandt mused. "But not anything good judging by the scent coming off that envelope. What did she say when she gave it to you?"

"That she was from the Chamber of Commerce and had a proposal for an event they wanted to hold on the grounds in a few months. She asked me to give it to the property manager. She didn't have a name, and I stupidly mentioned that I'd give it to Martine. Sorry." Crystal cringed. "And I'm also sorry I didn't recognize you."

Brandt smiled at her, and she realized he was as handsome as all those other werewolves. Tall, muscular, with a killer smile and even a dimple on one side of his face. If she'd been into dimples, she'd have been a goner. As it was, she could appreciate his handsomeness, but it didn't really stir her. No, since she'd met Marco, he was the only man who invaded her dreams and made her breath catch in the most delicious way. Unprofessional as that was to admit.

"No problem. After all, we've only met once, and I didn't look like this that time." His smile faded as he looked at the envelope on the table once more. "I think Martine is in the dining room. Do me a favor and just go tell her what happened and that I think she should stay in the house for now. We're going to do a sweep of the estate, but if that woman was using magic to shield her presence—which she probably was—then we won't find much." He frowned. "That's a problem. Potentially, a really big problem. We'll have to get that package out of here, but I'm afraid none of my people will want to touch it."

"That's okay. I've already touched it. I'll take it wherever you tell me," she offered.

He looked back at her, his eyes narrowing. "I may take you up on that, but let's find something to put it in first. Nobody should be touching that directly, if we can help it."

Crystal was a bit shocked by his reaction, to be honest. He really did seem concerned about the fact that she had touched the big envelope. It hadn't felt that bad, though there was something... She just wasn't sure. She wasn't used to magic being used so flagrantly.

"You mean like a plastic bag, or something?" she asked.

114

CHAPTER 14

"Something made of a natural fiber would be better," Brandt told Crystal. "Like a canvas bag. A tote bag or a messenger bag. Leather would probably be better, if we could find something, but any sort of natural fiber or substance would help block some of the magic, possibly."

"Okay. I think there was a tote bag in the storeroom. I'll go get it." She got up from the chair and was about to head to the storeroom when she remembered he'd asked her to talk to Martine. "Or should I go to the dining room first to speak with Martine?"

He reached into his pocket and brought out a small cellphone. He started tapping on the screen.

"I'm messaging her right now. If you can put your hands on that bag, I'd appreciate it. I'd like to get that package out of the mansion as soon as we can." He looked up from his screen. "All you have to do is put it in the bag. I can take it from there."

She didn't wait to hear more. She jogged down the hallway

and into the storage room, which was, thankfully, nearby. She grabbed one of the tote bags she had seen and went back out, returning quickly to the Alpha. She didn't waste time. She just went up to the side table and nudged the envelope into the bag.

"Thanks." He took the straps but held the bag at arm's length as he headed for the door to the outside.

Crystal watched him leave then turned to find Martine behind her. She briefed the other woman on what had happened outside and walked back with her to the dining room. Crystal grabbed some food to take with her back to the office, and they spent the rest of the morning working and waiting to hear the results of the Alpha's search of the property.

He came in and escorted them both to lunch, briefing them along the way as to their lack of progress. None of the Pack members had found anyone on the grounds, though they had scented a trace of dark magic on the esplanade in the area where Crystal had encountered the woman. Brandt tried to be reassuring, but Crystal got the impression he was very troubled by the entire incident.

"I've got that envelope in the tote bag, in the metal storage case in back of my truck. I'm going to meet up with Marco tonight so he can examine it off-site. He may be a bit later than normal. I want to be able to assure him that you, Miss Crystal, won't leave the building until he gets here." Brandt winked at her, trying to make his words a bit lighter, but she understood. Marco wouldn't be happy if she came to harm.

Though why the Alpha wolf should think that, she wasn't sure. Had Marco said something to him? If so, what? And what did it mean?

She was puzzled the rest of the afternoon as she worked through her ideas for developing the mansion and the property. She looked at architectural drawings and maps of the estate, which also helped her plan out the next areas she wanted to search. There was definitely something evil left on site, and she needed to find it.

One interpretation of the strange woman's appearance this morning might be that she was also looking for whatever had captured Crystal's attention and troubled the trees so much. If so, Crystal couldn't believe that someone who left envelopes that *reeked of evil magic* according to a powerful Alpha wolf wanted whatever it was that troubled the estate grounds for any *good* reason. Likely, whatever she had planned would be evil, and Crystal couldn't let that happen.

So, they appeared to be in a race to find the object or whatever it was. The pressure had just been turned up a notch, now that she suspected there would be competition for it. She wondered if the danger had also increased. The fact that the woman had been able to get on the estate without anybody noticing sent shivers down Crystal's spine.

When Marco arrived, a little later than usual that night, he looked grim.

"Are you all right?" he asked her the moment he walked into the office, coming right around her desk and crouching down by her chair so they were on the same level.

Crystal swiveled her office chair to face him. "I'm fine. Did you open the envelope?"

Marco shook his head, taking one of her hands in his and making a minute inspection of her fingers. "I dared not. Not yet anyway." He shrugged and let go of that hand, only to capture the other and subject it to the same scrutiny. "Brandt helped me put it someplace safe. I have some specialist magical help arriving any day now, and I would prefer to leave examination of the envelope until they get here."

"What do you think it is? Any idea?" He didn't let go of her hand after checking it for damage—or whatever—but held it between both of his. She liked the way he touched her so gently and wasn't in any hurry to retrieve her hand.

"I suspect it encapsulates some sort of spy spell so that, when it is opened, it reveals information to the sender about where it is and who is around it. It could also deliver a killing spell or even something to mark everyone in the vicinity for later targeting. It could be other things as well. Which is why

I want to open it somewhere that can't hurt any of my people and under very controlled conditions. I also want a better mage than myself to oversee the process," he said, surprising Crystal with his statement.

She had thought he was a very potent mage if he had undertaken the cleansing of this land. The fact that he knew his own limitations was both surprising and enlightening. She liked that he didn't just assume he could handle anything that came his way. That was the mark of both humility and intelligence as far as she was concerned. It was an unexpectedly sexy combination.

Marco breathed a sigh of relief, finding no residual dark magic clinging to Crystal. When Brandt had told him what had transpired, his first impulse was to go to her immediately, but Brandt had assured him she was all right. The werewolf's nose was acute, and he hadn't scented anything sticking to Crystal, which was reassuring, but Marco didn't rest easy until he got to see her for himself.

They were under attack, though she probably didn't realize it yet. That someone had been able to infiltrate the estate wasn't entirely a surprise, considering the way they'd been working until this point. The wards were proof against most intruders, except those who could actively hide their presence magically. It wasn't easy to fox a ward, but it could be done, and it seemed these *Venifucus* had that ability.

The reliance on wards alone and the casual attitude toward security were all going to change. Marco had already tasked Brandt and his team with beefing up patrols of the grounds and buildings. They hadn't done it before—other than wolves casually walking or running through the woods as they roamed in their fur—because Marco had assumed the evil folk who had used the mansion and grounds before had been either killed outright or run off to pursue their evil intent elsewhere.

Apparently, not all of them had left the area.

Marco had been blindsided by this development.

Suddenly, he felt like there was a ticking clock, counting down the minutes until another attack. He had been lulled into a sense of security about the place, but he should have realized that the *Venifucus* wouldn't let this property go so easily. Marco and his allies had destroyed the group that was using it, but that didn't mean some other branch of the organization didn't want to try to regain it.

Especially in light of what Crystal had told him. If there still was some sort of magical artifact hidden somewhere on this land, it made sense that the *Venifucus* would try to reclaim it. He didn't know why he hadn't thought of it before. When so many months had passed without incident, Marco had figured the enemy had given up. He should have known better.

Of course, when it was just the werewolves and himself, he hadn't been too concerned. But with the arrival of Crystal, everything changed. They were going to have to work harder to find whatever it was that had drawn her here. They had to find it before the enemy did. Or before the enemy attacked. Either situation was possible, and he had to prepare for all contingencies.

That in mind, they didn't waste any time going out to search the grounds. Crystal had been busy as well. She had looked at maps of the estate and had decided on a course of action for the remainder of the search. It made sense to Marco when she explained it, so he was happy to entertain her plan. They went to the area near the maze that had played such a prominent role in the fight to free the estate.

Immediately, Crystal showed signs of disturbance. She frowned often as they walked, and shook her head.

"There's something really wrong on the other side of the hedges in this spot," she told him, pausing at a particular spot on the edge of the maze.

"This is the outer boundary of the maze. Inside it were statues placed along the pathways. The statues were imbued with evil spells that made them come to life and try to kill those who were going through the maze on their way to the pavilion. Numerous traps were sprung during the battle for this place. Perhaps you're feeling a residual of that?" The statues were long gone. He wasn't sure what else she could be feeling.

Crystal shook her head slowly. "No. There's something still there. What's on the other side of this hedge?"

Marco levitated himself into the air and took a look over the top of the hedge. "Just a pedestal. The statues are destroyed, and we took the pieces away and ground them into dust, dispersing the evil spells that had been cast upon them." He kept talking even as he lowered himself back to the ground. "Only the pedestals are left." Crystal was looking at him with wide eyes.

"I didn't know you could do that," she admitted, her voice holding both surprise and a bit of awe. She shook her head as if to clear it. "Sorry. I think you had better re-examine the pedestals. There's something not right here."

"Perhaps we should go into the maze itself. Get a closer look," he suggested.

She agreed, and they set off for the entrance to the maze. Even as they walked down the first leafy hallway toward a junction where only a pedestal stood now, Crystal tensed. She was shaking her head and almost turning away, though she still moved forward slowly.

"Oh, that has got to go," she said pointing at the pedestal. It was a squat square construction of bricks and mortar. Marco sensed nothing wrong with it, but if Crystal was reacting the strongly, there had to be something he was missing.

"What do the bushes tell you? Do they speak to you at all?"

She nodded. "There was blood mixed into the mortar." Her voice was filled with disgust and abhorrence. "The pedestal was used as an evil altar before the statue was placed. Each one of these constructions included the blood of an innocent, sacrificed to evil. It's all got to go, Marco." She turned her devastated gaze to him. "You would not believe the scenes these bushes are showing me. It's absolutely evil." She stumbled a little and seemed weakened by the exposure.

Marco took her by the hand and led her from the maze. "I'll have Brandt put a group to work dismantling each and every one of those pedestals. I'm sorry, my dear. I knew the statues were bad, but I had no idea what had gone into making them and what they stood on."

"It's not your fault," she told him, her tone gentle, touching deep inside his heart. "But it would be good to get rid of those things. Maybe just let the maze grow over completely, and let the bushes have their way with the land. Or, if we really want to keep the maze, then we could plant some things where those statues stood to try to counterbalance the evil that was done there and heal the land."

"I'll let you decide which is the best course of action once we have rid the area of those stone monuments." She was the expert in this area. He would let her have final say in what happened to the maze.

She stumbled again, and he couldn't help himself. He lifted her into his arms and carried her back to the mansion. Whatever she had seen... Whatever the bushes had shown her... It had affected her greatly. Much as they needed to search every inch of this property as quickly as possible, they were done for the night. She needed a break, and he couldn't watch her deplete herself this way.

She protested a little, but he carried her right up to her room and deposited her on the bed. He used his magic to open each door and close it behind them. He wasn't fooling around. He didn't have to hide his magic anymore. Not with her. As much as he could, he would be open and honest with her, even though she had yet to discover what he truly was.

The only thing holding him back from telling her he was a bloodletter, at this point, was fear. Fear that she would reject him once she knew. If not for that, he would've told her already. But she was too important to him to make a mistake by rushing too fast. He would have to be patient.

"I feel so silly," Crystal said weakly as he sat on the side of the bed. She sat up a little, facing him.

"You should not feel that way, *cara*," he told her gently, reaching out to take her hand. "Dark magic is a terrible thing and affects some of us more than others. All magic is individual. No one can predict how things will affect a person until they are experienced. We just learned that you are particularly susceptible to things concealed in brick and mortar. Earthen elements. Which makes sense given your heritage." He raised her hand to his lips and kissed the back of it gently. "I'm sorry I didn't realize how it would affect you, but I'm also glad that you are able to find things that the rest of us have missed." Marco heard the little hitch in her breath and the way her pulse sped up as he caressed her hand. She was susceptible to him, which gratified him to no end. He moved closer. "Nevertheless, I feel badly that this affected you so, and I fear we'll have to continue our search to find whatever you first sensed. That visitor earlier today worries me," he confided.

"Because she might be after whatever it is that the trees abhor?"

Marco was pleasantly surprised by Crystal's sharp wits. "Exactly so," he admitted. "We have to find whatever it is before she or her confederates do. The evil object needs to be nullified or put where the enemy cannot get it and use it against us."

Crystal nodded. "I was thinking the same thing. It's a race now. We have to get to it before that woman finds a way back onto the grounds and possibly steals it."

Marco moved closer. "You are right, my dear. Brandt and his people are beefing up security. I didn't realize the enemy was still interested in this place or that there was anything they wanted here. As a result, I didn't implement the tight security we will now be putting in place. We had some, but it was much more casual than it will be. Many of Brandt's people are ex-military, and they've already stepped up. I'm also going to call in some specialist help. Tomorrow, they will be doing more, and you will notice some changes. Hopefully, it'll be enough to keep you safe, but I must ask that you not go out of the house until I am here to accompany you. Will you give me your word?"

Crystal met his gaze and nodded once. "I promise," she said softly and so seriously that he couldn't resist. He moved in and placed a kiss on her lips.

CHAPTER 15

Thank goodness! Crystal thought with relief. This was no little peck on the cheek. Those little kisses had been leaving her wanting for the past two days, and now...finally...she was getting the kiss she'd wanted. The real kiss, involving lips and tongues and sensations that made her gasp.

And it was so much better than she had imagined. So much more exciting. Her blood bubbled happily in her veins as the magic of Marco caused her passion to rise to unprecedented heights. Never had a simple kiss rocked her world so greatly.

He took her into his arms and held her close, her body melting into his. If he'd asked her to give him anything in that moment, she would gladly have done so. Anything.

He pressed her back onto the bed and came down over her. His arms bracketed her head, trapping her within the cocoon of his warmth. He became the focus of her entire world as he kissed her, his hard body over hers from the waist up.

Then he readjusted, and she felt the length of him along her side a moment before he put one of his knees on either side of her legs. He lowered his weight onto her just slightly, rubbing against her, and she gasped into the ongoing kiss. She could feel the hardness of him rubbing against her, and he was…impressive, to say the least.

Hard. Ready. So masculine she felt dainty in response.

Crystal squirmed to get closer and felt him growl deep in his chest. That was sexy. His kiss roughened a little and then his mouth left her lips and traveled down to her neck. He licked and sucked, using his teeth to gently abrade the sensitive skin of her neck, and she found it an incredible turn on.

He spent a long time on her neck. More than any man she'd been with before—not that there had been all that many. Still, he made her feel things she never had before, and she wondered why she had never realized what wonderful sensations could be had from a man kissing her neck.

Marco moved on eventually, his hands cupping her breasts and playing with the hard peaks. As his head moved lower, he used his teeth to move the neckline of her soft, stretchy shirt out of the way. The lacy cup of her bra was visible but was no match for his pearly whites as he took hold of the fabric and tugged it down, dragging his stubbled chin over her soft skin and making gooseflesh break out all over her arms.

Damn. The man was potent. A moment later, his mouth opened over her taut peak, his tongue and teeth dancing around the tip, bringing her up off the bed to somehow get closer. But he held her at bay. He had total control of her at that moment, and she didn't mind one bit. He made her feel things with just these simple touches that couldn't compare with any of her previous experiences. Not in any way.

Marco was new and unexpected. Daring and delightful. Mischievous and masterful.

She wasn't sure she would survive if they ever took this all the way to its natural conclusion.

Crystal was drowning in bliss, her senses going wild until

suddenly…he was gone.

Her eyes blinked open to find Marco standing at the side of the bed, looking down at her, a pained expression on his handsome face.

"Forgive me, I should not have let that go so far," he said in a rough voice. "I will see you tomorrow night." He seemed to sway toward her, and she thought he might come back, but he moved toward the door. He paused, one hand on the doorknob, and before he opened it, he whispered. "Think of me."

Then he left, closing the door behind him with a final click that resounded through her soul.

Marco practically dragged himself away from her. Everything within him was begging him to stay, but he knew he could not. For one thing, she was in no condition for what his body was tempting him to do. The encounter with evil— or whatever residual magic was left in those pedestals—had taken a toll on her. Because of her affinity with the earth, whatever had been done to the bricks and mortar, which, after all, were also part of the earth, it had really knocked her for a loop. She needed to recover from that before he would press his suit any further.

For another thing, he was very aware that they were operating on borrowed time. The appearance of that woman on the esplanade earlier today had been a wake-up call, in more ways than one. He had been a fool to think that, just because the former owners of the estate had been routed in battle and killed, their followers who had escaped justice would not return. He hadn't really worried about it before because the only people here were werewolves, most of whom were well able to take care of themselves against any mage. Most magic tended to slide right off of werewolf fur, making them more than a match for human magic users.

Marco had also not realized that there was anything left on this estate worth risking an encounter with a strong werewolf Pack. However, Crystal's arrival and insistence that there was something here that beckoned to her and caused the trees to cry out for help to her made him reevaluate his thoughts. Not only was there still something here, but that woman's appearance made him think it was something the enemy wanted desperately to retrieve.

The woman, whoever she was, had taken a great risk coming here. She had chosen her time well, considering she probably knew that the new owner of the estate was a vampire. So, she had come during the day. How she had slipped past the werewolves, nobody could tell yet. It was possible, though not entirely probable, that she had some sort of ability to create a portal that would take her from place to place magically. That kind of magic, though, usually left ripples of disturbance in the energy of a place that Marco would have noticed. So far, he hadn't sensed anything of the kind.

More likely, she had some sort of spell or perhaps a native ability that allowed her to navigate around obstacles—including people she wanted to avoid. It wasn't unheard of, though it was rare to have that kind of talent. Whatever the case, she had made her way to the house, unseen. She had not entered, which would have set off all kinds of magical alarms that Marco would have heard, even in his deep sleep of the day.

There were wards around the property too, but a really good mage could circumvent those in particular circumstances. Again, such a skill was not common, but it did exist. Marco had seen it in action only once before in his long life. One of his own family had been born with the ability to walk through any ward with utter impunity. Thankfully, she had been *strega*, and not inclined to misuse her power. She was, after all, on the side of Light.

With grim determination, Marco left Crystal's room and headed down the stairs. He had a lot of work to do. There were battle plans to make.

The crews were busy at work when Crystal came

downstairs the next day close to noon. Hammering in the distance had woken her up finally, along with the sound of power tools in use. She met up with Martine in the dining room, and they sat together to eat.

"Do you know what's going on?" Crystal asked after a while. "I know I've only been here a short time, but usually, it's not this noisy."

"Oh, Marco and Brandt got together last night and decided to build a gatehouse, along with a few other improvements." Martine waved her hand absently toward the front of the house. "There are a bunch of new rules as well. Like, nobody is allowed on the grounds without prior approval, all deliveries have to come through the front gate, and there will now be someone manning it twenty-four seven, and all the mail is getting delivered to the new gatehouse. Not even the mailman is coming up the drive any longer. No more casual snoopers, which is a relief, in some ways. In others, it's a little concerning."

Crystal frowned. "What do you mean?"

"Well, the whole reason for it is a concern. That woman who just appeared outside yesterday. You may not realize it, but that's a big deal. It's incredibly difficult to sneak up on someone like me, and I'm not really trained for it. I just have my natural senses that are so much more acute than regular people. But the guys, many of whom have been training in stealth for years and were part of the Special Forces in the military—to get past them without anybody noticing, that's a huge deal. A few of them are really upset about it."

"So they're doing all of that building in response to that woman's appearance yesterday?" Crystal was both astounded and relieved. That woman had given her the creeps, and the fact that she had been able to come onto the grounds without anybody aware of her presence had frightened Crystal, after the fact.

Martine nodded as she chewed and then swallowed. "Yes, and implementing all kinds of new procedures." Martine shrugged as she buttered a piece of toast. "It makes sense.

We've been assuming this place's safe because the bad guys were defeated, but that was probably a mistake. Brandt held a little meeting with all of us who work here this morning. He said we'd been a little too complacent in our belief that, just because the enemy was defeated once, they would never come back. Apparently, Marco said much the same thing to him last night. They're both in agreement. We have to be a lot more serious about security. Especially since there might be something they still want here."

Crystal shook her head, feeling conflicting emotions. "I think…" She took a deep breath and tried again. "I think whatever it is that brought me here is probably what that woman was after. It's what the trees don't want here. It's something evil. I can't think of any other reason for someone with bad intentions to show up here uninvited. I've got to find that thing, whatever it is."

"You will," Martine said with infinite confidence. When she said it like that, Crystal almost believed her. Martine had a very strong personality and a will of iron, Crystal was coming to learn. She admired the other woman greatly.

"I hope you're right. It's just frustrating that I haven't been able to locate it yet." Crystal ate the last bite of her brunch and put down her fork.

"Give yourself a break. You've only been at this for a few days. You'll find it. I believe in you." The smile Martine bestowed on Crystal was full of confidence as she rose, and Crystal followed suit. They headed back down the hall to the office and set to work for the day.

Around midday, there was a bit of a commotion in the front hall that drew both women out of the office. A glamorous dark-haired woman stood like a statue—or a fashion model striking a pose—in the light of the open door as men brought in suitcases and boxes behind her. She looked around the large entry, as if sizing up the décor, then her eyes lit on Martine and Crystal in the door to the parlor that had been converted into their office.

"Ah, *bon giorno*. I am Philomena. I told Uncle Marco I

would come, and here I am." Her cultured voice held the lilt of a slight Italian accent that was altogether charming.

Martine stepped forward and held out her hand in greeting. "I'm Martine. Marco mentioned that you might be arriving." The two women shook hands and seemed to be sizing each other up. When they let go, Martine turned to Crystal. "And this is Crystal. She's new but has been shaking things up in a good way." Martine smiled reassuringly as she introduced her to the new arrival.

Philomena turned her full attention on Crystal, and she felt almost intimidated by the woman's dark gaze. They shook hands, and when their fingers met, there was a little spark of electricity that seem to jump between them. It didn't hurt, but it was a little startling. Philomena seemed to take it in stride, but her gaze suddenly turned approving. As if Crystal had passed some sort of test.

"I have come to help with a little redecoration in the parts of the building that cannot be reconstructed from old records. A little mix of the new with the old, no?" Philomena explained. "I also came to see Uncle Marco. It has been too long between visits."

"He's actually your uncle?" Martine asked, frowning slightly.

Philomena tilted her head. "He is definitely my uncle, though I do not know how many times removed. Is that what you say, in English?"

"Great," Martine supplied. "He's your great-uncle, we would say. A few times great, I imagine."

Crystal didn't really understand all of what they were talking about, but she had already decided that Marco was probably a lot older than he looked. The shaman had told her that magic affected different people in different ways. Some were granted much longer lives by the way their magic affected them. She assumed Marco was one of those. His mannerisms, his speech, the little ways he had of doing things all pointed to a bygone era. Crystal found it charming, though she had many questions about how it must be to outlive everything you know. And everyone.

But he seemed to be coping with that pretty well. She didn't want to pry into his personal affairs, but she had formed her own conclusions. She figured, as they got to know each other better, he might tell her more about his past and exactly how old he really was.

"Whatever the case, we are family. And we look out for each other." Philomena's words were very firm, and Martine nodded in response. "The men at the gate are doing a good job, but I would like to speak with your Alpha, if he is on the grounds."

Martine only looked a little surprised to hear such words and nodded again. "He's not here right now, that I know of, but he should be back on the estate shortly. What are your plans? I mean, do you need to rest after your journey, or do you want to take a look around the house or grounds? I can let him know you're here when he gets back, and he can find you if we have an idea of where you'll be."

"I'm not tired, but Uncle Marco said I could stay in one of the guest rooms. If the young gentlemen will just help me get everything into my room, I'd like to take a look around the house." Philomena smiled at the two young men who had been helping her. She had brought quite a bit of luggage with her, and they had only just finished bringing it all in.

"Yes, I believe Marco put you in the blue suite. Top of the stairs, take a right, and it's at the end of the hall on the left," Martine said. The two men lifted the bags and started up the stairs without being asked.

Crystal noticed that the blue suite was at the opposite end of the corridor from where she was staying. She filed that thought away for later pondering.

CHAPTER 16

The three women spent the rest of the afternoon together, going through each room in the house. Martine was very knowledgeable about the areas that had not yet been restored. She was also a wealth of knowledge about the restoration and vintage of everything in the rooms that had been finished. Philomena asked detailed questions, indicating to Crystal that she really knew quite a bit about interior design and antiques.

Crystal felt as if she was just along for the ride a few times, but she didn't mind. She had only been through some of these rooms once, and it was such a beautiful place she didn't mind seeing it again and learning even more about it.

Occasionally, they would come across some men installing what looked like tiny little cameras and microphones, though Crystal certainly wasn't any sort of expert. Mysterious little boxes were put on many of the windows in hidden locations, and Crystal assumed it was some sort of security system being installed.

Most of the places she had worked had had very obvious

security systems. By contrast, the technology that was going in here seemed very unobtrusive. She was surprised that there hadn't been something here before, but they were remedying that now. A few times, when she looked out the window, she saw men out on the grounds installing things out there as well. Quite a few of the people were new. Several faces belonged to people she had not met before.

When Crystal mentioned this to Martine, the other woman told her that they had acquired some specialist help overnight. The new guys, Martine explained, were ex-military shifters from a group out of Wyoming. They had arrived that morning at Brandt and Marco's combined request to help beef up security. She concluded her explanation by saying that Crystal would probably meet most of them at dinner later.

After the house tour, Philomena left them back at the office. She had explained that she was going to beef up the wards on the house before dinner and went off on her own. Crystal saw Martine nod to one of the young men who appeared to be loitering in the hall, and he went after Philomena.

"Don't you trust her?" Crystal asked as they walked back into their shared office.

Martine tilted her head in that very canine way she sometimes had. "I don't know her. Not yet. I'd like to see how she and Marco interact before I make any decisions about her. My first instinct is to like her a great deal. She's clearly a woman of power, and she knows how to use it. I didn't really realize that Marco was still in touch with his relatives."

"Yes, he told me many of them work for him in one capacity or another. I think he really misses his sisters," Crystal said, thinking only of the hint of loneliness she had heard in Marco's voice when he'd told her about his sisters.

"He spoke of his family with you?" Martine was looking at her oddly, and Crystal realized she'd probably spoken out of turn. She shouldn't be gossiping about what Marco had said to her. It just wasn't polite.

Crystal tried to shrug off the other woman's interest. "A bit," she replied as offhandedly as possible.

Crystal turned to her computer and set to work, hoping to let the topic drop right there. Thankfully, Martine went to her own desk and got back to work without further comment.

Just before dinner, Philomena returned to the office, and the three women went to the dining room together. Philomena's appearance caused a bit of a stir among the men. Quite a few of them were practically salivating at her feet. She was a gorgeous woman with lustrous long black hair that had an artful wave around her face. Her eyes were dark brown, and her features were strong. Romanesque, Crystal thought. It was clear a lot of the guys were impressed by her as well, and it didn't take long for her to make friends with everyone.

As the dining room emptied, Marco walked in with Brandt. Marco made a beeline for Philomena and took her into his arms for a hug and kisses on both cheeks.

"Mena! *Cara mia!* It is so good to see you again," he said with genuine emotion in his voice.

"Uncle Marco." She laughed as he lifted her easily in his arms and then set her down on the floor again as if she was a little girl.

Philomena was shorter than him, but something about her personality made her seem to have a greater stature than she really did. The spiked heels didn't hurt either, Crystal thought with an inward grin. It was good to see Marco so happy. Crystal's heart went out to him. He had seemed so solemn and quiet when they'd first met but as she got to know him, she realized he had a big heart that was loving and pure.

"You've met my friends already," Marco said, turning to include Crystal and Martine in the conversation. "But you have not met the Alpha of this Pack or the specialists we have called in to help."

Marco stepped back and let Brandt move closer to Philomena, making the introductions. It was at that point that Crystal realized there were a few men behind him. Some of the newcomers she'd seen working around the house and grounds during the tour. They hadn't been at dinner, but the buffet hadn't been cleared away yet, and now, she understood why. A few of them were eyeing the food but had manners enough to wait until they'd been introduced before descending on the buffet.

Brandt and Philomena seemed to strike sparks off each other in a very male-female way when they were introduced. The Alpha wolf's gaze sharpened, and his eyes sparkled with attraction, if Crystal was any judge. Philomena looked intrigued by Brandt as well. Crystal wondered if there might be romance in the air, but she didn't have long to ponder that as the werewolf Alpha introduced the other men.

"This is Arlo and Rusty from a Pack out west. The pertinent fact is that they are both security experts and part of a team of ex-Special Forces shifters who hire out their services on worthy missions," Brandt introduced the newcomers first to Philomena and then to Crystal and Martine.

"Even in Italy, we have heard of the Wraiths," Philomena said as she shook first Arlo and then Rusty's hands.

Arlo was a tall, rangy man with sharp eyes and a deceptively lazy stance that Crystal thought probably hid quick reflexes held in check with effort. Rusty had bright red hair that gave her an inkling of how he'd gotten his nickname. They shook her hand and nodded in turn, then greeted Martine politely as well.

Marco went into the kitchen and returned with a couple of bottles of wine and some glasses on a tray. He invited the newly arrived men to grab some food while motioning to the ladies to join him at one of the smaller tables that had not been used.

"Would you join me in a glass of wine?" Marco asked the women politely. All three answered in the affirmative, and he opened a bottle and poured glasses for Philomena, Crystal, Martine and himself.

The kitchen staff worked quietly around the room,

clearing away the refuse from the main dinner and making sure the latecomers had everything they needed. Once the room was empty, save for the three women and four men, and all were seated, discussion began. Brandt, Arlo and Rusty were eating, but it didn't detract from their input into the conversation.

They reported on the progress that had been made that day in installing new security measures. Arlo mentioned that the rest of his team would be working through the night on rotation. Some of the Wraiths would be on duty during the day and some at night. They were splitting shifts and organizing themselves so that there was always coverage. Brandt reported that his Pack was doing the same in conjunction with Arlo's guys, and nobody was getting onto the grounds without divine intervention, as he put it.

Marco approved as he sipped the wine, and Crystal took a tentative taste, wowed by the vintage. This had to be a very expensive wine, though her palate wasn't as sophisticated as some. Working in the hospitality industry, she'd learned a bit about wine, though she wasn't quite an expert. She peered over at the label and was impressed to see the famous Maxwell Vineyards logo. Expensive wine, indeed.

"I am concerned especially for Crystal and Martine," Marco said, turning toward them. "Crystal because she had contact with the woman today and is also the least familiar of all of us with her own abilities. Forgive me, my dear, but our allies need to know that you are relatively new to your power and not really trained. That said, I'm certain you have some formidable abilities, but you may not be aware of them, and they may not come when you need them. In which case, I'd like the others to keep an eye on you, in particular. As for you, Martine," he turned his attention to the other woman, "you are the point of contact for this project with the outside world. Even if Crystal had not named you to the intruder, it wouldn't be hard for anyone to learn your name since it's on a lot of the paperwork we had to file with the mortal authorities to do the work on this property. For that reason, you could be targeted by the enemy, and I'd like you to take special precautions. Perhaps you would consider moving into the mansion temporarily, so you wouldn't have to commute? I know it's probably not as safe as your Pack lands, but the problem I see is you being grabbed or attacked during your commute from there to here. Alternatively, you might be able to work from home for a while? Either way, I want you to be more vigilant."

Brandt frowned and seconded Marco's wishes. He spoke in low tones to Martine. "I know you probably want in on any fight that might be coming this way, but remember your obligations, little one. Your family needs you more than the warriors of the Pack need an extra set of hands on this mission. We've got you covered if you want to try working from home for a day and see if it works out."

Martine looked torn and more than a bit angry at her Alpha's words, but she bit her lip and nodded, uncharacteristically docile. "It's true my folks need me, and I'm not really a trained fighter, but I don't like the idea of hiding while you all are facing possible danger."

"It's not hiding," Brandt told her. "Not really. It's choosing the better option and being true to your family obligations. We all understand that. It just makes sense that you retire from the field until it's safe again, if at all possible."

"I still don't like it, but I'll acceded to your wishes, Alpha." Martine gave in grudgingly, but she did give in.

Surprisingly, it was Philomena who reached out to cover Martine's hand on the table, drawing her attention. "Family is all important. If yours needs you, then that is more important than putting yourself in the line of fire here. We all respect that." Her low words seemed to take the tension from Martine's shoulders, and she smiled softly at the Italian witch.

"My parents are elderly, and though our kind don't often get ill, they are both frail, and I help care for them. When I leave here each night, I go to their house and sleep in the spare room, so I'll be there if they need help in the night. My father has fallen a few times in the past year, and my mother isn't strong enough anymore to lift him to his feet."

Philomena patted Martine's hand. "You are a good daughter." She drew back, and Martine seemed to realize she'd said a bit more than she'd wanted to say about her personal situation. She blushed and took her hands off the table, sitting back in her chair.

The meeting went on and the men described specifics of their new security system and the additional measures that would be put in place. When they wound down, it was Philomena's turn.

"As you know, I only arrived today, but already I have noticed a few places where I can contribute stronger spells of protection. I have begun constructing stronger wards on the entrances to this house—doors, windows, and the like. I would be happy to work with you, Crystal, on discovering what we could do for the grounds. I am no dryad, but I know a bit of earth magic that might be useful, and if you would like to work on basic things, I would be happy to teach you what I know that might help you."

Crystal was floored by the offer. "Thank you," she said immediately. "I'd like that."

Coming here had, indeed, been the hand of Fate stepping in to help, Crystal thought. She'd already learned more about the magical world in just a few days than she had in all the time she'd been aware of it. And now, this cultured, classy, powerful woman was going to give her magic lessons? It seemed unreal. And a once-in-a-lifetime kind of opportunity.

Although Philomena intimidated Crystal a bit, she sensed no ill will from the other woman. Philomena was beautiful and very sure of herself. She was elegant and quite obviously, incredibly wealthy. Her luggage was designer, and her clothes were like nothing Crystal had ever seen, except on the rich and famous. Philomena was part of the jet set, and Crystal was very aware that she had always worked for a living, but Philomena wasn't a snob, and she seemed very genuinely willing to help.

"Then it is settled." Marco took control of the meeting

once more. "The new security system is going in, nobody will be allowed to casually come onto the property anymore, Martine will try working from home, Mena will work with Crystal during the day, and I will continue to escort her around the grounds as she searches for whatever it is the enemy left here, at night. Did I miss anything?"

Everybody shook their heads, and the meeting broke up shortly thereafter. Philomena yawned and announced that she was heading to bed. She stopped to kiss Marco on the cheek and bid the others a goodnight, then headed out of the dining room. Brandt engaged Martine in conversation about the logistics of getting her safely to her parents' house that night, and the other men concentrated on filling their bellies. Crystal marveled again at how much these werewolves could *eat*.

Marco finished his wine and stood. Crystal followed suit. "Do you want to change before we take our walk?" Marco asked.

Crystal nodded. "I'll just be a few minutes."

"I'll wait for you at the foot of the stairs," he told her agreeably.

Crystal said goodbye to the others and went out of the dining room, quickly ascending the stairs to her room. She changed and rejoined Marco a few minutes later.

CHAPTER 17

Crystal was dressed all in soft, stretchy black knit jersey when she descended the stairs. Marco held his breath. She was regal as a queen, though she didn't know it, and that was even more impressive. Her beauty shone through the casual clothing and simple ponytail in which she confined her gloriously wavy, long golden hair. She looked both determined and a little unsure of herself, but to him, she was beauty itself.

The more he was around her, the more he was convinced he was going to spend the rest of his eternal life with her. He was taking his time, though it was killing him, because he didn't want to scare her off, but things were starting to come to a boil, and he knew he would have to advance his intentions soon, or explode. She had allowed him to kiss her, but he wanted to do so much more. No. He *needed* to do a hell of a lot more, or he was going to go out of his mind. Perhaps tonight. He would have to read the signs and do his best not to rush her into anything. He didn't want to begin their relationship on a bad note. All had to be as perfect as he could make it for his mate.

He breathed out on that thought. *Mate.* Someone he'd never thought to meet. Someone he'd all but given up on ever finding... And there she was. His mate. His One. The answer to prayers he'd thought he'd forsaken long ago.

She stopped in front of him at the bottom of the stairs, looking at him quizzically. "Ready?" she asked, smiling invitingly.

"Ready," he confirmed, turning to allow her to precede him toward the door. They walked out into the night together.

Exploration of the grounds proceeded much as it had the previous nights, only this time, they came across some people in the woods. Marco recognized members of the Wraiths installing hidden cameras and sensors in the trees and along the perimeter of the property. They nodded when they saw him, and they exchanged quiet greetings but otherwise didn't stop their work. Marco was glad to see they were putting in overtime to get the system up and running.

It had been a huge oversight of his not to have installed something already, but he'd honestly thought the threat of enemy action was over. He hadn't suspected there would be ongoing interest in the lands. If he had, he would have taken steps long ago. He cursed himself for a fool in assuming the enemy had given up on this place. He should have known better, but at least he'd been able to get help in rectifying the situation.

The Wraiths didn't work for just anyone. He'd been lucky to have connections with the group's leader. Maria and Jesse had been at the center of a battle that had been fought in the pavilion to free two bear shifters who had been kidnapped and drained of their energy almost to death during an evil ceremony. It had been the last evil event to take place on the grounds, and once it had gotten dark enough, Marco had flown in to help mop up the bad guys.

They had become friends during that time and allies as well. Jesse knew the layout of the estate, and he'd been instrumental in helping Marco convince the local wolves to work for him in the cleanup phase. After they'd established that relationship, Marco had been able to take it a step further and form an alliance with the Alpha and his Pack. That was a big step, and he knew it would not have come about if not for Jesse's endorsement.

They checked the woods along the perimeter first, out beyond the pavilion, but found nothing. Marco suggested a trip into the pavilion itself. The place had changed a lot from the evil pit of despair the former owners of the estate had turned it into. Now, it was cleansed of their taint and almost back to the grandeur it had once boasted when it was first built. A Victorian-style pavilion for outdoor entertainment with comfortable places to sit or recline.

"I feel like I lost the scent or something," Crystal said morosely as they entered the pavilion. "I can't believe we haven't found anything yet."

"Have faith, my dear," he told her gently. "You came here for a reason, and you will succeed. It just might take a bit more time."

"But we may not have the luxury of time," she reminded him, sounding stressed as they came to the outer ring of chaise lounges. A few were double-sized and upholstered in fabric that could withstand the outdoors but was still soft and supple to the touch.

"You need to relax," he told her decisively. "Come. Sit for a minute with me." He took her hand and led her to one of the large loungers and sat them both on the edge. Then he turned her slightly and put his hands on her shoulders from behind, beginning a slow, gentle massage. "You are very tense, *cara*. This tension is probably blocking your natural magical senses. It is no good for you or your quest."

He rubbed her shoulders, caressing her supple neck when she didn't object. She leaned into his touch, and her breath eased.

"Does that feel good, my love?" he whispered near her ear. He was hard as a rock inside his trousers, his desire reaching new heights as he felt her warmth under his hands.

"It does," she answered, dropping her head to the side, exposing the pulse that drew him so strongly. Damn. She didn't realize the temptation she posed. He wanted to lick and suck…and bite.

He knew it was probably way too soon, but he couldn't resist. The small taste he'd had of her the night before had only made him want her more. Need was riding him, and he couldn't deny himself even as he hoped he had enough control to not scare her away.

Marco dipped his head and nibbled on her earlobe. When she didn't move away, he lowered his head farther and licked a line down over the speeding pulse in her neck, putting his lips on her and kissing the area he would love to bite one day. Just not today.

That thought sobered him before he lost his mind and allowed his fangs to drop. She didn't know what he was yet. He couldn't let her find out this way. He had to be in control when she learned what he was, or he'd scare her off. The poor baby had only just started learning about the magical world. He couldn't take the risk that she would run, screaming into the night, if confronted with a hungry vampire who wanted to bite her and drink her blood.

He counselled himself to calm, but he couldn't stop touching her. Especially when she leaned back into his chest and moaned her compliance. She was as hot for him as he was for her.

Moving swiftly, he lifted and turned her so that she lay on the wide divan, facing him. Her breath caught in her throat at his quick move, but she didn't draw away. Her gaze was molten, focused on him.

"You are my sun, my moon and stars, Crystal," he whispered as he moved to lay next to her on the wide cushion. "I have wanted to make love to you since almost the first moment I saw you." He reached out to stroke her cheek with a light touch of his hand. She turned into his touch, enchanting him further. "Do you want me too?"

"I do," she breathed after only a moment's hesitation. She shook her head slightly. "I know it's probably not right. You're my boss, but—"

He put one finger over her lips. "I'm not your boss. You are your own boss. I might employ you at the moment, technically," he smiled down at her as he rested on one elbow beside her, "but that has no effect on what is between us here and now. We are just male and female. Attracted to each other. Brought together by Fate. Do you agree?"

Slowly, she nodded.

It was crazy. No, it was downright insane, but she wanted Marco like she had never wanted any other man. He might be her *employer*, as he put it, but that didn't matter. This wasn't any kind of sexual harassment or misconduct on his part. This was raw, primal attraction that could no longer be denied.

She'd gone just about crazy these past days—or rather, *nights*—when he'd left her at her door with a peck on the cheek. She'd wondered if she'd imagined those other kisses, that stark need she'd seen in his eyes on those other memorable occasions when he'd lost control and kissed her the way she wanted him to kiss her.

It might not be proper conduct in the employee handbook, but she'd wanted to jump his bones for a while, and right this minute, there was nothing stopping them. She wanted to grab on to this chance and not let go. She wanted to know what his lovemaking would feel like. She wanted to be cherished the way she believed he would cherish her, going by no more than the look in his eyes and the care with which he'd been treating her.

She didn't know what tomorrow would bring. It could be heartbreak, or it could be love everlasting. Or it could be something in the middle. Right now, she didn't care. She just knew she wanted to experience this night with Marco. She was going to put her heart on the line and wish on a star that it all worked out in the end, but right now, she was going to take that leap of faith.

"I want you to make love to me, Marco," she whispered, holding his gaze. She thought she saw flames leap in his eyes at her words, but she figured she had to be imagining things. A moment later, his head lowered, and his lips were on hers.

He had kissed her before, but that dizzying experience was nothing compared to this. Marco let loose with his desire, and she felt scorched in the heat of his passion.

Long moments later, his lips left hers to trail over her cheek and down to her neck. Once again, she learned how incredibly erotic it felt to have him kiss her there. It was a pleasure she had never experienced with anyone else. No other man had ever bothered to kiss her neck, and she felt sure no one else could ever evoke this kind of headlong response in her but Marco.

"Be certain, *cara*. For, I think, if I give you what you want, neither of us will ever be the same."

Was he just teasing or was he serious? His words felt serious, and they echoed in her soul. She definitely felt the way he described, but she still couldn't be sure if he was just saying things or really meant them. Regardless, she wanted to know, once and for all, what it would feel like to be possessed by him. She wanted to give him everything...anything...all that he asked for and would demand. She could deny him nothing, yet he seemed intent on making sure she was certain of her wants.

She was. Crystal moaned as he nipped at the hypersensitive skin of her neck with gentle nibbles. Oh, that felt amazing. A fire started in her core that only seemed to grow.

"I'm certain," she told him on a sigh as he licked the skin over her pulse. "Please, Marco, don't make me wait any longer."

He groaned, and his teeth bit down a little harder than before, but it didn't hurt. Far from it. His momentary loss of control excited her. She wanted to push him farther. She wanted to dare to make him want her as much as she wanted him. Making a bold decision, she lowered her hand to his abdomen, running her fingers over his tight stomach. She could feel the ridges of his abdominal muscles even through the fabric of his shirt.

Hubba hubba. She hadn't realized Marco was so ripped. Damn.

He sucked in a breath as her hand dared to roam lower, over his belt buckle and down over the zipper of his dress pants. She traced the hardness she found there and then cupped and squeezed, loving his reaction as his head fell back, his eyes closed, and his teeth ground together. His expression was tight with pleasure and restraint, and she loved the knowledge that she had brought that look to his handsome face.

His hand covered hers and pressed for just a moment before he moved her hand away, twining his fingers with hers. His touch was gentle, but she felt the slightest tremor in his grasp. She was affecting him, and he wasn't afraid to let her know it.

He positioned them so that she lay beneath his hard body. Just as he had when he'd left her aching for more. This time, she wouldn't let him get away. This time, she was going to see this through to the end if she had to hogtie him to the chaise lounge.

The thought made her feel an odd sense of glee. This man was so magical, but then again, so was she. He'd already brought out so much of her hidden facets that she hadn't even known existed. He'd taught her about the desire that was never far from the surface whenever he was near. She hadn't known she could feel so much or so…hot…when a man just looked at her a certain way.

Like he wanted to eat her alive. And not in a bad way. Mm-mm.

She was ready for him and wanted to skip the rest of the foreplay. They could get back to that later. After he had slaked the thirst he had created in her yearning body. First, she wanted—no, she *needed*—to experience all there was to being with him. She needed him inside her. She needed…him.

She pushed at his clothing, and he seemed to get the idea of what she wanted because he paused long enough to take off his shirt and unbutton the top button on his dress pants. Marco was always impeccably dressed, but right now, she wished he was naked.

She had made room for him between her thighs, bending her knees and rubbing against him, but that wasn't enough. It wasn't nearly enough. She needed to get rid of all this fabric separating them. Right now.

"Clothes…" she whispered raggedly, her senses going wild as Marco's hard body lay over her own, tantalizing her, driving her passions higher. "Gone…" she added, in case her message wasn't clear. It was all she could get out. She hoped he understood.

Marco chuckled darkly, lifting up enough to run his fingers down her ribcage, reaching for the hem of her shirt. *Hallelujah!*

He pushed the stretchy shirt up slowly, and she squirmed and wriggled to make it easier for him to get the soft fabric out from under her. When he reached her breasts, he moved more slowly, meeting her gaze as his hands trailed over her breasts, still covered by the cream-colored bra she wore. That needed to go too, but she enjoyed the sensations he caused with his talented fingers against the slippery fabric.

When she could take no more of his teasing, she moaned, and he seemed to understand. He rid her of the shirt completely, lifting her up slightly to tug it out from under her. When she wished he would remove the bra, he left it, and she was disappointed, but he had her pinned to the chaise. She couldn't get her arms up under her to undo the clasp on her own. But then he simply pulled the straps down from her shoulders, trapping her arms with the heavy elastic. The cups started to peel downward, and he helped them along with his teeth and tongue as he teased her tender skin.

Sweet heaven, that felt good, she thought. She lost track of time while he kissed and sucked, eventually making his way to her tender peaks. He used just the tiniest touch of his teeth to make things exciting, and she wasn't sure what to think at first, except that it was like nothing she'd ever felt before, and it was amazing.

"Now, Marco," she pleaded with him in gasping moans as he brought her to a peak of pleasure.

She knew there was more, and she didn't want to wait. No. The waiting time was over. She would have him tonight. That was a certainty in her mind.

"Your wish is my command," he rasped, and she was glad to hear that note in his voice that told her without words that he was as strongly affected as she was.

CHAPTER 18

The rest of their clothing disappeared more quickly, and she was glad to finally be skin-to-skin with the man who had been driving her absolutely wild for days.

He came back to her and...hesitated. His gaze searched hers, and he seemed to be waiting for some kind of sign. Or maybe he just wanted to make sure she was still on board with his plans. She didn't know how he could think otherwise, but she wanted to make sure nothing delayed the ecstasy she knew she would feel with Marco. She was too close to the edge now to wait much longer. She met his gaze with all the boldness she could muster and licked her lips.

"Please..." she whispered, and it seemed to be enough.

His eyes flared hot, and his lips captured hers as his lower body aligned into the perfect position. He was kissing her senseless when he joined his body to hers, and she gasped into the kiss, almost overwhelmed by sensation for a moment.

Then he began to move, and the motion lulled her into a

state of utter bliss that rolled over her like waves on the ocean, building…building…

She was surrounded by him. Enveloped in his warm embrace. His kiss drove her higher even as his body commanded hers. He broke the kiss and dragged his lips down to her neck, nibbling and then biting the cords of her neck in a way that made her cry out. Her voice echoed in the open air, but she didn't care. The night was dark, and it was only the two of them in this big space. If some peeping werewolf was out there listening to them, then so be it. She refused to be embarrassed, and in fact, it sort of made it a little more exciting. Daring, even. When she had never really been a daring type of woman.

He bit down a little harder, but she was up for it. The small pain prefaced a wave of pleasure the likes of which she had never known. She spasmed around him, her eyes shut tight in ecstasy, her head thrown back, giving him full access to whatever he wanted.

The pleasure went on and on. He tensed and turned his head away violently from her neck, in the throes of his own climax. He groaned, and she could feel the warmth of him inside her as he came as hard as she had, which spurred more aftershocks for her.

Crystal felt so good, she could barely catch her breath when things finally started winding down. She clung to him as his breathing came ragged, at first, then slowed, as hers did. They were so perfectly in tune. So perfectly matched.

He slid to one side, moving so that he spooned her from behind. The night air was chilly, but she didn't feel at all uncomfortable. Marco had her. He would keep her safe and secure. She felt that to the depths of her bones.

He stroked her arm from behind, had hands touching her reverently.

"We should go back to the house where you can be warm," he whispered, licking the shell of her ear.

"I don't want to move," she told him honestly. If they moved, he might leave, and she wanted to bask in this for a bit longer. Even if she couldn't have him permanently—or even temporarily—she had him now, and she wanted to enjoy it for as long as she could. "I don't want this to end."

He kissed her throat. "It doesn't have to end, *cara mia*. We can continue where we left off, but under more private conditions where I don't have to worry about you catching a chill."

"Me? What about you?" she quipped.

"I am impervious to such things," he told her, and she couldn't quite tell if he was serious or just teasing.

"All right. Let me up. I'd rather not streak from here to the house, so we'd better get dressed," she groused, but he chuckled and let her sit up, though his touch lingered on her waist.

She put on her shirt and was holding the rest of her clothing when Marco's arms came around her from behind. She leaned back into him and smiled. She loved the feel of his touch.

"I've got a better idea than walking," he whispered into her ear. "I hope you're not afraid of heights."

"What?" Her eyes were closed, but she opened them and realized they were already several yards above the ground.

Marco was flying with her in his arms? This was a lot more than the little rise to the top of the bushes he'd done before. Just what kind of magic did this man have, anyway?

He carried her up and over the roof of the pavilion and then over the treetops. She was still clutching her clothes in her hands as he flew them to the small balcony right outside her bedroom. He put her down then snapped his fingers and the latch on the balcony door came open, allowing him to open it and usher her inside. Her legs were bare, with only the thin shirt covering her body. She had her underwear, shoes and pants in her hands but hadn't managed to snag her socks before he'd taken her on her first flight.

Amazing.

"I didn't know you could fly like that," she told him as she walked into her room from the balcony.

"There are many things you still do not know about me," he answered somewhat mysteriously. Again, she couldn't tell if he was serious or teasing, or some combination of the two.

He was fully dressed, but he began to disrobe as he walked toward her with a devilish gleam in his eyes. Oh, yes. She was about to get what she'd wished for. More time with Marco. Her lover.

"Why don't we warm up in the bath and make slippery, soapy love until the dawn?" he asked, stripping off his shirt and making her salivate with the sexy display.

Oh, it looked like Marco was definitely in a playful mood. She liked that very much. She traipsed ahead of him into the large attached bath, looking over her shoulder to grin at him as he followed eagerly behind.

The bathtub was grand and more than big enough for two. Marco kissed her all over as the air filled with steam and they waited for the tub to start to fill. He sat her on the bathroom counter, which was at a perfect height for him to take her again in a quick move that left her gasping with pleasure.

Then he lifted her into the bath, never letting her feet touch the floor even once. He took great pleasure in soaping her up and running his fingers and hands all over her body. She tried to do the same, but he fended her off, claiming that things would be over before they began if he let her touch him too much.

They made love in the bath, and by the time he lifted her out, she was limp as an overcooked noodle. He dried her, rousing her passions again with the soft terrycloth of the towel abrading her skin, and then carried her into the bedroom. He placed her in the center of the large bed and proceeded to prove to her all over again how incredibly compatible they were in passion.

She dozed off in his arms, more sated than she had ever been. Marco had delivered on every sensual promise his eyes had ever made, and then some. She drifted off with a satisfied smile on her face and knew nothing more until morning.

*

The hardest thing Marco had ever done was to turn his fangs away from Crystal's supple neck and deny himself the pleasure of biting her while they were having sex. He was very much afraid that one drop of her blood would change him for all time.

The thing was, he had to be sure of her commitment before he took that final step. If he bound himself to her and she turned out not to feel the same about him, then he would truly run mad and could destroy a lot of innocent souls along with his own. He couldn't let that happen. He had to be certain of Crystal—and she had to be certain of him—before he would take that step.

She also had to know what he was. He couldn't believe she hadn't figured it out already, but she'd been very ignorant of the magical world when he'd first met her. Perhaps, even after meeting numerous werewolves, she didn't believe vampires were real.

Or maybe his cover story of having to work elsewhere during the day to keep his business empire running was more convincing than he'd realized. Whatever the case, she still didn't seem to fully understand what he was or what he would ask of her if they were to be mates.

He would have to tell her. Somehow, he'd have to find a way to break it to her that he was immortal and needed blood to survive. According to legend, once a bloodletter like him had found his One, he would only need to bite her for the rest of their lives. The mate's blood sustained like no other. It was a magical, soul-deep union that sustained them both for as long as they lived, which could be very long, indeed, barring some unfortunate event.

People were always hunting them. Regular humans always tried to kill what they did not understand.

His greatest fear was that she would reject him once she learned what he was. He would have to pick his moment and pray to the Mother of All that Crystal would understand and accept him. Only then would he have the right to taste Crystal's blood and make her his own completely. How he longed for that moment with all his reawakened heart.

For now, he had to leave her. Dawn was coming, and he had to be safe in his lair before the sun kissed the sky to the east. Leaving through the balcony door, he flew back to his hideaway and secured himself for the day, a smile on his lips as he remembered the previous hours spent with the most beautiful woman he had ever known.

*

Crystal woke briefly at dawn, her body aching in the most delicious ways. Memory returned in a rush, and she looked around for Marco, but he was gone. Disappointment flooded her for a moment as she sat up in the big bed and looked at the place she had last seen him…beside her.

That's when she saw it. A single blood-red rose on the pillow beside her, laying on top of a folded slip of paper. She reached for it, taking a moment to sniff the luscious scent of the rose and feel the softness of its petals against her cheek before opening the paper to see Marco's bold scrawl inside. He'd left her a note.

Cara mia,

Duty calls me away from you, but I will see you tonight to continue our search.

Think of me,
M.

Crystal clutched the note to her heart and sniffed the strong scent of the rose again, smiling as she got out of bed. The sheets were a disaster. She would have to do a little pre-cleaning unless she wanted the staff talking about her wild romp with the boss.

Even thinking of being the source of gossip and conjecture didn't dampen her mood. Let them talk. They would never know the kind of bliss she had achieved with Marco last night. They would never experience what she had.

Crystal felt like gloating but reined in her suddenly haughty thoughts. That wasn't like her. She didn't ever gloat. But then again, she'd never had a lover like Marco to gloat over before. She felt a tiny bit justified in her thoughts, though she would attempt to not look like the cat who had swallowed the canary when she went downstairs. Her relationship with Marco was too new and still uncertain, though he'd certainly seemed serious enough last night.

She hadn't had much sleep, but she didn't need much usually, and after being with Marco, she felt energized in a whole new way. As if being with him had topped up her internal batteries in some way she couldn't define. She got up and took a long shower, getting ready to face the day.

Crystal found a small group of men in the dining room, enjoying breakfast when she got there. She nodded to them in a friendly way and headed for the buffet, filling her plate with scrambled eggs and toast. When she turned to find a seat, Arlo motioned her over, and she joined the table of newcomers, curious to learn more about the Wraiths.

What followed was a fascinating conversation about her newfound relatives, Maria and Sally. Apparently, the Wraiths had been involved in discovering their true natures, and both women had urged Arlo to befriend Crystal and fill her in about life in the Wyoming Pack and among the Wraiths. They'd given him *carte blanche* to talk about them and answer any questions she might have, which was pretty amazing.

She learned all about how both Sally and Maria had met their mates and the harrowing experiences that had led up to their joining the Pack. Crystal had to hand it to them. They both sounded like brave, adventurous women. She hoped she could live up to their ideal, but she knew she'd led a boring corporate life up to this point.

After breakfast, she went to the office and began drawing up ideas for improvements to the estate. That led her to looking at maps, and she spent a happy few hours lost in study. Martine didn't come to work, but Philomena popped in just before lunch, and they went down to the dining room together.

Philomena held court at the large table, seeming to enchant every unattached male in the place while Crystal watched, amused. Everything made her happy today. She walked about as if in a dream, remembering the night before at odd times with a secret smile.

After lunch, Philomena took Crystal to the ballroom and set about teaching her about magic. It was a fascinating afternoon, learning the history and roots of magic, and how many different cultures had many different roads to using magic in various ways. Philomena told her all she knew about dryads, though it wasn't much, but it was more than Crystal had known before.

They were getting to the point of trying some rudimentary magic when Crystal noticed the time. It was almost time for dinner, but Philomena—who had asked Crystal to call her Mena—brought over a small potted plant. Crystal took it and used her magic to make it grow. It took little effort, and the little lavender plant wanted to please her, so it did as she asked. She made friends with it and learned that it liked the sun and was a bit thirsty.

Crystal took the much larger and blooming plant with her to the kitchen when they went in for dinner and watered it, happy when the plant giggled in delight in a way that only she could hear. Marci was happy to keep the plant in the kitchen, near the window so it would get plenty of light. She was a particular fan of lavender, as it turned out, so it was a good solution. Crystal let the plant go to Marci's grateful hands and then went into the dining room to eat.

At some point, Crystal realized that this place was beginning to feel like home. The thought stopped her in her tracks, but then the world moved on, and she began filling her plate in the buffet line again. These people felt like friends and even family, and Marco... He felt like the future. Her future.

CHAPTER 19

Marco arrived as they were finishing dinner and greeted her with a kiss in front of everybody. He accepted a glass of wine and sat with them while Crystal finished a decadent dessert of lemon merengue pie smothered in whipped cream. Tart and sweet, she enjoyed the pie while Marco stared hotly at her over the rim of his wine glass. He poured her a glass, and it was, once again, one of those pricey vintages from Maxwell's famous vineyard.

"This wine is fantastic," she complimented him. "I've only had Maxwell wine once before, and I liked it then as well."

"Atticus Maxwell is an old friend of mine," Marco told her. "I get most of my private stock from him, and I suspect he saves some of his best vintages for his friends."

Crystal was impressed. The famous vintner was said to be reclusive in the extreme, though she had read in the society pages when he had gotten married a few years ago.

"I didn't know you mingled with celebrities," she teased Marco. "Were you at the infamous private wedding?"

Marco shook his head. "Not I, but I did send the happy couple a gift to commemorate the occasion." He set down his empty glass and poured himself another.

If the wolves could eat tremendous amounts of food, Crystal was learning that Marco could drink quite a bit of wine with seemingly no ill effects. He never slurred his words or looked the least bit tipsy, though she had to stop at just one glass, and the warm, mellow feeling it inspired in her body. Any more and she might be singing tunelessly and making a fool of herself.

When she was done with both the pie and her single glass of wine, they stood and went out together. Mena winked at her as they left but remained behind with Arlo and the other men. She had hit it off with the Wraiths earlier in the day and appeared to be deep in conversation with their commander as Marco and Crystal headed out. The others were lingering over their dinners, and more than a few pointed looks were sent their way, but Crystal ignored it all. She was with Marco, and that's all that mattered.

"Want to make a stop upstairs before we begin our search for the evening?" Marco asked with a hungry purr in his voice as they walked down the empty hall.

Crystal knew darn well what would happen if they went upstairs. In fact, she had thought about little else all day.

"Yes," she replied with a wicked grin.

She felt decadent and a bit sultry, which wasn't something she had ever felt with any other man. Not that there had been many, but enough so that she knew this—whatever it was— with Marco was incredibly rare and special.

They walked a little faster, taking the stairs at a quick pace. Once inside her room, Marco didn't waste any time. He had her up against the wall even before the door closed completely, his lips devouring hers, his hands divesting her of her clothing.

She pushed at his dark jacket with clumsy hands. She wanted to touch his bare skin. She wanted his possession. His mastery. She wanted *him*. Period.

He joined with her after only the barest of preliminaries, but she was more than ready for him. She wrapped her legs around him as his body kept her pinned against the wall. His thrusts drove her higher, her back arching and her inner muscles clenching around him.

It was hard, fast and absolutely amazing. The most intense sexual experience she'd ever had. When she came, she sobbed his name, loving the grunt of animalistic pleasure that seemed ripped from his throat as he tensed within and around her. His arms caged her, his body pinning her in place, his masculine presence surrounding her in every possible way. It was sheer bliss and exactly what she'd needed all day as she went about her tasks, missing him.

Marco was breathing hard, his head buried in the curve of her neck as they both came down from the pinnacle, together. His tongue licked over the pulse in her neck, exciting her all over again.

"I'm sorry that was so fast," he whispered, kissing her neck. "Shall I make it up to you?"

"You have nothing to apologize for," she whispered back, gasping when he lifted her away from the wall, her legs still wrapped around his hips, and walked them to the bathroom. "But if you want to…"

She couldn't finish what she'd intended to be a playful gibe. He was growing hard within her once more, which shouldn't really be possible. But, she was learning, a lot of things she'd thought were impossible were old hat to this magic man she had discovered.

He walked them into the bathroom, which was as luxurious as the rest of the mansion and went directly into the spacious walk-in shower. He let her down and then turned her around, reaching down to turn on the water while they were still out of the spray, to let it warm up a bit before placing them both beneath the streaming rainfall of warm water.

He soaped her up, taking great pleasure in dragging out the process, sliding his slick hands all around her body, cupping, molding, squeezing and probing. She squeaked a few times when he hit particularly sensitive spots, but not in protest. Far from it.

He was making up for the lack of foreplay, but really, it hadn't been necessary. Still, she was enjoying every moment of this sensual torture. He seemed to delight in touching every last inch of her skin and learning her curves as his body pressed into her, then away, brushing against her bottom with tantalizing earnestness.

She was panting with need by the time he allowed her to step under the full spray of water to rinse off the suds. Then he turned her, directing her to bend forward from the waist and lean her hands against the built-in seat along one end of the enormous shower stall as he entered her from behind. Water streamed over her back and between their bodies from the overhead rain fixture, a warm pelting that only added to her excitement.

Her body was on fire that even the water couldn't put out. Only Marco and his pounding passion had a chance at slaking the need within her. He moved swiftly, his motions sure and commanding, his desire a palpable thing. She cried out as a small climax hit her, but he kept going, riding her throughout, driving her toward another precipice.

When she peaked again, a keening sound forced its way out of her lungs to echo in the damp chamber, but she didn't care. Marco was moving hard and fast, coming to the close of his own race to the precipice. And then they were together, falling, falling, through the stars and into the ocean of pleasure that awaited them.

She was dimly aware of Marco lifting her and carrying her out of the shower sometime later. He'd shut off the water and then dried her body with a warm towel while she tried to gather her wits, a happy, satisfied lethargy overtaking her body. The man was potent, she'd give him that. And he took impeccable care of her. Never had she had such a considerate lover.

She feared she never would again. Marco had just about

ruined her for anyone else. Her goal now was to stay with him for as long as she could. She would enjoy this while it lasted, she decided, and worry about tomorrow when it came.

Sometime later, they finally got outside and started searching the right side of the house. Marco held her hand as they walked along, and the night would have been lovely except for the frustration Crystal felt about not being able to pinpoint the location of the trouble on the grounds. She tried to not let it get to her, but her tension rose as they walked until Marco stopped and turned toward her.

"What's wrong? You're stretched as tight as a drum." His dark gaze searched hers.

"I don't like failure," she ground out.

Understanding dawned on his face. A moment later, he tugged her into his arms for a hug.

"You're not failing. We're just eliminating all the areas that aren't a problem. You already found the pedestals, which I had dismissed. I have faith in you, my heart. You will discover the place. If not tonight, then tomorrow. At some point, when the time is right, you will find what you seek."

Buoyed by his confidence in her abilities, she brushed her cheek against his. "You're a good man, Marco," she whispered before leaving his embrace. She squared her shoulders and looked at the dark forest in front of them. "Let's keep going."

Her perseverance paid off a few minutes later. Crystal held out her hand like a bar across Marco's chest, stopping him from going any farther.

"Do you feel that?" she asked, spooked by the malevolent power that pulsed through the ground toward them.

It wasn't strong, but it was there. They were on the edges of it right now, and the trees ahead looked…misshapen in small ways. Bent at odd angles with jutting sharp angles that were not normal for those varieties of trees. It looked unnatural to her eyes and felt sinister to her magical senses.

"Feel what, my love?" Marco asked, stilling immediately.

"There's a pulsing power in the earth. We're on the edge

of it, but it's not…um…friendly. It's a bit scary actually," she admitted. "Scary strong too, but muted by the earth. The trees have been trying to hide it. See the way they are misshapen for their efforts?"

She pointed to the small grove just ahead and saw Marco narrow his eyes at the trees they could see. He shook his head after a while.

"I'm sorry. This is not my specialty. One tree looks much like another to me, I'm afraid," he told her honestly. "But I believe you when you say there's something wrong. Your instincts are what matter here. You are the expert."

That was a lot of weight to put on her shoulders, but she knew he was right.

"Let's move closer, but carefully," Crystal said after a moment's thought. She didn't want to go closer to whatever it was out there in the woods, but she knew she had to.

One part of her mind felt triumph over finally finding what she had been searching for all this time while another part held fear of what they would uncover. She moved cautiously closer and noticed that Marco stepped where she stepped. Smart man.

"It's getting stronger," she told him in a quavering voice as her tension mounted. She reached back and grasped his hand for both comfort and strength. He didn't let her down.

Edging closer, she felt with her magical senses the deep disturbance in the earth all around here. Looking up, she examined the trees. They were getting more twisted the closer they came to the center of the disturbance.

Then she saw it. A very old tree, stooped into an unnatural shape, its growth stunted by whatever was going on beneath the soil. She crouched and put her hand on the ground, sending her senses out to see if she could figure out what was going on beneath the surface.

A picture came back to her. A suggestion of tree roots warped and mangled around something. Something it had grabbed in order to protect the rest of the forest. This tree was noble. An oak, she saw when she opened her eyes again.

It had grabbed onto whatever that was beneath the surface. A rectangular shape. It had grabbed it to protect everything around itself. The very thought brought a tear to her eye as she looked up to meet Marco's gaze.

"It's just there," she told him in a whisper. "That gnarled tree has it trapped in its roots. That noble oak grabbed it and is hiding it from the enemy, and protecting the rest of the forest with its sacrifice." Tears ran down her face as she spoke the words.

Marco reached out and brush them away with gentle fingers. "How do you think we should proceed?"

She loved that he was letting her take the lead. She might feel a bit unequipped to deal with the situation, but since she appeared to be the only person who could sense what was really going on underneath the surface, she needed to figure it out.

"Whatever it is, it's shaped sort of like a box. A rectangle, maybe about this big." She held up her hands to indicate the size of the box, roughly a foot long, maybe half a foot wide and the same deep. It was only a rough estimate, but that was the impression she got. "It's all tangled up in the roots of the oak. I don't want to hurt the tree. It's done such a great job at great detriment to itself. I would rather try to tease the box out of its roots without damaging the tree. But we may still need to do a little digging."

"All right." Marco reached into his pocket and took out his cellphone. "I think maybe we should call in a few of the wolves to stand guard and maybe help, if needed."

Crystal wasn't going to argue with that idea. A few big burly men with lethal skills might help her feel a little safer. Then again, the strength of the evil the oak was hiding might be too intense for her to handle, regardless. In which case, at least someone would be around to catch her when she fell. Not that Marco wouldn't be there for her, but somebody had to take control of the artifact when it came out of the ground. Marco couldn't do it all by himself.

"I think that's a really good idea," she told Marco. "And

maybe ask somebody to bring a bag or something to contain the box once we get it out of the ground. Oh, and if there is such a thing as fertilizer spikes somewhere on the property, I'd like to put some around the base of the oak. The poor thing has starved itself in order to keep the artifact hidden. I'd like to help it, if I can."

Seeding the area with fertilizer was only a small first step. If everything went as planned, Crystal already knew she was going to come out here again, and again to help restore this tree to what it should be. She would give of her own energy if she had to. This noble oak had given so much of itself to protect the rest of its forest brethren and the people now working on the estate. She would like to see it restored to health and no longer suffering for its sacrifice.

But that was in the future. Right now, she had to figure out how to get that box untangled from the tree roots and up from the ground. She had never undertaken a project so big, though on a smaller scale she knew she had skills that might do the trick. She had untangled the roots of pot-bound plants and moved dirt around with her magic. This was just on a massively larger scale. She wondered if she had the ability. Shaking her head, she squared her shoulders. The only way to find out was to try.

"Okay. I'm going closer, but I want you to stay well back of the area where I'm working. I'm going to be moving the dirt around under the surface, and it's just possible a sinkhole could form somewhere in about a fifteen-foot radius from the bottom of the tree."

"Will you be safe?" Marco's voice was tinged with concern, and she felt warmed by his worry for her safety.

"The earth is my friend. It will not harm me." She knew that without a doubt but wasn't really sure why she was so confident. She only knew the truth of her belief.

Marco looked uncertain but finally nodded. He had finally stopped tapping on the screen of his phone and looked ready for action.

"Some of the Wraiths, as well as a few of the local Pack

members, will be here shortly. Do you want to wait for them before you begin? Or shall I brief them when they get here so you can start working now?"

The confidence in his voice warmed her. It was confidence in *her*. A confidence she didn't necessarily feel but was becoming stronger as he treated her with respect for her abilities. He made her feel as if she could do anything. Maybe she could. As long as Marco was by her side.

"This could take a while," she told him. "I'm going to start now. You run interference with the shifters. Just keep them out of my work area. This is all underground work. At least at the beginning. You may see some ripples in the earth. I'm not sure honestly. I've never tried anything this big before."

"You have until dawn, *cara*," he told her with his stern expression. "If you need longer than that, we'll have to come back tomorrow. I don't want you overextending yourself too far."

His concern for her was sweet. Nobody had ever worried too much about how she was doing. She'd never had that kind of care in her life before and found that she craved it now. Being with Marco had changed her. He had made her aware of all the things she had missed in her solitary life. He had taught her things about herself, and about the world, that she would always remember. And she was coming to dread the thought that he would leave her one day.

"Just bear with me. It may not look like I'm doing much, but I need total concentration to get this started," she told him. She refused to think about the future right now. Not when there was such an enormous task in front of her and danger on the other end of it.

He stepped right up to her in a quick move, taking her in his arms and placing a hot kiss on her lips. He moved so fast he had taken her totally by surprise. She was just getting into the kiss when he released her.

"Be careful." The intense look in his eyes made her almost believe that she truly was his. His love. What she wouldn't give for those words to be true in the deepest sense.

She nodded, unable to speak for a moment. He backed off to the perimeter she had named, holding her gaze all the while, then nodded. She took a deep breath and lowered herself to the ground. She sat tailor fashion, her spine straight her legs folded in front of her. She bent forward placing both palms firmly on the ground and closed her eyes.

CHAPTER 20

Marco couldn't see much of anything, but he definitely felt an enormous magical wave happening in this immediate area. He saw the ground ripple a few times, but it looked like Crystal was working at depth, and it barely made an undulation on the surface. At first.

The others arrived, and he gave them instructions and told them what to watch for and what area to avoid in quiet tones. They all moved quietly, so as not to disturb Crystal at her work. Brandt had come with Mena, for which Marco was grateful. Mena stood opposite Marco, taking up a position to protect Crystal from the opposite side of the circle, which made Marco feel much better. Brandt took the perimeter position on Marco's right, halfway between himself and Mena, and Arlo mirrored Brandt on Marco's left. All four quarters were covered by one of them should the enemy attack while Crystal was doing her thing—or should Crystal unleash something that she could not control.

Marco grimaced as he thought that last bit. Hopefully, the

simple equipment Arlo had brought would be enough to transport the item, whatever it was. He noted a crate and a shovel next to the werewolf and was glad the Wraith mission commander had come prepared.

A few of the other wolves were prowling around an outer perimeter, and Brandt had told Marco that everyone on the estate was on high alert. It was hard to keep up such tense alertness when the magic took hours to perform. Crystal didn't move for a long time, but Marco could see the movements under the earth around her growing more violent as she worked something toward the surface. He could just imagine the expenditure of energy this was taking from her and was glad there were others here who could see to the artifact while he looked after Crystal, once she had revealed it.

He had no doubt about her ability to free whatever it was from the earth. She was a dryad after all. This was her element. The earth and forests were her native habitat over which she had vast powers. He was glad to see her claiming those abilities at last.

It was hours later when things finally became really noticeable. Great ripples appeared in the earth around the gnarled tree, and violent movements of the dirt and debris of the forest floor happened every few seconds until finally, with a wrenching pull of magic that even Marco felt, something popped free onto the surface of the ground. It was directly in front of Crystal.

She sat back, removing her hands from the ground and reaching for the object. Marco moved to get a better look, and his heart stuttered in his chest.

"Don't touch it!" he shouted, making Crystal pause in the act of reaching out for the box. The damnable box. He'd seen that box just once before in his life and would never forget the havoc it had wreaked.

It was an ancient object. One older than himself by eons. It was one of the legendary magical artifacts that had been used in many battles over many thousands of years in the battle of good versus evil. And this one was undoubtedly evil.

Crystal looked up at him, her expression questioning and her eyes so very weary. She was clearly close to burnout of her magical power. What she had just done had taken almost all of her energy.

"Is the ground stable enough to walk on?" he asked, needing the answer not for himself, but for the werewolves who could not fly out of danger should the earth give way suddenly.

Crystal nodded slowly, as if every movement cost her. "I packed it all back down as I went along so nobody would get hurt," she told him.

Relieved, Marco walked out to her and signaled for the three other guardians to join him. He had to get to Crystal, but that box had to be seen to as well. They couldn't leave that horrid thing out in the open. A thought occurred.

"Mena, are you shielding?" he asked as they all neared Crystal.

Mena nodded. "I may have missed a few seconds when it first appeared, but I've got it now."

Marco frowned. Even a few seconds could have alerted the enemy to the location of the box, but it couldn't be helped now. They would move the thing as soon as possible. As soon as it was safe to do so. And to make it safe, he had to tell the others exactly what they were dealing with.

"Whatever you do, don't touch that vile thing," he warned them all in a stern voice. "We must guard it and shield it as best we can, using all our powers, for if the enemy gets its hand on that thing, chaos will reign in these lands once more."

"What is it?" Brandt asked, frowning at the box. It had all sorts of engraving on it and appeared to be made out of some kind of metal that gleamed dully even after being buried for so long. The dirt simply didn't cling to it.

"Have you heard of the box once belonging to a woman named Pandora?" Marco asked quietly as they all stood around Crystal.

Several of the Wraiths backed up their mission

commander, carrying equipment of various kinds. Marco was satisfied to see shock and horror on several faces. Grim determination on others. Now they began to understand what they must guard against and keep from their enemies.

"You're claiming that's *the* Pandora's box? Seriously?" Brandt demanded in a quiet voice.

"The one and only. Thank the Mother of All," Marco replied, crouching to help Crystal to her feet. She was so weak that he put his arm around her waist and urged her to lean against him.

"You're sure?" Brandt asked.

"I have seen it once before, centuries ago. It was used by the enemy to unleash countless horrors on my homeland and others during the time known as the Dark Ages." Marco frowned. "By no means should anybody touch it and don't even think about cracking it open to take a peek."

A few of the Wraiths chuckled at that admonition. Arlo stepped forward with an empty crate in his hands. Marco recognized it as one of the wooden boxes that had come from Maxwell's winery. It had held bottles of wine and packing material, but now, it was empty and nicely sized to hold the evil box. Another of the Wraiths held a shovel, but that wouldn't work.

"You'll have to use a stick or something to push the box into the crate. Don't touch metal to the metal of the box or bad things could happen," Marco advised. Crystal sagged against him, and he lifted her into his arms.

Marco waited until Arlo and one of his men maneuvered the box into the empty wine crate using a couple of fallen tree limbs and a whole lot of patience. Once the box was safely in the crate, he turned to Mena.

"I'll meet you all back at the house. Don't come in. I'm not sure we should put that thing inside the house, but I want to get Crystal settled in bed first. I'll help you find a spot for the box on the estate. I'm thinking maybe the pavilion would be a good place since we cleansed it thoroughly after the last battle."

"That could work. We'll meet you at the side of the mansion closest to the pavilion," Mena replied. "Take care of Crystal. We will safeguard the artifact."

Marco was glad to have Mena there, as well as the others. They could be trusted not to do anything rash. Right now, he was concerned for Crystal. She had expended a lot of her energy in working the box free and would be unconscious for hours. He didn't think it was any worse than that. Her breathing was regular, and her spirit was strong. Her power had grown tremendously even in just the past few days.

Marco had to get her settled safely in her bed before he could do anything else. He had to see to his One before any other consideration—even that blasted box. It had come back from the past to haunt him, he swore.

His one encounter with it in the distant past had been more than enough. He'd never wanted to see that thing again, but here it was. Turning up like a bad penny. The worst penny imaginable.

How he was going to neutralize that thing, or even just hide it from their enemies, he did not know. He was going to have to consult with powers greater than his own. He would have to place some very delicate calls. First, though, he had to make sure Crystal was comfortable.

Marco was confident that she would recover given enough rest. She was really growing into her power and blossoming into something exquisite. The way she had finessed that box out of the ground had been amazing to watch. He'd been monitoring her energy levels carefully to make sure she didn't overextend herself too much, but she'd been handling it like a pro. She had learned from her past mistakes and siphoned out her energy a little at a time, being careful not to give too much at any part in the process. She was a natural.

He flew her to the mansion, using his magic to open the doors in his path and set her on the bed with the utmost care. He caressed her hair away from her face, realizing she was already fast asleep. Safe in his arms, she had given herself up to exhaustion, secure in the knowledge that he would take care of her.

Marco was touched that she would trust him so much. Especially when he was still keeping secrets from her. He knew the time was fast approaching when he would have to come clean with her and explain about his immortal existence. It was getting harder and harder to be near her—to be with her—without biting. He longed so much to taste of her essence and seal their bond, but he didn't dare. Not without telling her first. He just had to scrape up the courage, which wasn't something he was used to. There was very little left in this world that could scare him. But the very idea that his One might reject him was the scariest thing he could think of. Even worse than somebody opening that blasted box again.

Marco left her with a kiss and went out into the night, to meet up with the rest of the group. They were going to have to come up with some sort of temporary solution to keeping the box out of enemy hands. Dawn was approaching, and they had little choice. The pavilion would have to do, at least for today.

He met up with the small group as they neared the house on their way to the pavilion, and joined them. He walked next to Mena, watching Arlo and one of his men who held either end of the wooden wine crate between them. They were all somber and on guard as they entered the structure, walking downward toward the center of the amphitheater beneath the pavilion's roof. There was a small stage down there that the enemy had used for their evil ceremonies.

Everything in here had been cleansed to a high degree, both physically and magically. Furthermore, protective spells had been woven into everything and around everything under the pavilion's roof. Marco had never wanted to see evil in this place again, but this couldn't be helped. Right now, this was the safest place on the estate for Pandora's box.

The stage at the center of the pavilion was made of concrete and stone. Unbeknownst to most, there were cavities beneath the heavy flagstones. Some were merely storage compartments. Some held the wiring and cables necessary for modern amenities like the spotlights and electrical outlets. Nothing was being stored beneath the stage at this time. Nothing had been in the storage compartments when Marco took over the estate. He wasn't even sure if the former owners knew about the compartments under the stage. They were as good a place as any to hide something, at least for a little while.

Marco lifted the heavy flagstone covering the largest of the storage compartments with one hand. Even the shifters would've had to make more of an effort to lift the slab of granite, which was another reason for choosing this particular place to hide the box. It would take someone either very strong or very magical, or both, to lift the slab with the same kind of ease.

"Put it in there," Marco directed Arlo and his companion. "Just make sure it's not going to tip over or anything. Some of these compartments have irregular bases."

Marco watched as the Wraiths put the crate into the compartment and made sure it was steady. Satisfied, Marco replaced the heavy slab of stone and settled it into place.

"That should be good for today," Marco said with concerned satisfaction. "I'm going to make a few calls before I have to sleep. Arlo, I want to keep this as quiet as possible, but I wouldn't object to your discussing this development with Jesse and Jason and their mates. Brandt, likewise I wouldn't object if you were willing to reach out to the Lords, and perhaps the High Priestess. I've seen what this artifact can do, and we need to call in all the experts we can find to help us figure out what to do about it. But keep in mind that the enemy is most probably looking for it, and we don't want word to spread that we have found it. I fear that would precipitate an immediate attack, and I don't think we're ready for that just yet. Arlo, if you can perhaps ask your commanding officer to send a few more of your number as backup, I am more than happy to extend the contract, and Jesse knows I'm good for the money. Both Mena and Martine have access to my accounts and can provide any funds needed to get your people here as quickly as possible, if Jesse is agreeable."

"I can't see how he would not be," Arlo said in his quiet, firm voice. "You know we are all sworn to serve the Light. This is the kind of problem our group was designed to combat. The battle against evil is always our battle, and right now, this is the front line."

Marco nodded. "I'm glad you understand. Thank you," he said, meaning every word.

"I'll call the Lords," Brandt volunteered. "This is way bigger than I expected, and I'm glad you're seeking specialist help. I've never encountered any of the legendary artifacts, but of course I've heard about them and their effects. I can't say I'm happy to have to deal with this kind of thing, but if we have to, we have to. We'll get the job done."

"Good man," Marco said to his werewolf ally. "I'm leaving now, but Mena is here as my representative. She can authorize just about anything you might need without having to wait for me to rise tonight. Hopefully, by then, I'll have some responses from the people I'll be calling. Let's plan to meet in the office just after dark. Bring what you have, and we can formulate a battle plan."

Without much further ado, Marco said goodbye to the other men and walked up the aisle with Mena at his side. They spoke in low tones that even the werewolves couldn't hear.

"I'm going to cast even more protections on this place. I'll be busy today doing that, but I'll also watch over Crystal for you. Don't worry," Mena reassured him. "She was amazing, Uncle. Your One is a brave and resourceful woman. Powerful too." Mena smiled as she walked beside him. "At first, I confess, I wasn't sure she was a match for you, but now I understand. Her dryad blood may be dilute, but she is a strong elemental. Her powers over the earth are like nothing I've ever seen before. She is also kind, and I believe she loves you very much. I like the way she looks at you, Uncle Marco, and I will do everything in my power to keep her safe for you. I wonder if she'll squeak if I call her auntie?"

Mena was chuckling now, and Marco joined in, despite the serious circumstances in which they now found themselves. Never in a million years would he have thought to see that blighted box again. Yet, here it was, on land he owned. He didn't like this coincidence. Not at all.

Marco took his leave of his niece many times over and flew into the night to his secret lair, racing the dawn, which was coming ever closer. Despite his fatigue, he had to make a few phone calls before he could rest. He just hoped he could get through to the other masters he needed to talk to before they went to sleep for the day as well. It helped that they were both on the West Coast. He'd have an extra hour or so before dawn reached them.

CHAPTER 21

Crystal slept the entire day away. She wasn't really surprised when she woke up just before dark. Getting that box out from the tree roots had been the biggest thing she'd ever attempted to do magically. It had tired her out, but honestly, it had also given her confidence in her own abilities. The more she manipulated those energies, the better she felt she was getting at it.

It was also taking less out of her each time. That little bit of magic she had done when she first arrived had knocked her out. If she tried to do that now, after gaining some experience, she believed it wouldn't cause that much fatigue. The more she used her magical muscles, the stronger they became.

Crystal yawned as she went into the bathroom, showered and dressed for the evening in comfortable clothes. She had a feeling tonight was going to be another night filled with action and activity rather than something requiring business clothes. She put on the dark stretchy fabrics that she particularly liked and the hiking shoes she had picked out of the storeroom on that first day. They were quickly becoming favorites. Comfortable and high quality, they were also gray green and brown, the mottled colors of the forest. She liked that.

She left her room a few minutes later and went down the stairs at a jaunty trot, her energy fully restored. The only thing she needed now was a good meal to top up her energy levels. She headed for the dining room, encountering Mena on the way. The other woman looked tired, and Crystal felt instantly contrite. While she'd been sleeping, Mena had been working hard to keep the place secure.

"Is there anything I can do to help?" Crystal asked as she and Mena walked toward the dining room.

"Kind of you to ask, but you did your part last night," Mena told her. "Of course, I'm pretty sure Uncle Marco will have some ideas for you to assist with tonight. Your brand of power is unique and very welcome in this situation." Mena looked her over as if searching for something. "How are you feeling? Are you fully recovered after the outlay of power?"

Crystal smiled. "I feel fine. Just very hungry."

"That's to be expected with any expenditure of magical energy. You'll find, as you use your powers more, you'll need to eat more. The fuel has to come from somewhere." They entered the dining room to find others already present.

Everyone they passed on the way to the buffet greeted them warmly, and Crystal started to feel as if this place was her home in some inexplicable way. The shifters were welcoming in a way she had not expected.

They started to fill plates at the buffet, and Mena continued talking. "You know, it's a good way to spot magic users. If you see someone who can eat a lot and never gets fat, that's a pretty good tipoff." She grinned as she loaded her plate with calorie-dense items.

They sat together and ate while the rest of the room flowed around them. Crystal was still in just a tiny bit of a daze, but as she ate, she started to feel more in the moment.

More awake. Mena was good company. She kept the conversation going, without it being too intrusive. Both women were clearly hungry and eating a lot more than Crystal usually did.

"There's one thing I'm really concerned about," Mena said as they began slowing down a little on their consumption of calories. "I'm not really sure if I acted quickly enough to cloak the presence of the box last night. There was a short moment in time when the box was not really hidden, I believe." Her dark brows knit in a frown. "If I understand it correctly, the tree was actively hiding it from everyone. When you freed it from the tree, there was a moment before I picked up the protection, where it may have been broadcasting its presence to exactly the wrong people. If they were alert and looking for it, it might've been seen."

Crystal didn't like the sound of that. She waited for Mena to continue. The other woman was taking a sip of her drink and put it down carefully before she went on.

"If the enemy noticed it, they could be planning an attack, even now," Mena said in a low voice, concern clear in her expression. "I've been working all day on strengthening the protections around the house and the pavilion, where we hid the box. I won't try to pretend it didn't take a lot out of me. I'm going to be no good to anyone until I've had some sleep. But Uncle Marco will take the night shift while I recoup my energy. And I'll be good as new tomorrow to take the watch while he rests." Mena looked around at the other people in the big room, seated at other tables. "And, of course, there are the wolves and other shifters. I believe more of the military shifters will be arriving at any moment to supplement those already here. And Brandt has brought in more of his Pack to help. With all of them keeping watch, we should have ample warning of any attack. The only question is if we have enough firepower on our side to counteract anything they might bring against us." Mena shrugged expressively. "In the end, we will just have to do our best."

"I'm not sure what I can do, but whatever it is, I'm happy

to assist," Crystal offered. She wasn't a mage. She wasn't a fighter. She had no idea what she could contribute, but she knew that if they all came under attack, she would try her best to be of use.

They were finished eating and heading back to the office when Marco arrived. He greeted them as they approached the bottom of the main staircase in the entry hall.

He kissed Mena on both cheeks then took Crystal into his arms and hugged her close while nuzzling her neck. She giggled, a bit breathless, but flowed into him as if her body had been made to fit his. As, indeed, she was coming to believe it had.

If such a thing as a true mate really did exist for people like her, she was about ready to believe that Marco was hers. He hadn't said anything yet, but if he broached the subject, she was going to hop on that as quickly as possible. Right now, she couldn't imagine her life without him in it. She wanted to keep him...forever.

But he hadn't said anything. And they had a lot of work to do tonight before they could concentrate on their growing relationship.

When he finally set her away from him, he didn't let her go far. He kept one arm at her waist while he spoke, and Mena watched them indulgently, one foot on the bottom step of the stairs. She looked so tired. Crystal assumed she would be heading upstairs to rest in short order.

"Thank you for watching over things today, my dear," Marco addressed Mena.

"You're very welcome, Uncle, but if you don't mind," she paused to yawn, covering her mouth with her hand politely, "I need to sleep. Crystal will tell you of my worries, and I hope things stay quiet for you tonight. Call if you need me. Even tired, I can still help if trouble arises."

Marco bowed his head in an old-world style. "I will call only in direst need, and I thank you for being willing to expend so much of your energy on my behalf."

Mena met his gaze and smiled fondly. "You're family,

Uncle Marco. Blood is thicker than water, after all." She winked at him and started walking slowly up the stairs. "Good night, you two."

After she left, Marco turned his full attention to Crystal, holding her at arm's length, his hands around her waist and her hands held loosely around his shoulders.

"I've been thinking that maybe you should take a closer look at the box tonight. I racked my brain about my last encounter with it, and if I recall correctly, when the box was closed, it was undetectable. The fact that you can feel it and that the tree needed to hide it to damp its power could mean that the lid is not on securely. That it is feeding evil energy into the world. We need to examine it in detail to make sure it's shut and bound, so it will not be easy to open, even if it falls into enemy hands," he told her.

"That's what Mena was talking about earlier. She was concerned that there might've been a few moments when I freed it from the tree roots that it was unshielded. Before she got her own protections up around it. She's afraid that the enemy might have been watching and might now know that we've found the box. If so, she's afraid they might attack," Crystal reported.

Marco frowned and moved to her side, keeping hold of her hand as he led her toward the door. "We should get on with the work then, much as I'd like to go upstairs and demonstrate my desire for you again right this minute." He winked at her, and she laughed, feeling sexy and wanted. No man had ever made her feel this combination of desire and playfulness. Only Marco. Sexy, inventive, delicious Marco.

They went outside, and he led her toward the pavilion. They bypassed the maze this time, which bordered one side of the amphitheater, instead heading for the more direct approach. Crystal slowed her steps as they headed downward toward the center stage area under the pavilion's large, sloping roof.

"You put it down there, right?" Crystal asked, eyeing the stage warily. She couldn't see the box, but she could definitely feel it.

"There are chambers under the stage. We put it in one of those temporarily," he confirmed. "I erected wards of protection last night, and Mena added to them today. It probably can't be sensed from a distance, though close up, there is little any of us can do to hide that kind of power."

"Yet, you said when the box is completely closed, it should be undetectable," she countered.

Marco nodded. "Yes. I suspect it is just cracked open the tiniest bit. If it were all the way open, we couldn't be standing so close. What we need to do is reseal it so that not even that little trickle of evil energy can come through."

"Through from where?" Crystal asked as they walked ever closer.

"The box is an interdimensional portal to another realm. One where evil reigns."

Marco's words were shocking. She hadn't really known that such things as other dimensions really existed. It was a neat theory, but he spoke as if it was really a thing. Judging by recent events and the things she had learned to do with her own powers, it probably was. She just didn't really know anything about it.

"So, how do we seal the box shut? I'm guessing rubber bands won't work." She tried for levity even as her heart raced at approaching the box's hiding place.

Crystal could almost feel malevolence pulsing outward from under the stage. Or maybe it was her imagination. Then again, maybe not.

It went against Marco's every instinct to let Crystal get near the box's hiding place. He'd had only one run-in with that devilish artifact in the distant past, but once was enough. He had a healthy respect for the danger involved and didn't want to go anywhere near it, much less allow the woman he believed was his true mate near it. Again.

She had been magnificent. Not only in finding something that even he could not sense, but also in the way she had labored to free it from the earth. Her elemental power was still somewhat nascent, but she was growing stronger every time she used her abilities. He counted it a privilege to watch her magic unfurl like a flower bud blooming into full grandeur.

"Shutting the box may not be as difficult as you might think. We must interrupt the connection between the box and the evil realm from which it is siphoning energy. Then we add a protective spell. One of the oldest and simplest of spells should work for something this ancient."

"That all sounds simple enough, but I get the feeling it's not going to be that easy," Crystal muttered, coming to a halt at the edge of the stage area at the center of the pavilion.

"I have lived long enough to know that a positive attitude is always the beginning of success," he told her with a wink before turning to the stage.

Marco lifted the section of floor necessary, and the box was there, still safe in the wine crate. Not that he'd doubted it. He had felt the malevolence of the box in the back of his mind ever since they'd entered the pavilion. It really wasn't hidden very well, but if they did this right, it would be easier to hide once they sealed it shut and cut off the flow of energy.

"I feel it," Crystal said, eyeing the box as if it might explode at any moment. "I didn't understand last night, but I feel it now. There's a little trickle." She tilted her head, as if trying to find it with her senses. The werewolves were rubbing off on her. That little head tilt was a very common position for the denizens of the mansion at the moment.

"Can you tell where it's coming from?" Marco stood next to her, looking down at the box. "Is there a specific spot on the circumference that I should aim for?"

She looked at him sharply. "What are you planning to do?"

"What I must," he answered grimly.

"Wait a minute." She turned to face him. "Why do I get the impression that whatever it is you have planned is going to hurt you in some way?"

"The feed of power must be interrupted some way," he tried to explain patiently. "I plan to block its path physically."

"But you told everybody not to touch it," she reminded him. "What will that do to you, if you *block its path physically?*" she reiterated his exact words.

"I will never lie to you, *cara*," he replied candidly. "It's going to cause me some damage, but I don't see another way, and this must be done."

She shook her head and rolled her eyes skyward, blowing out a frustrated sigh. "I can think of a *bunch* of other ways to do this. You really need to work on your communication skills, Marco. If we could just talk this over, I'm sure we can come up with a way that won't *damage* you."

The sarcasm in her voice was tinged with fear. For him? His thawing heart was touched.

"All right," he gentled his voice and tried to tamp down the instinct that wanted to protect her from this and just do it all himself, "what do you have in mind?"

"Well…" She looked at the box, and her gaze narrowed in thought. "You want to lift the box without anybody touching it, close it all the way, and then do some kind of binding spell to keep it shut?"

"Essentially," Marco agreed.

"If we take it out of there and get near a tree—an oak or, better yet, a rowan would do well for this—I could ask the tree to hold it for us, so nobody has to touch it. I might even be able to get the tree to give up one or two of its boughs to bind the box securely after it's closed so it can't be reopened easily," she suggested.

"All right. We can give that a try. Now, we just need to get the crate out of the storage area. I'll get one of the wolves because I dare not go close to the box, lest it overwhelm me." He was nervous about being overly influenced by the evil nature of the box.

"Oh, that's no problem," Crystal said, moving closer to the storage compartment and reaching in. "I can get it."

CHAPTER 22

Marco reached out as if to stop her, but she was already in motion. She plucked up the wine crate as if it were nothing and started walking up the ramp and out of the pavilion. He went after her, caught by surprise by her decisive actions. The little dryad was surprisingly fast, even to a man who could move with preternatural speed whenever he wished. Or maybe it was just his reactions were slowed because he was enamored by her beauty and intelligence. Whatever the reason, she had a slowing effect on his senses that he was keenly aware of at the moment.

Crystal walked out from under the pavilion's roof and into the nearby tree line. She walked slowly, searching for a particular tree as he followed closely behind. Both of them could see clearly in the dark, and the moon shone down through the leaves and branches, dappling the woods with reflected light, making the place even more magical.

Apparently finding the spot she wanted, Crystal set down the wine crate with great care at the base of a small tree.

Marco recognized it as one of the rowan saplings he had planted a few years ago. He had peppered the woodlands on the estate, even before he became the rightful owner of the land, with oak and rowan saplings on purpose. He knew from his family tradition that both of those species of trees were capable of cleansing the earth of evil energy.

The rowan had quite the reputation in magical circles. Sometimes called the mountain ash, it had a long history of magical uses, and many different names. One of which was the portal tree, indicating the belief that the rowan tree could form a bridge between realms. In which case, this might be the perfect choice for what they intended to do. For the rowan was also known to protect from evil. For centuries, people carried twigs of rowan tied with red string to protect themselves from sorcerous spells and the evil eye.

Crystal left the crate and went up to the sapling, which was a lot larger than when Marcus had planted it, but it was still a very young tree. She touched the trunk of the eight-foot sapling and seemed to communicate with it for a moment, then stepped back.

"It's willing to help us," she reported to Marco, smiling faintly. "The rest of the forest is giving it encouragement, and I'll do what I can for it afterward, but this is going to be a little tricky, I think."

"I think you're right, but it's a good plan, and I apologize for leaving you out of the planning earlier," he said, feeling contrite. He had to remember that his One was a woman of power in her own right. He had to think of her more as a partner than a subordinate or this would never work. The last thing he wanted to do was stifle her in any way.

She smiled up at him. "You are forgiven." She nudged him in the ribs with an elbow as she turned back to contemplate the box. "Just don't let it happen again." She looked from the box to the tree and back again. "Now…how to do this…"

Crystal made a gesture with her hands, and one of the supple lower limbs of the sapling began to move slowly forward, its delicate leaves rustling slightly. It reached downward, joined by another one of the lower limbs Marco had not seen move, as it was on the other side from where he was standing.

Just like two hands, he thought, as the leafy limbs reached into the wine crate and lifted out the box without the slightest wobble. A third tree limb joined its fellows, studying Pandora's box from above, as if making sure the lid didn't have room to wiggle open any farther. Marco thought that was a nice touch.

"Do you want me to turn it so we can figure out where the leak is coming from?" Crystal asked.

"Please do, as long as it doesn't drain you too much," Marco added, breaking his examination of the box to look her over and make sure she wasn't straining.

She seemed all right and merely shrugged off his suggestion. He looked back at the box, and the trio of tree limbs was moving it around slowly so he could examine it from every angle.

"Stop there a moment, if you can," Marco asked, noting something different about one side of the box that he had not spotted before. "Do you see that?"

Crystal stepped a little closer, peering at the box minutely. "It's like a little nick where the upper part of the lid meets the lower rim? Is that what you're talking about?"

Marco nodded with grim satisfaction. "Precisely. I believe that is our problem. But I'm not sure how we can fix it. The metal the box is made of supposedly does not exist in this realm."

"Really? It feels like an alloy of copper, zinc, and a trace of gold to me."

Her analysis astounded him, and he looked at her in shock. "How do you know that?"

She shrugged. "I don't know exactly how, but it's come in handy in my hobbies. I used to do metal work and still dabble in a little jewelry making on occasion. One of my foster parents was into the lapidary arts and taught me how to grind and polish stones and do simple metalsmithing. I put myself through school by selling jewelry at craft fairs."

"You are, indeed, a woman of many talents. I had no idea you were so gifted."

"It's just a hobby," she said, a slight flush heating her cheeks in a becoming way. "But my magical senses have been getting stronger, and I've always been able to tell what something was made of, as long as they were natural materials. Metals are something I learned in that foster home. Once I got a feel for each metal, I was always able to identify them afterward. The box feels like ordinary terrestrial metals to me, with the flavor of something else that I don't recognize. That could be whatever it is from the other realm, but if we want to plug up this little nick with a similar metal, I can probably cobble something together that might work. All I need is a torch and a crucible. Oh, and some oven mitts. The kitchen probably has a small torch that's used to make *crème brûlée* and maybe a stone mortar and pestle. That could work in a pinch. And my bracelet is made of copper. My little stud earrings are a gold alloy that also contains zinc. I could sacrifice an earring and a few links of my bracelet to experiment with. If it doesn't work, I'll be out an earring, and I'll need to fix my bracelet, which is easy enough since I made it to begin with. That's not too bad. And if it works, well then, we'll be one step closer to solving our evil little box problem."

He took out his cellphone and started dialing. "It's worth a try."

Marco had the number for the security room they had set up in the mansion. One of the Wraiths was always standing by in that room, watching the cameras and sensors. Sure enough, Arlo answered on the first ring. Marco told the ex-military werewolf what they needed from the kitchen and where to find them, asking Arlo to send one of his men on the double with the items.

Marco sensed Arlo wanted to ask what they were up to, but he refrained. Marco appreciated the man's discretion and reminded himself to thank the Wraith's field commander later. He ended the call and put the phone away.

"Someone is coming with the items you requested," Marco told Crystal. "It shouldn't take long. Are you okay to hold the box like that?"

Crystal shrugged. "The tree is doing most of the work. I feel no strain. I'll let you know if it starts to get to be too much."

"You do that, milady. I would remind you that, as much as you didn't want to see me come to harm tonight in this task, I feel the same about you." He met her gaze, allowing some of the emotion he was feeling to show in his expression.

When she smiled softly at him, his heart bloomed with joy. It had been so long since he had felt so strongly for anyone or anything. Especially, the tender emotions. He'd been so focused for so long on fighting evil that he had not realized how much of the beauty of the world he had missed. But Crystal was bringing it all back to him. He could not love her any more than he already did, but in moments like this, making new discoveries, it all felt new again. And that was significant for a man his age.

In even less time than he had expected, Arlo himself arrived. He had the items in his hands.

"I left my second-in-command in charge. I get the feeling you two might need a little backup. Will it disturb anything if I stay?" Arlo asked.

Crystal shook her head when Marco looked at her. "I don't mind. As a matter of fact, you can help a little bit. See that flat stone over there?" She indicated a flat, level rock about five yards away. When Arlo nodded, she went on, "Bring the mortar over here, and I'll fill it with the things we need to melt."

Arlo approached, holding out the stone mortar. Crystal quickly took out one small earring and put it in the bottom of the bowl, then took off her bracelet and, using her fingers, opened some of the large rings that made up the design. She put a few of them into the bowl with the earring and accepted the torch from Arlo.

"You might want to put on those oven mitts," she recommended with a small grin.

Flicking the little flame to life, she adjusted the settings until she had a hot central flame, which she pointed directly at the copper links and gold alloy earring in the mortar, which was acting as a crucible. Arlo was holding it in his mitted hand. The mortar was carved from heavy stone which easily accepted the heat.

"You see how I'm moving the flame around?" Crystal asked Arlo. He nodded, and she stopped. "The mortar is going to really heat up as the metal melts, so you should probably put it on that stone over there, just in case it gets too hot to hold. If you will, I'd like for you to continue melting the metal for me. Is that okay with you?"

"No problem, ma'am," Arlo replied politely. He accepted the little torch back from her and went over to the flat stone, placing the mortar down gently. He then set to work, doing what she had shown him.

"That will take just a few minutes," Crystal told both Marco and Arlo. "We should probably do whatever we need to do to prepare the box, so we're ready to go when it's melted. Any thoughts on that, Marco?"

"If your tree will hold the box with that damaged side face up, you can pour the metal while I speak the binding spell," he suggested.

"Okay. Hold on a moment. I'm going to coax those limbs around the box a bit more. The tree has already agreed to sacrifice them," she told him. He could hear the seriousness in her tone, and Marco continued to be impressed with her ability to talk to trees and manipulate the earth.

As Marco watched, the tree limbs wound slowly around the box. All three limbs slowly wrapped around the box, three times each. Whether Crystal realized it or not, three times three was a potent number for magical work. Her instincts were as spot-on as ever.

When she was done, the box was held upward on its side, exposing the spot where the little nick had been taken out of the lid. It was perfectly level and also perfectly still. Ready for action.

"How's the metal coming along?" Marco asked Arlo, who looked up from his work and shut off the torch.

"It's melted," he reported.

"Great," Crystal replied, walking toward Arlo, who was only a few feet away.

Crystal took the oven mitts off the stone and put them on. A moment later, she lifted the hot crucible containing the tiny bead of melted ore from the stone and walked slowly back to the tree that still held Pandora's infamous box in its leafy grip.

She paused in front of the box, as if thinking. "If I try to pour from this thing, it's just going to make a mess," she observed. "I think I can direct it with my mind—my magic. Let's see…"

Marco watched as Crystal's eyebrows drew together in a frown of concentration. A moment later, a bright stream of molten metal lifted from the crucible to form a neat droplet hovering in the air above the stone mortar. As he watched, it moved through the air, heading for the box, then halted a few inches above the nick.

"Are you ready?" she asked in a breathless voice, watching the liquid metal intently.

"Ready when you are, *cara mia*."

Marco knew Crystal didn't understand the incredible level of ability she was displaying. She had grown so much in just the past few days. Her instincts led her in the right direction every time. It was humbling to watch her learn this way. So natural. So impressive. So powerful.

"Okay. I'm going to start filling in the nick before the metal cools too much. Starting in three…two…one…"

Marco timed his words with the first touch of molten metal to the box. He chose a simple spell from days of old that held power in its antiquity. After all, they were dealing with something much older than himself. Simpler was usually better in such instances. He called his power—not the power that came with what he had become, but the power that was his by birthright—and cast the spell.

*"I bind thee in the name of the Light.
What once was wrong I now make right."*

So quickly he might almost have missed it, as the liquid metal touched the box, it glowed fiercely. The slight nick in the lid filled in, and then the tiny bit of excess metal seemed to stream like fire around the circumference of the box, just at the line where the lid met the body. It shone bright for a split-second, then the glow faded.

It didn't take long. The nick in the lid, after all, was tiny. It didn't take much metal to fill it in. But Marco felt it down to his bones when the box was finally sealed. A pressure he had not known he was feeling suddenly eased. The flow of evil energy from that other dimension was cut off. Even he could feel the earth relaxing around him.

Crystal sagged, her shoulders losing the tension that had tightened them almost up around her ears. She was holding the hot crucible in both oven-mitted hands, and she sighed heavily.

"I'm glad that's done," she whispered, still looking at the box. "The trees are much happier now. You feel it too, right?" Crystal looked up at him, her eyes wide.

He had to clear his throat before he could speak. She was such an amazing woman. She had just commanded more magic than he had seen in years, and seemed to think nothing of it.

"Oh, most definitely. It is sealed. Now, we must find a place to hide it temporarily until a more permanent solution can be devised. And we can also expect some attempt at retaliation from our enemies. There's no way they would've missed this. Especially if they were feeding off the energy coming from the box. They're going to be mad that it has been cut off."

"Well, that's not good, but I guess we'll just deal with it if it happens. Now, let me just…" She walked over and put the mortar back on the stone near where Arlo still stood. She took off the oven mitts and placed them next to the mortar, sending Arlo a small smile.

"Now for the rowan. It's been very brave and steadfast," she said, praising the tree as she returned to stand before it. "Its sacrifice is great and much appreciated."

Crystal motioned with her hands gently, and those three limbs seemed to age and grow around the box. The leaves on just those limbs disappeared as the aging accelerated and the size of the bands around the box increased until the metal of the box was all but hidden by hard wood growing around it. Then the limbs cracked off the tree, and the box lay on the ground, encased in the wood around it.

Crystal went up to it and tipped the empty wine crate on its side, using her foot to shove the wood-covered box into the crate once more. Then she tilted the crate up again so that it could be carried easily and looked up to meet Marco's gaze.

"Where do you think we should put it?" she asked, blinking up at him.

"I think back in the pavilion for now."

CHAPTER 23

After returning the crate to the hollow beneath the stage and replacing the heavy stone over it, Crystal breathed a sigh of relief. Marco put his arm around her shoulders as he walked with her back to the house.

"I think we're safe enough for now, but we can expect trouble sooner, rather than later," Marco murmured as they mounted the steps. Once they were inside, he stopped and turned to her, taking her into a loose embrace. "You know, you've come a very long way from the woman who fainted from expending too much energy a few nights ago. Are you even tired right now?"

Crystal thought about it and realized he was right. "I don't really feel tired. Just a little weary but also kind of satisfied with what we have accomplished. I was feeling like such a failure when I wasn't finding anything. I'm just relieved to have discovered the problem and done something about it." She moved closer and rested her head on his shoulder. "We should check over whatever parts of the forest we missed, just to be sure, but the trees are a lot happier, so I think there probably isn't anything else out there that could cause a problem."

"Your power keeps growing. Did you realize that?" he asked softly, placing a kiss on her hair.

"Mm. I feel it. It's like something that was sleeping all my life has been waking up and unfurling within me. Every time I use it, my magic gets stronger. At least, that's how it feels right now. I'm sure, at some point, it'll slow down, but being here, around you and all the other magical folk on this estate is making me aware of things in a whole new way," she admitted. "I never knew much about the magical world. I found out a little when I talked to that shaman I told you about, but he couldn't really tell me what I was or what I could do. He wasn't sure either. It's only now that I know what I am that I can really tap into abilities. They feel like they've always been inside me, just waiting to be called."

"You're amazing, *cara mia*," he whispered, stroking his hand down her back. She felt cherished in that moment. He just held her for a long time before finally drawing back a little to meet her gaze. "What do you want to do with what's left of the night?"

His flashing dark eyes challenged her, and she was up for anything. She was glad she didn't feel too tired to play with her handsome lover.

"What do you think?" She grinned at him, feeling daring, excitement building at the thought of spending the rest of the night in Marco's strong arms. Naked.

"I think, perhaps, that great minds think alike," he told her, teasing. Then he picked her up and floated them rapidly up the stairs and into her bedroom. Thank heaven.

This time, the mood was slow and leisurely. He took his time undressing, dragging out his own disrobing in a way that made her mouth water. It wasn't quite a floor show, but he was definitely watching her reaction as he removed his shirt and then his trousers. Dear Lord, the man was honed like a marble statue—and about as hard as one too.

She reached for him, but he stood back, just out of reach. His expression was both teasing and disciplinary. *Oh, goodie. He wants to play.*

"Now, you," he instructed her, waiting for her compliance.

Her mouth went dry as she sat up on the bed. He had placed her there then moved back to disrobe, holding her gaze all the while.

Slowly, she reached for the hem of her shirt, dragging it up her torso inch by inch. She'd never done a striptease before, but she was getting into the spirit of things. Crystal pulled the shirt off and then eased her legs over the side of the bed to deal with her pants in the same way—removing them an inch at a time while Marco watched with rapt attention.

Left in bra and panties, she would have gone on with the tantalizing torture, but Marco moved, coming to her and staying her hands. He took over, removing her underwear with delicate strength that gave her no doubt about the level of his desire.

When she was bare, he flipped her onto her stomach and slapped her butt lightly when she tried to object. Oddly, the little love tap only heightened her anticipation for whatever he had coming next. She was happy to let him be in charge of this encounter. She already knew he was a generous lover, and she was more than willing to play along with whatever he had in mind.

He blanketed her from above with his hard body, his hands resting on the mattress next to her head. He didn't press his full weight onto her, just let her feel the power of him above and behind her. It felt delicious.

He bent to kiss the side of her throat, and she tilted her head for him, granting him access. Shivers went down her spine as she felt the slight rasp of his teeth against her sensitive skin, but they were gone almost before the sensation had registered. He moved then, lifting up to position her on her knees, ass up in the air.

A moment later, he joined with her, taking her from behind in a penetration that she felt down to the soles of her feet. Pleasure. Pure, unadulterated pleasure wracked her body as he seated himself within her. She felt…complete. For the first time in her life, she felt as if some missing part of her had come back to make her whole.

A silly thought, but one that would not be silenced. She let her mind wander as Marco began to move within her. Slow, at first, then increasing in speed and depth until she was keening his name in a litany of desire.

She came in a rush, ecstasy swamping her as he shuddered into her, finding his own climax.

When they were able to move, he lay them down on the soft mattress, spooning her from behind, his hand running over her arm in a soothing, possessive gesture that touched her deeply. Never had she been with a man who was so tactile, so loving even after he'd gotten what he wanted. Marco was one of a kind. She faded into sleep on that happy thought.

*

When Crystal woke the next morning, Marco was, once again, gone with the light. There was another rose on her pillow, and she held it to her nose as she remembered with joy the night before. They had worked together so well, and then after they'd shut the box and put it away, they'd come together in a pleasure even more satisfying than anything they'd shared before.

She had really wanted Marco to be here when she woke up, but she knew he was running a business empire, and he couldn't really take too much time away during business hours. Mena was in the office when Crystal went downstairs sometime after lunch.

She'd expended a lot of energy the night before but didn't feel drained. It really was true. The more she used her magic, the better she got at it and the stronger it became.

Marco's strength had also been impressive. It seemed like he was the only one who could lift that enormous slab of rock over the box's hiding place. The werewolves were strong, but none of them even attempted to raise the heavy slab that Marco lifted with a simple wave of his hand.

Magic. The man was pure magic. He had power and strength to spare, it seemed, and she had never—and would never—know another man like him. As far as she was concerned, he was the ultimate man. The one she wanted to be with for the rest of her life. If that's what he wanted.

She got the distinct impression that he was leaning that way, but he hadn't said it outright. Their communication wasn't as clear as she wanted it to be, but she was playing it cautious. She didn't want to make assumptions and ruin what they had. Even if it was driving her nuts not to know exactly where she stood with him.

Crystal missed having Martine in the office. After just a few days, she'd come to appreciate the werewolf woman's sense of humor and believed she had made a good friend, but Crystal understood why she was working remotely for the time being.

Mena was there, and she was larger than life but also really down to earth. Her style was flamboyant, to say the least, but she had a big heart and a cunning humor that spoke of her love for life and high energy. She was always bustling about during the day, sketching in a large book she carried around with her as she went into parts of the mansion that were not yet under renovation.

She had the dash of an artist and the aplomb of a runway model. The unmarried men were uniformly under her spell, and many of the women had already sought her advice on clothing and décor.

Crystal began to realize that Mena wasn't just Marco's relative. She was a power in her own right. They were sharing the office, and Mena answered a ringing phone with her name. Suddenly, it came clear in Crystal's mind. When Mena ended the call, Crystal spoke with dawning realization.

"You're Philomena Modesti. You own PhilMode, Inc." Crystal could have smacked herself on the forehead but didn't want to look even sillier.

PhilMode was a world leader in design. Its famous CEO was a fashion icon and trend setter. She was often pictured in the society pages and had designed for the royal families of several countries as well as movie stars and business leaders. She was famous and incredibly wealthy, and Crystal had to have been crazy not to recognize her before this.

"I thought you had not recognized me. It was nice to be incognito for a while," Mena said with a laugh.

"I'm an idiot," Crystal said candidly. "I guess I just never imagined I would ever meet someone at your level of society, and I didn't expect to find a world-class designer in the middle of Nebraska, of all places."

Mena laughed outright. "I will admit, Nebraska is not normally on my short list of the fashion capitals of the world, but it is where my family is, so it is where I am." She shrugged elegantly. "I would go anywhere to help Uncle Marco. He staked my company when I was just starting out. PhilMode would not exist but for his help. And besides that, I love him. He is the patriarch of my family, and we Italians take family very seriously, you know."

"He's very lucky to have you," Crystal remarked with brutal honesty. She had longed for family when she was younger.

"And I am blessed to have him," Mena agreed. "All of us are. He takes care of everyone in his bloodline. Whether they know it or not, every one of our relations is employed by one of his companies, and he makes sure we are all able to live comfortably. A certain number of us have more direct ties to him."

Crystal was about to ask more when Mena's phone rang, and she answered it, launching into a rolling spate of Italian. It was clear she was on a business call that might go on for some time, so Crystal set to her own work. She was working on plans for revitalizing the maze near the pavilion. She needed to consult the bushes growing there to find out if they wanted to continue to keep the maze formation or if they'd be happier growing more wild. At this point, they'd had to witness so much evil in their midst that she was inclined to let them do as they wished rather than force them to keep a shape they might abhor.

She needed to go outside to consult with them. Crystal thought twice about going outdoors unaccompanied, but they'd dealt with the box, and the werewolves had all sorts of new security in place. Still, she didn't think Marco would be pleased if she left the house and went all the way down to the maze. Maybe she could just stick her head outside the door and see if she could make contact that way? She didn't want to make any more plans without consulting the living things that would have to abide by whatever she designed.

Mena was still heavily involved in her phone call, so Crystal just left the office quietly and headed for the door nearest the maze. It was one of the back doors on the side of the mansion, in the opposite direction from the well-traveled hallway that contained the kitchen and dining room. This end of the house was quieter and hadn't really undergone much repair or renovation yet. In fact, she didn't pass anyone as she made her way down the hall toward the door that was her goal.

Crystal just opened the door and poked her head outside. Nobody was out there, and all seemed quiet. She stepped outside and let the door close behind her. So far, so good.

Then all hell broke loose.

Between one eye blink and the next, the forest erupted in a cacophony of pain, fear and noise as it was attacked on several fronts at once. She was moving even before she thought about it, cursing the fact that she'd left her cellphone on her desk, attached to the charger. She would have to hope she ran into one of the werewolf patrols, or maybe she could trip one of the new sensors on purpose and bring the cavalry running, but she couldn't stop. There were major problems in her forest, and her tree friends were suffering.

A fire had been set in one part of the forest, and in another, someone was busy with an axe, chopping down oak and rowan saplings with wild abandon. She didn't know where to turn first, but she had to stop them!

Crystal took off at a run across the esplanade and down the steps toward the pavilion. She avoided the maze area and headed for the tree line but didn't make it. The woman she'd confronted on the esplanade previously stepped into her path, and Crystal was brought up short several feet from her.

"Ah. Happy to see I was right about your nature, little dryad. Snap a twig and make the wood nymph come running. Works every time, according to the history of our Order," the woman said, smiling evilly. "Was it you who found the box?"

Crystal froze, not knowing what to do. Could she bluff her way out of this?

"I thought you were from the Chamber of Commerce or something. If you're trying to submit another proposal, you should go up to the office." Crystal tried to edge away from the other woman, but she kept moving closer. As Crystal backed up, the woman moved forward.

"Really? I think we're beyond that now. If you don't know that I am one of the *Venifucus*, then you have to be pretty stupid. And I don't think someone that dumb could actually find the box for which we've been searching for so long."

The woman nodded to someone over Crystal's shoulder, and only then did she realize she was being herded. There was a man behind her. Much too close. She tried to run, but it was too late. He grabbed her arms, immobilizing her with ridiculous ease. *Damn.* She had been a fool, and if she made it out of this alive, Marco was going to kill her.

CHAPTER 24

Arlo was running the perimeter in his human form when he realized something was wrong. He saw a crumpled form in the distance. One of his guys. On the ground, either dead or unconscious. Either one was bad, because it meant somebody with serious skills or magic, or both, had infiltrated past the point his man had been guarding.

On full alert, Arlo tapped out a sequence over his tactical radio. His guys would get the message and disseminate it around the estate. Even as he approached his fallen comrade, Arlo kept his head on a swivel, anticipating more trouble.

It didn't take long for an axe-wielding maniac to come running out of the woods, swinging for him. Arlo dodged, but the guy with the axe had more than just momentum on his side. He had magic. *Shit.*

The gloves were off once the assailant showed his true colors. Arlo wasn't going to waste any more time than he had to on this guy. It had to be a feint. The guy with the axe was likely just a distraction. Something else was happening on the estate. Something bad. He could feel it in his bones and every instinct of his wolf nature howled in alarm.

His opponent might be throwing magic around, but Arlo was a trained operative. And sometimes, even magic users had trouble dodging bullets. Arlo pulled out his weapon and began firing.

The little shit hadn't been expecting that, and Arlo winged him within the first round fired. The man went down, the look on his face surprised. Arlo went closer to see what he'd do.

"You want to tell me what you're doing here? This is private property." Arlo wanted to hear what the man had to say before he took further action.

"This was our land," the man spat, holding his injured arm and rocking back and forth on the ground in pain. "We came for what was ours. You can't stop us."

Arlo realized the rocking was part of some kind of ritual gesture when the bullet popped out of the guy's arm. The little rat was doing magic to heal himself so he could attack Arlo again.

Not likely. Arlo raised the butt of his gun and tapped the guy hard on the temple, expertly knocking him out. The mage crumpled on the ground, unconscious. He wouldn't wake for a long time.

Arlo scanned the surrounding woods even as he spoke over the radio to his team. He reported his encounter briefly and waited to hear what else was going on as each of his men checked in. They did it by the numbers, man by man, going around the perimeter of the property.

It wasn't until they got around to the opposite end of the estate from where he was standing that another of his men failed to check in. Arlo immediately sent the closest guys to check on the one who was probably down.

He then ordered some of the guys from the house to come collect the prisoner and their fallen comrade—a recent addition to the Wraiths named Luke. Arlo had discovered Luke was just unconscious, not dead, though he had a nasty burn on the side of his face. A magical burn.

That was going to leave a mark. Then again, Luke was already pretty enough. The scar would give him character.

Arlo stayed put, much as he wanted to be on the move, until he sighted his relief coming through the trees. Once he saw them, he took off running. They would take care of the prisoner and Luke while Arlo found out exactly what the hell was happening. He was very much afraid he had totally fucked up, and somehow, the enemy was already past the perimeter and wreaking havoc within the estate's boundaries. Exactly what he'd been brought here to prevent. *Dammit.*

He ran a straight route, dodging through the trees with all agility of his wolf side, though he remained in human form. He was listening to reports from his men over the radio as he made his way toward them. There was some kind of fire on the opposite side of the estate and a fire mage that had been treed by a pair of his guys who were currently dodging fireballs.

He talked to his control room back in the mansion and asked them to call Philomena and get her help with the fire mage. The wolves could keep the mage in one place, because magic had a tendency to roll off a wolf's fur whether he was in wolf or human form, but they probably needed another mage to take that one down without causing more damage. That's where the Italian bombshell came in, or so she had promised.

Arlo kept running, swinging around the curve of the pavilion just in time to see a familiar blonde head disappear into the trees with two strangers.

Fuck. What was Crystal doing outside? Marco was going to have his balls for letting his lady be captured by these creeps. There had been a big man holding her by the arm and dragging her along. The woman had been overseeing the operation and had to be a mage. Otherwise, they wouldn't have been able to disappear so quickly or completely, right in front of Arlo's eyes. The mage had to be cloaking their presence somehow.

But Arlo was a werewolf, and he had a super keen nose. He entered the trees some distance from where he'd seen them disappear and alerted the guy manning the command center in the mansion as to the situation. Then Arlo went on the hunt.

Marco woke suddenly with the sense that something was terribly wrong. He reached for the tablet on his bedside table and tapped to see the various security cam views. He could see the sun was hidden behind a cloud, riding low on the horizon, but it was still out.

Over the centuries, he had built up a small tolerance to daylight. For example, he was no longer debilitatingly tired by it or unable to move around during daylight hours. He was not at his energetic best, it was true, but he could be awake during the day for a few hours, as long as he didn't go out in direct sunlight, which would burn him to a crisp in minutes.

The fact was that the longer a bloodletter lived, the more powerful he became. Marco had been a bloodletter for centuries and had come from a magical family as well. He had always been a bit more magical than the others of his kind who had started life without the magical heritage of his bloodline. It was that magic that told him there were major problems at the estate right now, and he had to help.

Last night, he had elected to stay in a secret room he'd built off the wine cellar in the extensive basements of the mansion for just such circumstances. He'd wanted to be on the grounds in case there was more trouble. He'd wanted to be near Crystal, even though he'd had to leave her bed in that above-ground bedroom where the sun would stream in the windows during the day.

He raced through the lower levels of the house, stopping in the security room where one of the Wraiths was manning the monitors. He was Arlo's second-in-command on this op, a newer operative named Jericho. He seemed surprised to see Marco, but only for a split second before delivering a concise situation report. There was a fire on one side of the property and a guy with an axe on the other.

"Tell Arlo I'm going to do what I can to get out there and help," Marco told him.

"You are?" Jericho's eyes widened. "But—"

"I'm older than I look, and I have a few tricks up my sleeve," Marco told the man.

Before Jericho could reply, Arlo made another report over the radio. Two intruders had captured Crystal.

Marco heard the transmission and cursed, even as he took flight toward the hidden tunnel he'd put in after taking possession of the property. It would let him out under cover of the pavilion. From there, he'd be on his own. He paused to grab two bottles of wine on his way out of the cellars. He might need it if his skin was exposed to the sun.

Most people didn't know that wine actually healed bloodletters. It was bottled sunshine. The fermented fruit of the vine was the last and only link he had with the sun, and it was one of the few substances he could ingest. If he got sunburned or otherwise injured, the wine would help heal him.

He'd leave it in the pavilion, just in case. He could always retrieve it later if he didn't need it. At the moment, he was near-frantic at the thought of Crystal in the hands of the intruders. Arlo had said they were cloaking their presence magically, but Arlo was a wolf. He'd find them.

As would Marco. And then they'd be sorry they were ever born. He'd make certain of it. How dare they touch his One?

Outrage filled him as he flowed down the secret tunnel and came out in one of the anterooms of the pavilion. He was in darkness. He'd chosen the outlet of this tunnel very carefully. He'd have a secure path to the edge of the woods that would keep him out of direct sunlight. If the sky cooperated, he might be able to take advantage of some cloud cover to limit his exposure as he dashed from the cover of the pavilion's roof to the sheltering darkness under the trees.

As long as he kept to the denser part of the forest where the leafy canopy kept almost all of the light out, he should be all right. He had to be all right. He had to get to Crystal. There was no question of him not rushing to her aid, no matter the cost to himself. Her life was vital to his continued existence. He'd rather die, shriveled to dust in the sun, than go on without her.

In fact, he could not. He would die if she did, and gladly so. He would not continue without her light in his life. It was just not possible. He loved her too deeply already.

If he was to continue in this realm, then she must be saved. There was no other choice. And if he died in the process, then so be it. He was a better man for having known her, and he would take the memory of her love with him to the next realm.

Marco gauged the sky and the cloud cover, then made a dash for the densest part of the tree line.

Crystal couldn't believe what was happening. She had been duped into coming outside and gotten caught by these assholes. Inwardly, she was fuming. Angry at herself for being so stupid and enraged at what these trespassers had done to get her attention. The fact that they had attacked the forest in order to draw her out made her so mad she could spit.

Another part of her mind was really scared. She'd never really been in the sort of danger before. She had never been abducted or threatened bodily. No one had ever really raised a hand to her before in her life. The goon dragging her into the forest was hurting her arms, and try as she might, she couldn't break free of his hold. That was truly scary. As was the fact that nobody really knew where she was. She hadn't been smart enough to tell anybody where she was going when she left the office.

She could only hope that maybe Mena would notice when she didn't come back in a timely manner and come out searching for her. But Crystal couldn't really count on that. She knew she had to do something to help herself. The one good thing, as far as she was concerned, was that they hadn't taken her out of the forest yet. Among the trees, she had plenty of allies. She just had to figure out how to best utilize their assistance.

She started sending out little tendrils of her magic to the trees as they passed, trying to figure out what she could ask them to do to help her out of this mess. The trees were more than willing to help, but the people were moving too fast. Trees weren't exactly the quickest beings. Crystal had to hope that the people dragging her through the woodland would slow down a little bit at some point. Then, she might have a chance.

Up ahead, she saw a break in the trees. They were on a part of the estate that she and Marco had not yet searched. There was a little clearing up ahead, and she could hear the sound of flowing water. She hadn't seen it in person, but there was a small lake on the property that she remembered from the maps of the estate. The forest had been cleared well around the lake so that the water could be accessed more easily. That's where they were heading. She'd bet on it.

Were they going to try to drown her? If so, as long as that was a natural lake with things growing in it, she didn't think she would be into much trouble. She could always coax living things to grow and maybe lift her out of the water. She was a little more concerned about the fact that the trees were so far away. She had hoped to tangle her abductors up in branches whose growth she could accelerate to bind them, but if they were too far away, that wasn't going to be an option.

She sent a little tendril of her magic ahead of her and queried the earth around the lake. Sure enough, it was a natural lake. Oh, maybe it had been dug, but there was no barrier between the water and the earth, and there were plants growing along the shore and at the bottom. Plants she could communicate with. Maybe they could be of some help.

As they drew closer to the opening in the tree canopy, the woman slowed, allowing the man who was manhandling Crystal to catch up. The three of them stood side-by-side at the edge of the trees, her two captors coming to a halt and allowing her to stop as well. The woman was looking around, her expression angry.

"Where are the others? Don't tell me those two idiots got caught." The woman stomped forward aggressively. "Well, we can easily do this without them. More magic for us." The man started moving again, dragging Crystal along with him. "But we have to get this done before nightfall. Otherwise, we'll have that blasted vampire to deal with."

"I'm still not convinced he's on the other side," the man said unexpectedly. "His kind usually allies with us, not with the goody two shoes."

"I don't know, Chester. This one stepped in to buy the estate awfully fast. We didn't even know it was up for sale, and he'd already purchased it. That tells me there's some kind of insider information in play, and where would he have gotten that? From the bastards who killed our friends."

"I still think you're wrong about that, Lissette. He's got connections all over the place. I'm not surprised he found out about the sale long before we did. For one thing, we weren't looking for it. For another, he's got all kinds of real estate investments all over the world, and people dedicated to looking for just these kinds of properties to add to his empire." The man stopped as his friend Lissette came to a halt in front of them. They were only a few feet from the edge of the lake, out in the open sun.

"There's really no way to be sure, Chester. Not until one of us confronts him face-to-face, and I'd much rather not do that, myself. He's one of the really old ones. I don't want to take any chance that he might be a do-gooder. So, let's get this over with. Drain her power and be on our way before he wakes up for the night."

Two things about this conversation shocked Crystal. First, they were talking about a vampire, for goodness' sake. Vampires weren't real.

Were they?

These people certainly seem to believe that there was one in the vicinity. And if she was hearing them right, they thought it was Marco. Marco! How could that be? She had seen him drinking wine. Plenty of it, as a matter of fact. She had drunk from the same bottle, so she knew it was just wine and not something...else.

If he was really a vampire, wouldn't he have to drink blood? Then again, she couldn't remember ever seeing him eat anything. Just the wine. Maybe that was some kind of exception?

While it was true he didn't really show up until after dark, he didn't look or feel undead. His skin was warm, his complexion was vibrantly Italian. She had seen him in the bathroom mirror and hadn't had to invite him into her domain as far she could remember. It didn't add up, and frankly, the whole idea just confused her. Marco, a vampire? It seemed a little ridiculous, but then again...

The second thing about their conversation that set her alarm bells ringing was that part about draining her power and being on their way. Marco had alluded to this kind of thing when he was explaining about the *Venifucus*. He had told her that there were certain evil magic users who stole their power from other people. They preyed on the magical races and often killed their victims in heinous rites, draining their magical energy to take for their own.

It sounded as if that's what they had planned for her. Maybe jumping in the lake was a better option. She'd rather drown—or, at least, *pretend* to drown—rather than let these two idiots steal the magic she was only just discovering.

She looked around as best she could, trying to locate the nearest trees. They were about ten yards away. Was that too far? She just wasn't sure.

Then she caught movement in the trees. Somebody else was out there. Who? She sent the thought to that part of the forest and the answer came back immediately. *The Protector.*

Thank heavens! Marco was there. And, if he was out and about in the daylight, then he couldn't be a vampire. Could he?

CHAPTER 25

Marco saw Crystal through the trees. She was alive, but there were two people—a man and a woman—holding her prisoner. One of them might be the one who had set the fires on this side of the property, or there still might be more intruders who would be joining these two any minute now. Marco wasn't sure.

The man with the ax had been stopped, but the person, or persons, who had set the fire had not. Not yet, at any rate. If it was one of those two he could see, they would be dead soon, if he had his way. And he *would* have his way. They had threatened Crystal. They had abducted her. They would die for that alone. Nobody had the right to manhandle his One and put her in danger. Nobody.

He looked at Crystal through the trees and realized that she had spotted him. Their eyes met, and she nodded just the tiniest bit. He tried to send her reassurance but wasn't sure if he succeeded through the fury and cold, decisive anger riding him. He needed to act, but the sun was still up. While it was true that it was starting to dip closer to the treetops, it was still there. If only a stray cloud could give him a bit of cover.

Crystal wondered why Marco wasn't making a move. She saw him scanning the sky with a grim expression on his handsome face, and she thought again about the limitations a vampire would have.

If he really was a vampire, then shouldn't he not be out during the day? It was really dark under the trees where no sunlight came through. Perhaps that was enough to protect him. Though, she really didn't know enough about the whole vampire mythos to know what they could do and what they couldn't. All she knew was from popular culture, and she was pretty sure regular folks didn't really know what they were talking about—if such beings actually did exist.

But if he wasn't afraid of the sun, then what else could be causing him to just stand there? Maybe he really couldn't tolerate sunlight. Maybe he really was a vampire. Maybe if she figured out how to make the trees grow over to cover him, then he could come out and do his thing? She wasn't sure. She still wasn't one hundred percent convinced that he was a vampire, but if he wasn't, then why wasn't he acting?

Maybe he was just waiting for the right moment. And if that was the case, Crystal felt that she should do something to help. She wasn't some damsel in distress waiting for the big man to come and save her. Although, she admitted it did kind of look that way right now. But she had abilities. She had magic of her own. She had been learning by leaps and bounds the past few days about how to use it and what she could do with it.

Crystal decided she was going to be part of her own rescue. She wasn't going to just sit here idly, waiting to figure out what was going on and why he wasn't acting. Perhaps he was waiting for her to take the lead. There were two of them, and only one of him. Perhaps he was just waiting for his moment.

If so, she was going to do everything she could to provide

that perfect moment to intervene. Crystal wasn't sure what she was going to do, but she was going to do something. Starting right now.

"You're not going to get away with this, you know," she said to her captors, drawing their attention.

Crystal had been silent up to now, thinking hard and wondering what their goals were. She had collected enough information. These people didn't have anything good in mind. That was enough. It was time to act.

"Oh, I think we're doing just fine," the woman— Lissette—said smugly. "And, in just a few minutes, nothing will matter to you ever again." Her smile was evil, and Crystal suppressed a shudder.

"I don't think you'll find me that easy to kill." Crystal drew on every molecule of bravado she could possibly muster, though inside she was shaking a little.

Lissette looked her up and down, as if considering Crystal's ability to resist. "I think not."

As the woman turned away from Crystal dismissively, she struck. Or, rather, Crystal's underwater plant friends slithered out of the water, reaching their tendrils toward Lissette's ankles. All at Crystal's direction, of course. The underwater plants were very willing to answer her call.

As were the trees. They were struggling mightily the whole while, to grow just a little more of their canopy out toward the water. Crystal didn't dare look, but she felt Marco's advance through the edge of the trees. He was under the shadow of the canopy but now standing out in the open.

Crystal's two captors noticed him, but they still hadn't noticed the vines that were growing steadily closer from the lake. This might just work. She might have enough time to coax those vines into position while Marco distracted Lissette and Chester.

"How?" Lisette sounded very confused, looking at Marco. He didn't dignify her query with an answer. He just kept walking.

Then he outpaced the leaf growth and ended up in the

sun. His skin smoked, and he stepped hastily back into the shadows. Crystal could've cried. He was a vampire. Oddly, that didn't bother her as much as the fact that he had put himself into such danger on her behalf. If the legends were true, he was weak during the day. The fact that he had come out here—even stepped into the sunlight and burned himself—to try to save her... It touched her deeply. She hadn't fully realized how much he really cared.

"Get him!" Lissette screamed at Chester. "He's weak during the day. If we could get his power, we would be invincible."

Chester set off at a run, barreling toward Marco, his hands flailing in the air as he seemed to be working some sort of spell. Crystal opened her mouth to warn Marco but said nothing as he seemed to just sort of sidestep Chester's headlong rush—and his magic. A pulse of it pounded against the nearest trees, but they absorbed it with little damage. Trees were good like that. They could take a lot of magical energy and just ground it into the earth.

While Chester was attacking Marco rather ineffectually, Lissette came up behind Crystal, a gleaming silver knife in her hand. Crystal didn't have any self-defense skills to speak of. She really regretted that right now. If she survived this, she was going to take up martial arts. That was for sure. As it was, she wasn't nimble enough to escape Lissette and that evil knife of hers.

It was an...athame? Crystal thought that's what witches called their ritual cutlery. She suspected such items started out neither good nor bad. It was the people who used them that made them go one way or the other. The kind of magic the knife had been exposed to over the years it had belonged to Lissette made it reek of evil to Crystal's awakening magical senses.

She didn't want that thing anywhere near her, but Lissette seemed to have more physical skills than Crystal did. She grabbed her in some kind of kung fu hold and press that sickening blade against her neck.

Crystal really was going to find a martial arts school after all this was over. She hated how inept she was. And this maneuver had kept moving them farther away from the shore of the lake, and the vines were really struggling to reach them. But Crystal wasn't giving up on her green and growing friends. If this dragged on long enough, they might still be of some help.

Lissette was taller and stronger than Crystal. The evil witch held Crystal securely with that blade way too close for comfort while they watched Marco dispatch Chester with ease.

Under cover of the trees, in their comforting darkness, Marco was still a lot stronger than Chester. Even with the sun still shining just a few feet away. The moment Chester entered the shadow of the trees, he was toast.

Crystal took some comfort watching Chester fall. At least he wouldn't be threatening her or Marco again. She wasn't sure if he was alive or dead, and frankly, she didn't care. As long as he was out of the action, that's all that mattered.

Now, all they had to deal with was Lissette. Two against one, in the opposite direction. Despite her disadvantageous position, Crystal started to feel better about the situation. She kept pouring her magic into the little tendrils of lake vines and the trees that were still filling in above to allow Marco to get closer.

Marco was pleased when the male rushed him. It was easy enough to take out that one, leaving him only the woman to deal with. But then the woman pulled a knife and held it to Crystal's throat. Marco grimaced and steeled his will. He had to stay calm and make sure Crystal lived through this or they would all die.

He had no doubt that Crystal was working her magic on the trees, allowing him to move closer a little bit at a time. It was excruciating, but he had to go slow. So far, the witch didn't seem to notice the green tendrils working their way out of the lake toward her ankles. Crystal was working overtime to try to help, bless her. Marco was duly impressed with his One. She had courage he hadn't quite anticipated, but that made him love her all the more. He was thrilled with the way she could surprise him. So few could, these days.

"I'll kill her!" the woman who held Crystal at knifepoint screamed, her eyes wild.

"I suspect you will anyway," Marco said as he walked a step closer, his tone carefully neutral. It was killing him inside to see Crystal in such a situation, but he had to keep his cool. "Surely, there is more to barter with than the life of one insignificant part-dryad." He lifted one eyebrow. "The box, for example."

"How did you—?" The woman's eyes narrowed in anger. "So, *you're* the one who found it. We figured one of those do-gooder wolves had it."

Marco shook his head. "Not them, madam. It is I who hold the legacy of Pandora, though frankly, it is of little use to me." He shrugged elegantly, hiding his reaction to the woman's avid interest. "Perhaps I will give you the box, if you release the girl." Marco made his proposal sound as if it didn't much matter either way. He would not give this person any more information, particularly about his feelings for Crystal.

"You would give up my ancestress's box for the woman?"

Marco didn't like the speculative tone in the woman's voice. He was also appalled to learn that this woman thought she was descended of the original Pandora—the meddling harpy who just couldn't leave well alone. Marco hadn't been alive during Pandora's time, but he'd talked with a few ancients over his many years who had told him all about the meddlesome witch who had caused so much trouble.

"The artifact holds little appeal for one such as I." Marco shrugged, trying to maintain his casual air. "However, I have a thirst, and magical blood is more difficult to come by than most. Even just slightly magical blood."

Marco hoped Crystal understood. Saving her was the most important thing in his world, but he couldn't let the enemy realize how vital she was to him. Lady willing, he would have a chance to explain it to Crystal later. After this dangerous moron was dead.

"If I let you have her, how do I know you won't just kill me later?" Perhaps the woman was not as moronic as Marco had thought.

"Of course, that is a possibility," Marco replied offhandedly. "However, I find myself in a generous mood, and I weary of this confrontation. Your people provided enough sport for me today. Now, I merely wish for you to leave me in peace so I may dine." He licked his lips, allowing his fangs to elongate and show, hoping to unnerve the woman.

Judging by the way his opponent seemed to wobble, Marco believed he had achieved the desired effect. Good. Maybe they could get on with this now.

The woman seemed to come to a decision. "Where is the box?"

Dear sweet Mother of All, she was going to bargain with him. Marco breathed an invisible sigh of relief.

"I hid it in the pavilion," he admitted.

If he could get the woman under the roof of the pavilion—even if he could just get her under the cover of the trees—he would have a much better chance of getting Crystal out of this unharmed. But there were a few variables in play, and he wasn't sure what would happen next. The next move was up to the *Venifucus* witch.

"You go first," she told Marco. "Walk ahead, where I can see you, and we'll just follow along behind. If you try anything funny, she dies."

Marco held the woman's gaze. "Just so we're clear, if she dies, so do you. Right now, I'm humoring you because I'd like to play with the girl on my own terms. If she is taken off the table, then I have no use for you at all. Clear?"

The woman actually gulped, and Marco felt a stab of satisfaction. She nodded. "Clear."

He turned and started walking back toward the pavilion. He looked back occasionally, as casually as he could, gratified to see that the two females were following along behind. Crystal was cooperating, and so far, she was all right. Now, if he could only keep it that way.

As he walked through the woods, Marco became aware of the Wraiths shadowing his path on either side. They were living up to their name, keeping so far out of sight that he only noticed them because Arlo deliberately showed himself in such a way that only Marco could see him, then vanished into the forest. After that, Marco realized that more than just Arlo was escorting them toward the pavilion, and Marco had no doubt that Arlo would have arranged for backup to be waiting in the natural amphitheater for their arrival.

Marco made some hand gestures where the women couldn't see. He had kept up on military signs and believed he was telling Arlo and his guys to stay out of sight and let Marco take the lead on this. He hoped they got the message, or this could get confusing.

When he reached the edge of the woods and the short traverse he must make to get under cover of the pavilion, he turned back to the woman. He hated exposing his weaknesses, but then again, it was daylight. By rights—according to human legends—he shouldn't even be awake at all. Little did they understand his unique powers.

"I must go quickly here. I will meet you under the pavilion," he said.

"No tricks," the woman growled, prodding Crystal to move forward.

Marco held up his hands, palms outward. "No tricks," he agreed. "I expect you also to abide by the agreement," he reminded her. "Or all bets are off."

Slowly, the woman nodded.

Marco couldn't give Crystal the reassuring look he wanted to give. The enemy would see it and use it against them. Instead, he just shrugged and turned on his heel, biding his time and making a dash for the cover of the pavilion.

He waited, watching from the shadows while the women crossed the open area. So far, so good.

He began walking in front once more, heading for the box's hiding place under the stage. Not that he'd let her know where it really was if he could help it. But there was more room to maneuver down there, away from the seating area.

"Where's the box, vampire?" the woman shouted as he led them closer to the center of the building.

"Just down there, actually," he said, calmly turning and gesturing toward the stage, even as he met the woman's gaze.

"There's nothing down there," she countered, looking suspicious.

"That's where you are wrong," he replied, leaning one hip against one of the rows of chairs.

"Prove it," she spat.

CHAPTER 26

Marco sighed and pointed one finger behind him. This is where his family's magic and his centuries of study would come into play. He didn't usually display his abilities so openly, but this woman would die by his hand this day. That he vowed.

She'd already stepped way over the line in threatening Crystal, and he would not countenance the witch's continued existence. Not after she'd held his One at knifepoint. That could not ever be forgiven.

Marco didn't even have to look as he pointed one finger over his shoulder, allowing his family's magic to spill over and lift the slabs of rock off the stage. He'd lifted them all, exposing all the cavities beneath the stage.

"It's in there," he told the woman. "Go see for yourself. But I get the girl first."

"You want the girl?" she countered, giving him a cunning look. "Then take her!"

With her words, the little silver dagger sliced into the side of Crystal's throat, cutting the throbbing vein that pulsed with fear. The woman pushed Crystal away from herself, practically throwing her at Marco. He caught her gently, cursing the situation as Crystal's blood poured out of a mortal wound.

A wound made by silver. And worse—silver imbued with evil magic. Dammit!

With a stray thought, Marco used his power to lift the woman who was running for the stage off her feet. He slammed her into one of the concrete pillars, only mildly satisfied when he heard her skull crack on contact. She was dead, but he was very much afraid she had killed Crystal too.

"My love," Marco breathed, sinking to the ground with Crystal in his arms. She was bleeding so heavily, and the wound was poisoned with silver. His saliva could make wounds disappear, but not something like this. The silver would not let it heal, and it would poison him as well.

Marco felt his fangs drop in response to the blood, but he could not drink. For the first time, though, Crystal was seeing him as he was. He saw the wonder in her eyes.

"You really are a vampire," she said in a weak voice, even as he held his hand over her wound, trying without success to staunch the flow of blood.

"I am. And you are my One. My mate. I will not go on without you, my love." Marco held her close, knowing her life was draining away, his heart breaking. "Normally, I could seal the wound and restore you to health, but not a wound made by silver, but there is another way. You could become like me, but I will not do it unless it is your choice. Either we continue together in this realm, living only by night, or we both move on to eternity together. Make the choice, beloved. I will not sentence you to life in the darkness without your permission. What do you want?"

"Turn...me..." She could barely speak, her life force flowing quickly away, but he understood.

Wasting no more time, he did what he had to, slicing into his own wrist so that she might drink of his blood. He wasn't sure if it was going to work. Her magical heritage could interfere in some way. He had been very careful over the centuries to not make more of his kind. Only in very rare circumstances had he ever turned anyone, and he had not done so for a very, very long time.

Marco held his wrist to her mouth and encouraged her to drink. Her tongue tickled his skin, and as she swallowed, he felt a wave of relief. She had chosen life—and him. Goddess willing, this might work.

Marco gave her what he judged to be a bit more than enough of his blood then sealed his own wound with a quick swipe of his tongue. It was part of the vampire magic that wounds closed without a trace when he licked them. Otherwise, everybody would know when he'd been feeding.

He watched her carefully, noting when the wound on her neck began to seal itself. It was working! Thank the Goddess, it was working.

Marco knew they weren't completely safe yet, but they had passed the first hurdle. His blood was healing her, which was a very good sign.

He sent a prayer up to the Goddess then looked around. He'd been so focused on Crystal that he hadn't kept track of the other players in this little drama. He saw Arlo bending over the woman who had stabbed Crystal. He straightened and caught Marco's gaze, shaking his head. As Marco had thought, the woman was dead. Good.

Arlo came a little closer but seemed uncharacteristically hesitant. "Is there anything I can do?"

"My One lives," Marco reported, hanging on to the hope that her transformation would go well.

There was still some question about that in his mind, because he wasn't sure what his blood would do to a dryad. Would it continue to be compatible, or would she react badly and die anyway? He had to hold to the hope that she would be well.

"Thanks be to the Mother of All," Arlo replied with heartfelt sincerity. "Philomena dealt with the fire mage, but she took a little damage. I sent her back to the house when I got the sit rep that you had this under control," Arlo said softly. "The fire mage is dead, as is the ax man. We'll take care of the bodies unless you want them to get some special treatment."

"Burn them as quickly and quietly as possible. There's a spot down by the lake that should work nicely. It's cleared of trees, but the canopy has recently grown to cover the spot from any aerial surveillance." He felt pride in Crystal's ability to coax the trees to grow so he could get closer. She was one hell of a woman.

"I'll see to it," Arlo assured him. "Can we help you get her back to the house? Or is there anything else I can do?"

Marco met the man's gaze. "No, but thank you. You have been a good friend and ally, Arlo. I will not forget this."

Arlo shook his head. "No thanks necessary," he assured Marco. "I haven't been blessed enough to find a mate myself, but I see what she means to you, and I wish you both the best. You're a lucky man, Master Marco."

"Blessed," Marco corrected the other man gently. "The Goddess has surely smiled upon me at last. I pray that you find your One someday soon, my friend. It will change you forever, in the very best possible ways."

And with that, Marco stood, lifting Crystal in his arms. She was very weak from blood loss but no longer dying. He would take her back to the rooms under the mansion. She would stay there with him until her change was complete...or not. Whatever happened now, they would go through it together.

Crystal woke in Marco's strong arms and stretched. She felt so languid, and her body was sore, but she didn't know why. Then, all in a rush, she remembered, and her hand flew to her neck.

"The wound is gone, my love. You are healed." Marco's voice came to her, and she blinked open her eyes, looking at his beloved face.

"I didn't dream any of that, did I?" she asked. She was naked, but she didn't remember undressing. "What happened to my clothes?"

Marco chuckled, and a little thrill went down her spine despite her confusion. "Your clothes were covered in your blood. I took the liberty of taking them off and cleaning you up a bit before I put you to bed. You were only semi-conscious at the time, but I suspect my blood was having a little battle with your own and figuring out how the two were going to cohabit in your body. How do you feel? Are you thirsty?"

Crystal thought about that for a moment. "I'd really like a glass of water."

Marco frowned a bit, but got up and went into the attached bathroom, returning with a glass of water he'd gotten from the tap. He handed it to her with grave courtesy and watched as she gulped it down.

Boy, that hit the spot. She was so parched she'd really like another glass. Or maybe two or three more.

"Why are you looking at me so funny?" she asked after she finished the glass.

"Does it agree with you? No stomach complaints?" he asked in return.

"No. No problems. And I'd really like some more."

She wrapped the sheet around herself before getting up experimentally from the bed. She felt only a little wobbly and managed to walk into the bathroom and get herself some more water. Marco followed her, watching her carefully.

After she'd finished the third glass, she placed it on the countertop and turned to him. She leaned against the counter, feeling a bit odd but otherwise much better than she'd expected after being stabbed and nearly bleeding to death.

"What is it?" she asked again.

"It's just that—" For the first time she'd ever witnessed, Marco seemed at a loss for words. "You drank my blood. It healed you." She nodded, encouraging him silently to continue. "Technically, it should have changed you."

She remembered that dimly. She remembered him saying that he could turn her into a vampire, and she would live. Otherwise, he was going to follow her into death. She knew she hadn't dreamed that. She hadn't dreamed any of it.

"You would have died for me," she whispered, truly touched by the notion and the remembered emotion in his words and his expression. "You said you loved me."

Marco moved closer and put his hands around her waist. "I do love you, *cara*, with all my heart and soul. Forevermore."

"Oh, Marco, I love you too," she declared, reaching up to put her hands around his neck. She stood on tiptoe, and he accommodated her by bending down so she could kiss him.

Their kiss was slow and languid, speaking of the love they shared without words. It was a kiss of commitment. A kiss of forever.

It was both the sweetest and most passionate thing she had ever known, and she couldn't say how long it went on for, but when Marco raised his head and smiled at her, his presence lit her entire world. She hoped he knew that she felt the same. Somehow, deep down inside her, she felt a connection. As if she could almost hear what he was thinking.

"You're a vampire," she stated, confused. She hadn't dreamed any of that. She knew it was true, but she didn't understand how it could work.

Marco took both of her hands in his and brought them to his lips, kissing her knuckles then holding her hands to his chest, allowing her to feel the beat of his heart. He smiled again. She got the distinct impression that he had smiled more since meeting her than he had in centuries.

The thought ran through her mind like an echo from his. She tilted her head and squinted her eyes a little bit. How did she know such things? Was her imagination running overtime?

"I am immortal. Yes, this is true," Marco admitted. "After what happened, you should have become like me, but so far, I get the impression you are not." He looked bemused, not concerned. "Then again, my creation didn't quite go as planned either."

"So, you're saying that, by ingesting your blood, I should've woken up as a vampire too, right?" Her brows drew together as she tried to puzzle this out. "But I don't feel any different. I'm thirsty, but not for blood."

"Yes, that is odd in the extreme," he agreed. "Most bloodletters, when they are made, wake with an all-consuming thirst. It is the responsibility of the maker to be certain that their creations understand the responsibility of their new life and how to sustain themselves without hurting others unnecessarily."

"I don't feel like hurting anyone," Crystal said, still perplexed. "I'm thirsty for water, and I'm very hungry too. I'm sort of craving a nice juicy steak, which isn't something I normally crave. But that's about it. I don't want any more blood. Although I'm very grateful for the healing yours gave me. That's what did it, right?"

"The blood of magical creatures is quite different. Immortal blood can heal almost anyone or anything, even mortal wounds, such as the one you suffered. But, usually, it carries a price. It changes the receiver forevermore. However, I myself know that the changes depend on the receiver. Normal people can become immortal. That's what happened to me, to a certain extent. But I came from a long line of magic users. My maker didn't know that when I was changed. You probably don't realize this, but the magical races don't often mix. At least, they haven't for many centuries. The only times we seem to band together and interact with each other—forming alliances and such—is when we are faced with a common threat," he told her.

"So, normally, you wouldn't have such close alliances with the wolf Pack. Is that what you mean?" she asked.

"Just so," he agreed, nodding slightly. "Likewise, without my connections to the family, an immortal such as myself would not usually have any dealings with magic users like Mena and the other *strega* in my extended family. When I was made immortal, my maker did not know that I had come from a line of powerful *strega*. I suspect if they had, they would have just let me die. But they didn't, and when I awoke, I craved not only blood, but magic itself."

"You're a magical vampire? Does that mean you siphon off magic from other people to keep going?" Crystal didn't like the thought of that.

"Not so much people, as places. It's why I often buy properties that have magical pasts. You should know, places can have just as much magic as people do. Oftentimes, more. As long as I'm in such a place, the magical need is met. I'll be the first to admit, it could have gone the other way. I could have easily become like the *Venifucus* we faced here hours ago. They steal other people's magic, killing them in the process. It would have been easy to become that kind of vampire."

"But you're not like that," she insisted. She was certain he had more integrity than that.

"I have fought long and hard to never become like that," he told her. "My mother and sisters were women of integrity, and I tried very hard to follow their example throughout my life, especially after I was changed."

"So, do you still have to bite people and drink their blood?" She knew she was making a face, but she couldn't help it. The thought didn't sit well with her.

"My requirements for blood were never as great as most of my brethren. Probably because I fulfill my needs with magic as well," he admitted. "What you have to understand is that now that I have found you, my dear, I will never have to bite anyone else ever again. That's what happens when my kind finds their perfect mate. Their One. You, Crystal, are my One. The only One I will ever love, and as we grow together, we will begin to share our hearts and minds. I suspect you are already beginning to pick up on my emotions and, perhaps, my thoughts as well. From what I understand, that will grow stronger as we do over the next centuries we have together, Goddess willing."

"Centuries?" The thought boggled her mind. She hadn't

even realized the implications of his being a vampire yet and what that might mean to her. "But I didn't change. At least, I don't think I changed."

"And yet, you are my One. There is no denying that." He seemed a little smug, but she supposed that was allowable.

He had been searching a very long time to find someone to share his life. A little smugness, now that he had achieved his goal, wasn't bad. Especially when it was her that he was so smug about. She tried to keep her smile to herself but failed.

"I still don't understand it all. How can I be immortal, like you, when I'm not...uh...changed?"

"But you are. Maybe not in the obvious way, but my blood healed you, and now, we are joined. Surely, you feel the bond between our souls? It's been growing every day since we met, but now, it's no longer a nebulous thing. It's rock solid, never to be broken. I can feel it. Can't you?"

"I feel something," she admitted. "But remember, all this magic stuff is new to me. I'm not always certain about what I'm sensing and what it means."

"That's all right," he told her reassuringly. "You will learn. I will be happy to teach you what I can, and the rest, we will learn together. It will be a delight to share my life, my magic, my home, and everything that I am now and ever will be with you. Forever."

Her heart swelled at his declaration, and she felt the truth of his words echoing through her mind. He was right. Their connection was growing stronger.

Her stomach growled very loudly, breaking the mood and making them both laugh. He let go of her hands and moved away.

"You will have to make do with some of my clothing for now. I didn't have anything put down here for you because I didn't expect to bring you here. Will exercise shorts and a T-shirt do for now?" he asked, gathering the items from a small chest to one side of the large bed.

Only then did Crystal look around enough to notice that the room they were in had no windows. She'd never seen this room before, and she'd thought she'd been all over the mansion.

"Where are we?" she asked as she accepted the clothes from him.

"I created this set of rooms when I bought the mansion. It was part of the wine cellar, but I created some hidden passageways and secret doors, just in case I ever needed them. Normally, I don't reside here, but when you came, I began to stay close and have been sleeping down here for the past few days." He shrugged and gave her a lopsided smile. "I wanted to be close to you."

Her heart melted even more. "That is so sweet, but I hope you're safe here. Does anybody else know about this place?"

"They didn't. But some of the Wraiths may suspect now," he admitted. "And a few of them definitely saw me use the secret passage to the pavilion, so that isn't much of a secret anymore."

She pulled the overlarge T-shirt over her head then pulled on the shorts. She might look a little frumpy, but it was better than parading through the house naked. Her stomach growled again, and she realized she was getting really, really hungry. As her body woke more, it was sort of coming back online and making demands. After the water, it now demanded food.

"What time is it?" She was wondering if the kitchen would be open, or if she would have to raid the fridge herself.

"It's just after dinner," he told her. "You woke much sooner than I had expected. I thought you would be out until morning, or even tomorrow night, but you bounced back much more quickly than anyone I've ever seen. Not that I make a habit of turning people. In fact, I can count on one hand the number of times I have turned someone, and still have fingers left over. This sort of life—this immortal life—is not easy. I would not condemn anyone to it lightly."

She looked up at him, understanding as she remembered. "You gave me a choice. If I hadn't chosen to stay and be turned, you would have died with me." It was still hard to imagine someone loving her that much, even though she felt as deeply about him. She had just never had someone care about her as much as she cared about them before. It was a novel—beautiful—concept.

Marco paused, meeting her gaze from across the room. He had put on black dress pants and a white dark shirt. He looked very much like the old-world gentlemen. A heartthrob for the ages.

"From now until the stars grow cold, wherever you go, I go too. We are One, Crystal. Forevermore."

She felt the certainty of his words ring through her soul. As if something clicked into place, never to be removed. She smiled at him, her heart on her sleeve, as usual. But she knew she could trust him with it.

"I really like the sound of that," she told him.

His answering smile lit her world with happiness.

CHAPTER 27

Marco was still bemused by the situation but prouder than he had ever been to walk into that dining room with Crystal on his arm. The shifters had already known, but there would never be a question again that Marco and Crystal were mates in the truest sense. They were One.

Most of the crowd had finished with their dinner and were on their way elsewhere, but a few still remained in the dining room. The buffet had not yet been cleared, and Crystal made a beeline for it.

Martine was back on-site, now that things were safer, and also at the buffet table. She greeted Crystal warmly and they chatted as they worked their way down the buffet together. Marco watched indulgently, catching the surprised glances on the faces of some of his werewolf friends as Crystal filled her plate.

Arlo was there with a few of his comrades. The Alpha of the local Pack was not, but Marco was sure he would hear all about this within minutes. In fact, Marco wouldn't be surprised if Brandt didn't show up sometime tonight to see for himself the dryad-turned-vampire… Or not.

Marco wasn't really sure himself what had happened to Crystal. The fact that she was still hungry for food had surprised him. Based on his own experience, he had expected her to wake up as a bloodletter. Every indication so far was that she had not.

Yet, his blood had healed her, and he knew his magic lived within her. He could feel it. His own change had been not quite normal, but it hadn't been anything like this. He would have to wait and see, but he suspected his One would remain more dryad than bloodletter. Personally, he was glad for that. She was a creature of the forest and of growing things. He didn't want to be the reason she could no longer face the sun. They would have to test that out tomorrow, though he expected she would be much more tolerant of sunlight than he was, based on the giant plate of food she was fixing for herself.

She filled her plate and sat down at one of the side tables, oblivious to everybody else's reaction. Martine had taken her plate out with her and Marco had heard the woman remark that she was going to eat at her desk while she caught up on everything she'd left hanging in the office. Crystal's stomach had growled loud enough for Marco to hear, and he knew she was very hungry, indeed. He watched her, glad that his blood had not caused too much disruption in her life.

Arlo sidled up to him, curiosity clear in his expression. They both watched Crystal with varying degrees of interest and puzzlement.

"I know what I saw," Arlo said in a low tone. "I didn't expect this."

"Frankly, neither did I," Marco admitted. "Her dryad magic seems to have superseded mine."

"Is that going to be a problem?" Arlo asked, his brow furrowed.

"Not for me," Marco said, delighted in his ultra-special mate. "I have always been a little different from my brothers anyway."

"I sort of noticed that," Arlo admitted with a lopsided grin. "I mean, I know you're pretty old, but you were way more awake and able today than I expected."

"You wish to know all my secrets, eh?" Marco joked, raising one brow even as he smiled. "But you know this one already. You have met Mena and know that she is of my bloodline. I am descended of one of the oldest and most powerful *strega* lines in Italy. I had magic blood even before I was turned. The turning affected me a little differently than most. It enhanced what magic I already had, and I have had centuries to perfect my skills. Now, by joining with my lovely dryad, I have changed again, as has she. We will not know the full extent of our changes until much later, but it will be exciting to discover them together."

"So long as you're playing for the right side," Arlo said, daring greatly to confront a Master on his own turf in such a way.

But Arlo was made of stern stuff and would have been a powerful Alpha in his own right had he not decided to follow the lead of the Wraiths' Alpha wolf. He had to have strong reasons to do so, but Marco had no need to pry into the werewolf's past. He was strong, but no match for Marco, though he had already proven to be a good ally.

"You have no cause to worry on that count, my friend," Marco assured him. "My own family would end me if I ever betrayed their trust in such a way. And, as you may have witnessed from Mena's skills, they are more than able to do so. If they ever ganged up on me, I'd be toast. But I, like them, have always served the Light. It is the path our family swore to back before the glory of Rome. I may be old, but my family's dedication to the Goddess is truly ancient. I would never betray that for any price."

Arlo nodded solemnly. "I can respect that, Master Marco." His use of the title was deliberate and meaningful. "I wish you well with your new mate. She is a brave one, that's for sure." Arlo gazed at Crystal then turned to pin Marco with his keen gaze. "I talked something over with my Alpha earlier that I'd like to run by you when you have time. It's about this estate. I know you were thinking to open it to guests at some point. We may have a better solution for you that involves your mate's extended family."

Marco was intrigued but realized he would no longer be making decisions alone. He wanted Crystal in on any decisions from now on. Partners.

"Wait until my lady has finished eating," Marco told Arlo. "Maybe we could meet in the office in, say, an hour? We can then both hear the proposal together."

Arlo gave Marco a cunning smile. "I see you're thinking like a mated man already. Good call, Master Marco. I'll see you both in an hour. Maybe I can get a conference call set up by then too."

"I look forward to it," Marco said as Arlo took his leave. Marco snagged a bottle of wine one of the kitchen staff had thoughtfully brought out to him and joined his mate at the table where she was already halfway through her meal. "How are you feeling, my dear?" he asked her as he sat down.

She paused to swallow the bite she had just taken then shook her head. "I was feeling hollow, but I'm starting to fill up. I guess I expended a lot more energy than I thought, and everything tastes so incredibly delicious." She took another bite even as she grinned.

"Heightened senses might be a result of my influence," he said, consideringly. "These things may continue to change over time." He opened his wine bottle and poured a glass. He offered her one, and she accepted. "Arlo has a proposition for us regarding the future of this estate. I told him we would meet him in the office in an hour, if that's all right with you."

She stopped eating and looked up at him. "Me? But it's your decision. It's your estate."

She looked so adorably confused he wanted to hug her but refrained. "No, my love. It is ours. All that I have, all that I am, is yours now. We will make any decisions together, and I want to start as I mean to go on. Besides, whatever it is that

Arlo has to propose has something to do with your extended family, he said, so I thought it best that we learn what he has to say together."

"My family?" She took a sip of the wine, savoring it before swallowing. "This wine is incredible," she said, pausing a moment to look at the glass. "I mean, it tasted good before, but now…"

Marco shrugged. "Perhaps another benefit of my magic rubbing off on you. To me, Maxwell's wines always taste like distilled sunlight. Or, at least, that's the way my romantic imagination tends to think of it."

"I like that," she replied, looking dreamily into his eyes. If they'd been alone at that moment, he would have taken her down to any convenient surface and showed her just how much he loved that she was now part of his immortal life.

"There you are." Mena's voice came to them from near the doorway to the dining room. She walked in and came right over to their table. She looked a bit worse for wear, but whole. "Are you both well?" She looked pointedly at Crystal's half-full plate of food and then at Marco.

"We are very well, indeed," Marco told her. Mena looked so much like his long-lost sister at that moment that he could almost believe in reincarnation.

"I thought—"

Marco knew what she was going to ask, but he didn't quite know how to answer. Instead, he took a good look at her and realized she was lacking her usual sparkle. She had battled a fire mage and come out the winner, but that could not have been a walk in the park.

"Perhaps you should join us, Mena. Maybe eat something?" he suggested.

She shook her head and looked around the room. The buffet was still out, and there were a few still eating at the big table at the center. She sighed and ran a hand through her hair.

"You're right. Give me a moment to get something. I used a lot of energy, and I need to refuel." She walked over to the buffet and began filling a plate.

Mena was back with them in short order, and Marco sat, bemused, as the two most important ladies in his life sat opposite him, stuffing their faces. He could never have predicted this sort of situation, but he was a happy man to be sitting here with not only a beloved member of his family who accepted him for what he was, but also his precious One.

Marco poured a glass of wine for Mena and placed it near her hand. He refilled Crystal's glass, seeing that she was handling the wine a lot better than she had just the day before. His blood *had* changed her in some ways. It was going to be fun discovering just how deep the changes went.

"Before you can ask what I have no doubt is on your mind," Marco said preemptively as Mena ate, "I will tell you that Crystal is my mate and was healed of a mortal wound by my blood, by her choice. As you can see, she has not changed completely, which I suppose has something to do with her elemental power as the descendant of a dryad."

Mena nodded and swallowed, taking a sip of water, which she had brought with her from the buffet. She paused in her consumption of calories to talk, and Marco had the impression she had given some thought to what might happen if they ever found themselves in this situation.

"Bloodletters seldom mix with other magical races, as you know, so there is little in the histories to confirm my ideas, but I think you are right. It is possible that an elemental power—which, after all, is what Crystal has—will supersede the magic of your blood, Uncle Marco." Mena took another sip of her water. "In fact, I would not be surprised to find that Crystal could retain the ability to live in the sun, though perhaps she might be a bit more susceptible to sunburns now than she was before. And, Uncle Marco, have you given thought to the changes that may happen to you?"

Marco shook his head. He didn't want to draw Crystal's attention to the fact that he had yet to drink of her blood. They were mates, but the final joining had not yet been accomplished. He had not wanted to push her when he wasn't certain how she would recover from her ordeal. Later, they would have time to complete the bond...and then they would see what they would see.

"I have not," he said, hoping to end the speculation there, but Mena forged ahead.

He didn't know why he'd expected anything else. His sister had been just the same, and Mena was just like her namesake.

"The dryad magic in Crystal's blood could make you even more able to withstand daylight than our family's innate magic already does. You could become a daywalker," Mena said enthusiastically. "I mean, such things are only the stuff of legend, but legends have to come from somewhere, no? Perhaps you will be the one to prove all those old tales correct."

Marco saw the moment realization dawned over Crystal's face. Her gaze turned to him, and she looked so sad and guilty he had to reach out to her. Their hands met on the tabletop, and she squeezed his fingers contritely.

"You haven't bitten me. Not ever," she whispered. "Oh, Marco. I'm so sorry. All I've done is take and take."

"Never, my love. Never think that," he told her, passion in his words. "I could not feed when you didn't even know what I was, and since you discovered, you have been in no shape. I want to be certain you are well and whole before we take the next step. If we ever do. It'll be solely up to you."

"Are you kidding me?" She seemed both upset and exasperated, surprising him. His One was a contradictory woman, and he loved every last quirk of her nature. "Of course, we're taking the next step. You have to be joking! I love you. You love me. We share everything, you just said, so there's no question of either of us holding out anything from each other. Am I right?"

He felt pinned by her gaze, and he had the oddest instinct to squirm. What a novel thought. He hadn't felt like this since he was a little boy. Crystal was good for him. Of that, he had no doubt. She brought him new experiences and memories of his younger self every few hours, which kept him on his toes. He loved that. Almost as much as he loved her.

"I defer to your desires, my One. Whatever you wish is my command," he said graciously, smiling indulgently at her.

"Marco, we're partners in this. That's the only way it can possibly work. I don't command you. You don't command me. We work through everything together." She squeezed his hand, and he was floored by the earnestness in her words.

He brought one of her hands to his lips and kissed the back of it. "As you wish, my love. My partner." As he spoke the words, they felt like a vow.

Mena raised her glass of wine to them both. "Congratulations, you two, and welcome to the family, Crystal. I can't wait to see what happens next."

CHAPTER 28

Crystal still couldn't quite believe how things had changed so quickly. When Arlo told them about Sunny's parents and how they ran a clandestine art school for non-combative mages, she knew she and Marco had to at least meet them. Opening the estate to the public—even if it was just limited to shifters and other magical folk—wasn't really that great of an idea anymore. Not now that they knew the place still had a ways to go in recovering from the evil that had been done here. What they needed were caretakers who would continue the essential work of keeping the place safe from evil while allowing the grounds the time they needed to fully recover.

And the family connection didn't hurt. Marco was all about family, after all, and Crystal was going to have to get used to being a part of two families now. Marco's and her own newly-discovered extended family of dryads and their people. It was a bit overwhelming, but very welcome. She'd gone from being alone in the truest sense of the word to having not only a lover who welcomed her into his life, but a large set of relatives as well. It was a blessing over and over again.

They set up a time for Sunny and her new mate to visit the estate with Sunny's parents so everybody could meet. The solution sounded like a good one, but they would all have to get to know each other first, to see if it really would work out.

Arlo also intimated that one of the other dryad descendants had experience with a legendary artifact. That piqued both Marco and Crystal's curiosity, and they agreed they should approach the other dryad relations cautiously about the topic. Maybe there was a better way to protect the box that they hadn't yet discovered. Of course, they would be careful about who they told what about the box that remained hidden on the estate. The fewer people who knew of its continued existence and hiding place, the better.

After that, Marco and Crystal cut the business side of the night short in order to go back to bed. They retired to Crystal's room upstairs with the idea that they would move below ground later, but they were in too much of a hurry to be together to wait much longer, and Crystal's room was closer. Besides, there was plenty of time left in the night.

They were barely inside the room when he pulled her into his arms and drew her close. His breath rasped past her ear as he whispered words of love and desire.

"I can't wait. I've tried so hard to give you time to get used to this but…"

She pressed against his chest so that she could meet his gaze. "You've been more than patient. You've been self-sacrificing beyond the point that I think is healthy for you, or wise. Let's just do this, and then we'll see what happens. As much as you want me to be whole and well, I want the same for you. Take me, Marco. I have complete faith in you."

Something changed in his eyes at that revelation, and they seemed to glow from within. Far from frightening, she found it incredibly sexy. Then he smiled, and she got to really see his fangs close up for the first time. Again, she would have assumed when confronted with a real-life vampire, she might have been scared, but shown the reality of Marco, she was…turned on to an incredible degree.

This was Marco, after all. She knew him better than she had known any man. She was beginning to feel as if they were sharing their thoughts on a limited basis, and nothing she had ever sensed from him gave her any cause for concern. Far from it. At every turn, he had sought what was best for her without regard to his own needs and desires. He was a special, special man and a gifted lover. She already knew that from first-hand experience. Nothing he could do to her would harm her. Of that, she was certain.

He lifted her off her feet and took her over to the bed. He rested his back against the upholstered headboard. She was on his lap and could feel the excitement in his body—and in one particular body part that prodded against her hip.

"I've been thinking about this since almost the moment I first saw you," he admitted, and she was gratified to learn that his fangs didn't impede his speech at all. She'd wondered idly about that since learning what he really was, but it was a nonsensical thought.

"Will it make us truly One?" she asked, her voice breathy.

"I believe so. From what I've heard, we will share each other's thoughts, in time. The bond formed with my kind is deeper and more complete than with other species, though it wouldn't do to tell the shifters that. But they don't share their mates' minds." Marco sounded a bit smug about that, and she had to grin.

"What will my magic do to you?" She loved being in his arms, and the anticipation of what was to come only made it that much sweeter.

But Crystal really was concerned about how her blood might affect him. They had discussed the possibilities in a vague way, but she suspected there were things he wasn't telling her about. Things that worried her.

"Have no fear, my love. While it is true that magical blood is something most bloodletters never really get the chance to sample except under rare circumstances, I come from a magical bloodline so I think it won't be as potent to me as it would be to others of my kind. I'm also…uh…rather old, and in bloodletters, age usually brings power and knowledge. Hopefully, wisdom as well." He grinned, and she smiled back.

"Well, then." Crystal started unbuttoning his silk shirt. "I think it's time we were skin-to-skin. We've both waited long enough, don't you think?"

With a laughing growl, he flipped her onto her back on the bed and straddled her thighs. He let her watch as he slowly unbuttoned the rest of his shirt and shrugged it off. Then his hands went to the fastening of his trousers and her mouth went dry.

He performed a decadent striptease for her then rid her of her clothing with slow, deliberate, sexy moves until they were, as she had said, skin-to-skin. He reached between her thighs and, finding she was ready for him, wasted no more time joining their bodies together. Then he paused and looked deep into her eyes.

His were glowing again, and the fire in them made her blood flow even hotter. He really was the sexiest man alive. He seemed to be hesitating when her body was crying out for more. What was he waiting for?

"I don't want to hurt you," he explained, as if he was already reading her thoughts. Maybe she'd just had that look on her face, and he'd interpreted it correctly. "I mean… My bite doesn't hurt. At least, not for long. The same magic that lets me close wounds without a trace also gives the person I'm biting a good experience."

"Then, prove it to me, lover," she said, clenching her inner muscles around him in a way that made him groan. She loved being daring with him. Never before had she felt so free with a man. Never before had she loved someone so completely, so fast…and had it feel so right.

"You are going to be the death of me," he muttered, lowering his body so that he could kiss her mouth, then move to her jaw, and eventually, to her neck.

His kiss drugged her into a fog of desire. She couldn't wait to learn everything there was to being with a bloodletter, as he called his kind. She had never believed vampires could be real, but here she was, with the living, loving proof. He began to move within her as she felt his lips on her pulse, then his teeth.

She was nearing a fast, hard precipice within moments, and then he bit down on her flesh, and her body was thrown into a whirlpool of ecstasy the likes of which she had never known before. Even with Marco. This was something altogether new and highly addictive.

She might have blacked out for a moment. She wasn't sure.

"Are you all right?" Marco asked after long moments of harsh breathing on both their parts.

"Never better," she gasped back as he lifted away and rolled to his back beside her, reaching for her hand and intertwining their fingers.

"Ain't that the truth," he muttered, then brought her hand to his mouth and kissed it tenderly. "That was amazing."

"It truly was," she replied, barely able to think, much less make intelligent conversation. "How do *you* feel?" She wondered if any changes her blood may have made to him would have taken effect already.

"Fine. If anything changes, I suspect we won't be completely aware of it until sometime later. For now," he rolled onto his side to look at her, putting hand around her waist, "I think we should try that again. What do you say?"

"I say, yes. Yes. Emphatically yes!" She leaned into his kiss and allowed him to position her above him this time.

She took him into her body, and they made love again, and then again. Each time, he drank just a little bit of her blood, heightening the sensations to a heretofore unknown level. It was like nothing she had ever even imagined... And it—he—was all hers. For the rest of their lives.

How had she become so blessed?

That thought would follow her into sleep, and when she woke hours later out of an exhausted, sated, languid repose,

Marco was there with her in bed…his hard body outlined in a shaft of sunlight coming in through the windows. She sat upright, worried for a moment, but he seemed all right. In fact, as she met his gaze, she saw tears in his luminous brown eyes as he looked at his hand, outlined in the bright light of a new day.

"Is it okay?" she whispered, worried when he didn't speak. His skin wasn't smoking like it had in the clearing. That had to be a good sign, right?

He met her gaze as a single tear rolled down his face, unchecked. "I never thought I would ever feel the sun on my skin without pain again. You have given me this gift, my love."

She moved closer to him, touching his cheek and wiping the tear away. "Will it last?" She was whispering. The moment was special.

"I believe so. Between my own inherited magic and the blessing of your elemental nature, I may have become something out of legend. A daywalker. A bloodletter that can stand in the light and not burn, whose power is undiminished by the rays of the sun. If so, you and I together will be powerful soldiers in the fight against the *Venifucus* and their leader, if she really has returned to this realm."

"Do you think that's why the Goddess brought us together?" She was still whispering, her thoughts filled with awe at the very idea.

"It is said She works in mysterious ways. I have heard through the grapevine that more than the usual number of what we might call *power couples* have found each other over the past few years." He was looking at the sunlight again, his eyes filled with wonder. She was so happy to see the breathtaking joy in his expression.

"Power couples?" she asked, settling her head against his shoulder and her hand against the steady beat of his heart.

"Unconventional mixes of powers and abilities. I know one of my brethren mated with a werewolf woman. Her blood gives him extraordinary powers. There are other uncommon combinations popping up way more than usual. As a rule, the magical races have not mixed like this since the last time Elspeth tried to assert dominion over this realm. The fact that her followers are becoming increasingly active and more power couples are being formed could very well be connected. It may be that our increased powers will be needed in the battles to come."

Crystal wasn't sure she liked the sound of that, but she could face just about anything with Marco as her partner. He made her feel so secure and so…loved. She'd never had this feeling before and vowed internally to never take it for granted. Just as she would never take *him* for granted.

"Whatever comes, we will face it together. You've changed my life for the better, Marco." She kissed his chest and lay her head back against his shoulder. "I love you," she said simply, knowing that covered everything that was in her heart that she didn't have words for at that exact moment.

He kissed her hair, and she felt deep stirrings in the bond that now connected them on a soul level. She didn't need the words, but she really enjoyed hearing them anyway.

"I love you too, Crystal. My One and Only."

EPILOGUE

That evening, Marco took Crystal on a tour of the wine cellar and the rooms he'd put in soon after obtaining ownership of the estate. Crystal realized the location wasn't much of a secret anymore, but she trusted the wolves who had seen Marco materialize from this part of the house the night before. Plus, Marco wasn't hampered by the need to stay out of sunlight anymore.

Marco paused by a rack of wine bottles that looked just like every other rack in the area and he touched a spot up near the top of the rack, then another in the center and one below. A little snick was the only indication of a lock coming undone, and then he pulled the rack outward on silent hidden hinges to show a small hallway with a steel door at the end. It was dark, but she could see the faint glow of a small amber LED at the end of the passage.

They entered, and he closed the wine rack-covered secret door behind them then advanced to the door on the opposite end. Here was a more conventional coded lock with a keypad that lit as he touched it. He entered some numbers, and the steel door opened.

Beyond it was a cozy room with a couch. It looked like a living room with bookshelves and comfortable seating for one. Well, that was going to change. Any place Marco lived would now have to accommodate two, Crystal thought with an inward grin.

"We can keep this as a safe room," Marco observed. "Kit it out with more electronics if we decide to live here. I actually own another property not far as the crow flies. I've lived there for the past century and a half and have built it to my own specifications. It has extensive underground living space, but if my condition continues as it started this morning, then I won't need to hide from the sun anymore, and we can live wherever you want, within my current territory, of course. It would take a bit of preparation and negotiation should you wish to live elsewhere. If there is already a bloodletter presence, I'd have to lay some groundwork, but it still might be possible." He sent her an inquiring look.

"I've lived all over. I have no particular attachment to any one place. I like Nebraska, and I'm happy in this area," she told him honestly. "We can stay here. Or move." She shrugged. "Wherever you want to live is fine with me."

He seemed relieved, and she believed he really would have moved—no matter how difficult it was—to accommodate her wishes. Marco was such a great guy.

"But one thing has got to change," she added, trying to lighten the mood as she continued. "No more single chairs. Wherever we end up, we're always going to be together from now on." As the words came out of her mouth, they sounded more like a promise than anything else. "So, we need at least two of everything. His and hers."

Marco reached out and pulled her into his arms. "I really like the sound of that."

She reached up and cupped his cheek, drawing his face closer to hers. "So do I," she murmured, just before his lips met hers, and that was the last word either of them spoke for quite some time.

Please enjoy this excerpt from the next book in the series:

Brotherhood of Blood ~ Wildwood 3

WILDWOOD IN WINTER

Chapter One

Winter in Northern Idaho…

Pam heard the song of the forest, as she always did. There was snow on the ground, but that was nothing new this time of year. She lived in the wilds by choice, up in the tall timber of the forest north and east of Coeur d'Alene, that had once been logged almost beyond all recognition. These days, a lot of it was protected in various ways and she made her home in one of the rare, unspoiled parts of the forest that had never been logged.

Not because of any physical impediment, though the slopes here were steep and logging was difficult, even with modern machinery, but because the place was protected…by magic. Somebody, long ago, had worked protective spells around a little piece of forest on the steep side of a mountain, and the homestead hidden within. It was Pamela's homestead now. She had inherited it from a friend who had done her best to teach Pam what little she knew of magic.

Her friend—an elderly lady named Sue, who had lived down the street from Pam when she'd made her home in Boise—had come from a magical family, or so she'd claimed. Sue knew a lot about the magical world, but didn't have much power of her own, except that she had an occasional prophetic vision of the future.

The old lady had never had children and her extended family had inherited the bulk of her estate, but Sue had left the cabin in the woods to Pam, much to Pam's surprise. The letter that had accompanied the bequest explained that Sue had received a vision about Pam living in that cabin and learning of her destiny there. Sue also claimed that Pam would find her true love there, as well.

Pam had never done well in the city, and even though it was a bit lonely out here in the middle of the forest, she loved it. She sent a prayer up every day in thanks to Sue, who had made it possible for Pam to get out of the hustle and bustle of city life and find some peace. There weren't a lot of other people around—none at all on her land—but there was plenty of wildlife, and the trees... The trees were amazing.

Pam had always had a way with growing things and Sue had been able to tell her stories about all sorts of beings that supposedly shared the world of man. Shapeshifters, bloodletters, mages of every description. These were the tales Sue would share in the afternoons when Pam brought over a bakery box stuffed with goodies, and they shared a pot of tea.

Pam had always found Sue's house calming. Sue claimed that she had just enough magic to set wards around her personal space and tried to teach Pam to do the same, but with mixed results. Pam's magic wasn't really like anything Sue had ever seen and she didn't know enough to teach things she didn't have personal experience with, unfortunately. But it was okay. Pam enjoyed the old lady's company and Sue was a calming presence to be around.

Sue's family didn't have much to do with her. Sue claimed it was because her magic had always been negligible, and Pam didn't like what that said about Sue's family at all. So, when the bequest had come to her, Pam took it as a sign of friendship, even though some of Sue's family had raised their eyebrows at the gesture. Still, they had inherited quite a bit of money and other properties from Sue, so they didn't contest it.

Pam had sold her little house in Boise, moved north, and had never looked back. The forest up here sang to her from the moment she had arrived, and she had learned more about herself and her power in the few short years she had been up here than in all the years she had kicked around in cities, not ever feeling as if she really belonged.

Pam had been on her own ever since her parents had died in a tragic traffic accident, shortly after moving to Boise. Pam was their only child, just turned eighteen and about to start college in Boise, which was why they had chosen to move there. Pam had known it wasn't quite normal for a family to uproot itself to move to where their child was going to college, but her family had never lived in one place very long. They'd spent only a few years in each place, never really making lasting friendships, preferring to keep their circle small.

She'd often wondered if it was because one or both of her folks had magic. She couldn't ask them now, of course. They had never spoken of it and her power had only manifested after they were gone. Maybe one of them had been like her and had been waiting for her to display the talent before talking to her about it. She liked to believe that, though she wasn't sure.

After their deaths, Pam had carried on with the plan to get her degree, though her heart wasn't really in it. Sue had been there for her in a way she never had expected. She'd arrived on Pam's doorstep the day after the funerals with a casserole dish and Pam had invited her in. They'd sat in Pam's kitchen and had tea while Sue listened to Pam, in her grief, and provided a steady shoulder to lean on.

Sue had become like Pam's grandmother and that summer, when Pam had tidied up Sue's back garden as a kindness, Sue had recognized Pam's abilities with plants and the earth as magic. That discovery had changed their relationship. Deepened it. Sue shared the secret of her own magic and the history of her family and her role in it.

Sue had opened up a whole new world of understanding for Pam, teaching her things about the world that she had never known. They'd run a bunch of different experiments, trying to figure out what kind of talent Pam had, but Sue hadn't been able to nail it down.

Pam had finished college and Sue had come to her graduation, cheering her on. Sue had never liked Brad, the boyfriend Pam had picked up her last year in college. They'd stayed together for a couple of years, and he'd really done a number on her self-esteem. When they'd finally broken up, Sue had been there to dry Pam's tears and listen to her tale of woe.

Then, that summer, Sue fell ill suddenly and passed away, leaving the house in the woods to Pam. Pam had grieved the loss of her dear friend, then followed Sue's final wish that Pam move into the house in the forest and find her destiny.

Pam had been here for a few years now, and hadn't yet found that promised destiny. She'd sort of given up on it altogether, but she enjoyed the house and the solitude, for the most part, so she stayed.

Here in the forest Pam had finally found peace within herself. She communed with the trees in a way that she still didn't fully understand and managed to live in harmony with the creatures that also lived among the trees. Even the predators. Somehow, she always knew when the dangerous ones were around, and she managed to avoid running into them unexpectedly.

Except for today. Much to Pam's surprise as she walked through her forest, she came face to face with the biggest timber wolf she had ever seen. It just stood there, head alert, watching her.

"Oh, boy," Pam muttered, feeling her heart start beating faster as adrenaline rushed through her veins in the classic fight or flight scenario. "Nice wolfie." She kept her tone as calm as possible, though her heart rate had just skyrocketed into the panic zone.

She tried to think her way out of this situation. She could climb a tree. Wolves didn't climb. But that would leave her stuck in a tree for an indefinite period and it was cold out.

She didn't see any other wolves around, though she believed wolves usually hunted in packs. Was this some kind of lone wolf? Was it hunting her? Or was this just some random meeting in the woods. And why hadn't the trees warned her? They always warned her about the big predators.

Why not this one? Maybe this wolf was friendly or something? Maybe the trees didn't see it as a threat to her? If so, why not?

That question was probably better left until she was out of this situation. The wolf didn't look too hungry. In fact, it seemed well fed and rather calm. Maybe she could walk past it and get safely back to her cabin. She could hope the wolf stayed where it was and didn't try to eat her as she sauntered past it.

Well, it was worth a try. If that didn't work, she could always climb a tree. If she wasn't too badly mauled by then to climb.

On that cheery thought, she began to move. Giving the wolf a wide berth, she sidled around, keeping as much distance between herself and the wolf as she could. It didn't move. It just sat there, watching her.

Until, that is, she got on its other side. She began to walk calmly toward her cabin and the wolf got up and trotted quietly after her.

Shit! Why was it following her?

She tried to breathe slowly and keep calm, but it was definitely following her. It didn't seem to be gaining on her, just following at a steady distance.

It was acting more like somebody's pet poodle than a huge, wild wolf. It kept up with her without crowding her, but it was definitely following her. The wolf's golden-brown eyes were trained on her, but she didn't feel like it was menacing her.

When the cabin came into view, she breathed a sigh of relief. She was almost there. Now, if the beast would just let her get to her home in safety. It didn't seem to be behaving at all aggressively, so she might just make it. What would happen then, she wasn't sure.

If the forest couldn't be relied on any longer to warn her of danger, that was going to seriously curtail her outdoor activities. She didn't like the idea of that at all. But if the forest didn't think this wolf was dangerous enough to warn her about, then maybe it wasn't.

She couldn't think about that right now, though. She had to get to safety first. The house was in sight. Each step brought her nearer to her back porch and the door that led to her kitchen. To safety.

Pam kept one eye on the wolf and noted that it stayed behind her, walking at that same measured distance. It wasn't growling or anything, but it definitely was watching her. The intelligence in its eyes seemed almost uncanny.

A sudden thought occurred to her. Was this wolf—this unnaturally enormous wolf—a shapeshifter? Sue had told her stories about shifters and how they were usually larger in their shifted forms than the regular creatures of their species. Not that Pam was going to stop and try to have a conversation with this deadly beast at that exact moment, but it was something to ponder.

She stepped onto her porch and reached for the door. The wolf sat at the bottom of the steps and just watched her. Breathing deeply, she opened the door and then stepped inside and closed it behind her.

Sheesh! She needed to calm down. Adrenaline was still coursing through her system.

"If you're a shifter, that was really uncool, dude," she said out loud.

Arlo heard the woman's words from inside and had to chuckle inwardly. He hadn't meant to intercept her like that. The wind had been blowing in the wrong direction, carrying her scent away from him. He'd just been doing a quick reconnaissance run around her property to get the lay of the land before he decided how best to approach.

Intel said this woman—Pamela Auerbach—was one of the missing dryad descendants. It had been really hard to track her, but eventually Sally's detective skills had come through and she'd asked for help making contact since the cabin where Pamela lived had no phone service. Sally suspected Pamela had some kind of mobile phone—cellular or even satellite—but Sally had been unable to trace it. They'd had to send somebody to see her and make sure she was the right person.

Jesse had asked Arlo to run the mission since he was familiar with dryad magic after having worked to guard several of the others that had been discovered so far. Arlo was Jesse Moore's right hand man these days in the shifter mercenary company he ran, known as the Wraiths. Arlo had been taking on more responsibility since Jesse had found his mate and preferred to stay close to home these days. As a result, Arlo had stepped up to run most of the high-level ops this past year or two.

He hadn't brought a team with him on this quick sneak and peek. He hadn't thought it would be necessary. All he had to do was check out one lone woman living in the middle of the forest. How hard could it be?

Arlo had planned to do a little recon, then, depending on what he found, approach her in as non-threatening a way as possible. He had contemplated engineering an encounter in the nearby town when she made a grocery run. Failing that, he had decided to just knock politely on her door.

He had been working up to that, in fact, but had wanted to check things out a little more first. Instead, he had run headlong into her in the woods, scaring her silly. Though, he had to admit, she had handled the situation better than he might have expected. She didn't panic, though she had been quite obviously frightened. She had kept a level head and had walked calmly back to her place, which told him she was good in a crisis.

Then she had surprised him again by muttering about shifters once she was safely inside her house. That told him a few additional things. First, she wasn't rattled easily, which was a point in her favor, as far as he was concerned. He respected that. Second, she had more knowledge of the magical world than most of the other dryads who had been discovered so far. Quite a few of them had been raised by humans and hadn't known much of anything about magic or even the existence of shifters.

Arlo made a quick decision and shifted back to his two-legged form. He was naked, but that couldn't be helped. His clothes were back where he had left his truck, down the mountain a ways.

"Sorry, ma'am. I didn't mean to sneak up on you like that. I didn't know you were there," he said loud enough for her to hear him inside the house. He knew she hadn't moved from the doorway. He could see her through the little window in the door.

The door flew open and she peered out. "You *are* a shifter?"

She looked right at him, her tone and look accusatory. She looked so angry. Arlo privately thought it was adorable.

"Guilty as charged, ma'am," he admitted, leaning against the railing that bordered the steps up to the porch.

He'd positioned himself to the side of the steps so as to appear as non-threatening as possible. She also couldn't see much more than his chest unless she walked farther out onto the porch, but she was staying by the door, for now.

"I don't believe it," she whispered, searching his eyes.

"I can shift back if it'll help you believe, but if you don't mind my asking, how do you know about my kind?"

She seemed to think about that for a moment before answering. "The lady who left me this house had a lot of knowledge and she passed some of it on to me before she died. She told me about a lot of different things, but you're the first shifter I've ever met," she admitted. "Why are you here?"

"I came to find you."

*To read more, get your copy of **Wildwood in Winter**.*

ABOUT THE AUTHOR

Bianca D'Arc has run a laboratory, climbed the corporate ladder in the shark-infested streets of lower Manhattan, studied and taught martial arts, and earned the right to put a whole bunch of letters after her name, but she's always enjoyed writing more than any of her other pursuits. She grew up and still lives on Long Island, where she keeps busy with an extensive garden, several aquariums full of very demanding fish, and writing her favorite genres of paranormal, fantasy and sci-fi romance.

Bianca loves to hear from readers and can be reached through Twitter (@BiancaDArc), Facebook (BiancaDArcAuthor) or through the various links on her website.

WELCOME TO THE D'ARC SIDE... WWW.BIANCADARC.COM

OTHER BOOKS BY BIANCA D'ARC

Brotherhood of Blood
One & Only
Rare Vintage
Phantom Desires
Sweeter Than Wine
Forever Valentine
Wolf Hills*
Wolf Quest

Brotherhood ~ Wildwood
Dance of the Dryad
Night of the Nymph
Wildwood in Winter
The Elven Star

Tales of the Were
Lords of the Were
Inferno
Rocky
Slade

Tales ~ String of Fate
Cat's Cradle
King's Throne
Jacob's Ladder
Her Warriors

Tales ~ Redstone Clan
The Purrfect Stranger
Grif
Red
Magnus
Bobcat
Matt

Tales ~ Grizzly Cove
All About the Bear
Mating Dance
Night Shift
Alpha Bear
Saving Grace
Bearliest Catch
The Bear's Healing Touch
The Luck of the Shifters
Badass Bear
Bounty Hunter Bear
Storm Bear
Bear Meets Girl
Spirit Bear
Lion in Waiting
Black Magic Bear
Wolf Tracks

Tales ~ Trident Trilogy
Waterborn
Fathom
Leviathan

Tales ~ Were-Fey
Lone Wolf
Snow Magic
Midnight Kiss

Tales ~ Lick of Fire
Phoenix Rising
Phoenix and the Wolf
Phoenix and the Dragon

Tales ~ Big Wolf
A Touch of Class
Perfect
The Werewolf Alpha's
Solstice Miracle

Tales ~ Jaguar Island
The Jaguar Tycoon
The Jaguar Bodyguard
The Jaguar's Secret Baby
The Jaguar Star

Guardians of the Dark
Simon Says
Once Bitten
Smoke on the Water
Night Shade
Shadow Play

Gifts of the Ancients
Warrior's Heart
Future Past
A Friend in Need
Heal the Healer

Tales ~Gemini Project
Tag Team
Doubling Down
Deuces Wild

Resonance Mates
Hara's Legacy**
Davin's Quest
Jaci's Experiment
Grady's Awakening
Harry's Sacrifice

Dragon Knights
Daughters of the Dragon
Maiden Flight*
Border Lair
The Ice Dragon**
Prince of Spies***

The Novellas
The Dragon Healer
Master at Arms
Wings of Change

Sons of Draconia
FireDrake
Dragon Storm
Keeper of the Flame
Hidden Dragons

The Sea Captain's Daughter
Book 1: Sea Dragon
Book 2: Dragon Fire
Book 3: Dragon Mates

The Captain's Dragon
Snow Dragon
Gatekeeper

Jit'Suku Chronicles
Arcana
King of Swords
King of Cups
King of Clubs
King of Stars
End of the Line
Diva

StarLords
Hidden Talent
Talent For Trouble
Shy Talent

Jit'Suku Chronicles
Sons of Amber
Angel in the Badlands
Master of Her Heart

Jit'Suku Chronicles
In the Stars
The Cyborg Next Door
Heart of the Machine

StarLords
Hidden Talent
Talent For Trouble
Shy Talent

Irish Lullaby
Bells Will Be Ringing
Wild Irish Rose

More than Mated
The Right Spot

* RT Book Reviews Awards Nominee
** EPPIE Award Winner
*** CAPA Award Winner

Welcome to Grizzly Cove, where bear shifters can be who they are - if the creatures of the deep will just leave them be. Wild magic, unexpected allies, a conflagration of sorcery and shifter magic the likes of which has not been seen in centuries... That's what awaits the peaceful town of Grizzly Cove. That, and love. Lots and lots of love.

This series begins with...

All About the Bear
Welcome to Grizzly Cove, where the sheriff has more than the peace to protect. The proprietor of the new bakery in town is clueless about the dual nature of her nearest neighbors, but not for long. It'll be up to Sheriff Brody to clue her in and convince her to stay calm—and in his bed—for the next fifty years or so.

Mating Dance
Tom, Grizzly Cove's only lawyer, is also a badass grizzly bear, but he's met his match in Ashley, the woman he just can't get out of his mind. She's got a dark secret, that only he knows. When ugliness from her past tracks her to her new home, can Tom protect the woman he is fast coming to believe is his mate?

Night Shift
Sheriff's Deputy Zak is one of the few black bear shifters in a colony of grizzlies. When his job takes him into closer proximity to the lovely Tina, though, he finds he can't resist her. Could it be he's finally found his mate? And when adversity strikes, will she turn to him, or run into the night? Zak will do all he can to make sure she chooses him.

Phoenix Rising

Lance is inexplicably drawn to the sun and doesn't understand why. Tina is a witch who remembers him from their high school days. She'd had a crush on the quiet boy who had an air of magic about him. Reunited by Fate, she wonders if she could be the one to ground him and make him want to stay even after the fire within him claims his soul...if only their love can be strong enough.

Phoenix and the Wolf

Diana is drawn to the sun and dreams of flying, but her elderly grandmother needs her feet firmly on the ground. When Diana's old clunker breaks down in front of a high-end car lot, she seeks help and finds herself ensnared by the sexy werewolf mechanic who runs the repair shop. Stone makes her want to forget all her responsibilities and take a walk on the wild side...with him.

Phoenix and the Dragon

He's a dragon shapeshifter in search of others like himself. She's a newly transformed phoenix shifter with a lot to learn and bad guys on her trail. Together, they will go on a dazzling adventure into the unknown, and fight against evil folk intent on subduing her immense power and using it for their own ends. They will face untold danger and find love that will last a lifetime.

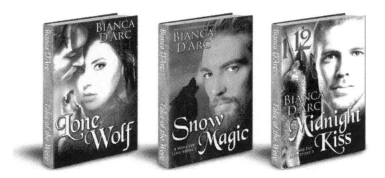

Lone Wolf

Josh is a werewolf who suddenly has extra, unexpected and totally untrained powers. He's not happy about it - or about the evil jackasses who keep attacking him, trying to steal his magic. Forced to seek help, Josh is sent to an unexpected ally for training.

Deena is a priestess with more than her share of magical power and a unique ability that has made her a target. She welcomes Josh, seeing a kindred soul in the lone werewolf. She knows she can help him... if they can survive their enemies long enough.

Snow Magic

Evie has been a lone wolf since the disappearance of her mate, Sir Rayburne, a fey knight from another realm. Left all alone with a young son to raise, Evie has become stronger than she ever was. But now her son is grown and suddenly Ray is back.

Ray never meant to leave Evie all those years ago but he's been caught in a magical trap, slowly being drained of magic all this time. Freed at last, he whisks Evie to the only place he knows in the mortal realm where they were happy and safe—the rustic cabin in the midst of a North Dakota winter where they had been newlyweds. He's used the last of his magic to get there and until he recovers a bit, they're stuck in the middle of nowhere with a blizzard coming and bad guys on their trail.

Can they pick up where they left off and rekindle the magic between them, or has it been extinguished forever?

Midnight Kiss

Margo is a werewolf on a mission...with a disruptively handsome mage named Gabe. She can't figure out where Gabe fits in the pecking order, but it doesn't seem to matter to the attraction driving her wild. Gabe knows he's going to have to prove himself in order to win Margo's heart. He wants her for his mate, but can she give her heart to a mage? And will their dangerous quest get in the way?

The Jaguar Tycoon

Mark may be the larger-than-life billionaire Alpha of the secretive Jaguar Clan, but he's a pussycat when it comes to the one women destined to be his mate. Shelly is an up-and-coming architect trying to drum up business at an elite dinner party at which Mark is the guest of honor. When shots ring out, the hunt for the gunman brings Mark into Shelly's path and their lives will never be the same.

The Jaguar Bodyguard

Sworn to protect his Clan, Nick heads to Hollywood to keep an eye on a rising star who has seen a little too much for her own good. Unexpectedly fame has made a circus of Sal's life, but when decapitated squirrels show up on her doorstep, she knows she needs professional help. Nick embeds himself in her security squad to keep an eye on her as sparks fly and passions rise between them. Can he keep her safe and prevent her from revealing what she knows?

The Jaguar's Secret Baby

Hank has never forgotten the wild woman with whom he spent one memorable night. He's dreamed of her for years now, but has never been back to the small airport in Texas owned and run by her werewolf Pack. Tracy was left with a delicious memory of her night in Hank's arms, and a beautiful baby girl who is the light of her life. She chose not to tell Hank about his daughter, but when he finally returns and he discovers the daughter he's never known, he'll do all he can to set things right.

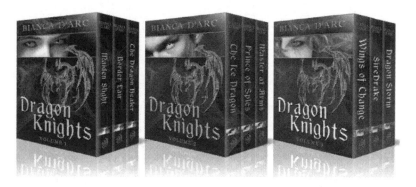

Dragon Knights

Two dragons, two knights, and one woman to complete their circle. That's the recipe for happiness in the land of fighting dragons. But there are a few special dragons that are more. They are the ruling family and they are half-dragon and half-human, able to change at will from one form to another.

Books in this series have won the EPPIE Award for Best Erotic Romance in the Fantasy/Paranormal category, and have been nominated for *RT Book Reviews Magazine* Reviewers Choice Awards among other honors.

Daughters of the Dragon
1. Maiden Flight
2. Border Lair
3. The Ice Dragon
4. Prince of Spies

The Novellas
1.5. The Dragon Healer
2.5. Master at Arms
4.5. Wings of Change

Sons of Draconia
5. FireDrake
6. Dragon Storm
7. Keeper of the Flame
8. Hidden Dragons

The Sea Captain's Daughter
9. Sea Dragon
10. Dragon Fire
11. Dragon Mates

WWW.BIANCADARC.COM

Made in the USA
Columbia, SC
16 January 2023

10418861R00150